Praise for the writing of Marie Harte

Tied and True

"Ask me how I'd describe this book by Ms. Harte and I'll tell you—Yum! Yum! And yum!"

—Dawn, *Enchanting Reviews*

"With a very well paced plot and two wonderfully developed characters I enjoyed this read more than imagined. Each character as complex as the reason as to their true motive, I was thoroughly amused at their genuine chemistry."

—Mila Bean, *Coffee Time Romance Reviews*

Reaper's Reward

"Bravo, Ms. Harte! *Reaper's Reward* was everything I hoped it would be and more! This was an excellent story, and I certainly look forward to Ms. Harte's next work."

—Maria, *Romance Junkies*

"*Reaper's Reward* is a story that will knock your socks off. Marie Harte has once again written a tale that you won't want to miss!"

—Trang Black, *eCataromance*

LooseId®

ISBN: 978-1-59632-881-5
TIED AND TRUE
Copyright © 2009 by Loose Id, LLC
Cover Art by April Martinez
Cover Design by April Martinez

Publisher acknowledges the authors and copyright holders of the individual works, as follows:
TIED AND TRUE
Copyright © June 2007 by Marie Harte
REAPER'S REWARD
Copyright © July 2007 by Marie Harte

Printed in the U.S.A. by
Lightning Source, Inc.
1246 Heil Quaker Blvd
La Vergne TN 37086
www.lightningsource.com

Contents

Tied and True
1

Reaper's Reward
97

TIED AND TRUE

Chapter One

"Well, friends, I finally did the unthinkable."

Lindsay Riordan froze behind the coffee station in the main office. The deep voice doing the bragging on the other side of the wall still had the unnerving ability to make her entire body throb. *Jared Hunt.* The new guy with a killer body and a to-die-for face, who continually asked her to dinner, taking her refusals with good-humored grace.

"Yeah, I had a piece of what you've only been dreaming about."

She blinked. That didn't sound like the Jared she knew at all. However, the whistles and derogatory comments that could only belong to the idiot twins Dale Maclearn and Ken Simmons made her head ache. Lindsay had been dodging those two jerks since she'd started with the company. Luckily, they both worked several floors below her in tech services, so she rarely had to put up with them.

Which begged the question, what were they doing up here on a Wednesday morning? And why were they so chummy with Jared Hunt?

"Come on, Hunt," Maclearn murmured. "Tell us what she was like. Those tits, they're real, aren't they?"

"I've got ten that says they're fake," Simmons encouraged.

She frowned. From Maclearn and Simmons she expected such juvenile behavior. Both were in their late twenties, they acted like they were God's gift to women, and they were anything but. Jared, however, seemed the complete opposite. He struck her as more reserved, despite his obvious appeal. The office wunderkind, in the last month he'd brought in two new clients that had the entire sales division abuzz. And if that weren't enough, Hunt possessed the charm, astonishingly good looks, and bearing of an office go-getter. His light green eyes promised heaven in the bedroom to any woman with a pulse.

Glaring down at her thundering chest, Lindsay wished she had some immunity to his appeal. But the best she'd been able to do thus far in his short tenure at Tron Corp was ignore him. Politely, but firmly, she'd declined several of Jared's invitations to dinner, having seen too many office relationships that hadn't worked. Lindsay couldn't say she hadn't been tempted, but now hearing him pal around with the idiot twins, she was glad she'd done her best to steer clear of him.

"Riordan is hell on wheels, I'll say that." Hunt laughed, a deep, throaty chuckle that momentarily distracted her from hearing her name on his lips. "That professional act is all fake."

"I knew it!" Simmons interrupted.

"She gives killer head, and those breasts, they're definitely real. And much more than a handful."

She blinked and lowered her coffee mug to the table. Had Hunt just said what she thought she'd heard?

"You should see what I have at home. You know how they say a picture is worth a thousand words?" Jared chuckled. "How much would a money shot of Riordan be worth?"

"No shit." Simmons whistled. "Jared, you are the man. So, when do we get to see it?"

"We'll see. For now I like keeping that treasure close by my bed, if you know what I mean. Maybe sometime we'll hang out, and I'll bring it with me. But you'll have to buy the beer."

"Come on, man. Have a heart."

"Is she a screamer?" Maclearn wanted to know. He sounded almost out of breath, pubescent excitement no doubt arousing the asshole.

She couldn't make out what Hunt said next since he lowered his voice, but two loud guffaws made her see red.

That creep! That sexist jerk! While she'd been politely rejecting him, he'd been making up stories to impress *those two!* She'd been right all along to be cautious of him.

Lindsay bit her lip. It made no sense for her to feel hurt by his crude comments. And what the hell was a money shot? She'd never been out on a date with him, so it couldn't have been an intimate photo. Unless Hunt had stalked her at home, he had to be making it up.

Debating whether to face him now and most likely scald him with hot coffee, or confront him later, Lindsay waited a minute too long. Nancy Clement, a sales supervisor, joined the men, and the discourse took a swift turn in another direction. Fuming that she'd lost her opportunity, Lindsay resolved to nip this situation in the bud.

Too bad her boss was as useless as, well, a snow shovel in Miami. He, like the rest of Tron Corp, held Hunt in high esteem, and Todd didn't have the fortitude to deal with bullies like Maclearn and Simmons. And frankly, Lindsay had never really considered either creep worth the effort.

But Hunt's blatant lies bothered her more than they should. Maybe it was because she had held a few secret fantasies about him she'd stubbornly refused to let go. Or maybe it irked her that a man who looked so perfect was far from the mark. Regardless, she wouldn't tolerate his behavior.

Sexual harassment has no place in the workplace. She huffed. As if that ideal applied. The last woman to complain about harassment had been transferred out of tech services to the corporate office in Maryland. Great deal for Susie Hutchins—more pay, a major move, a shift, and advancement. But Lindsay liked her job in Augusta. And damn it, she was one of the best logistics officers they had in the company. If anyone should move, it should be Hunt or his buddies.

Clenching her jaw, she listened as the foursome on the other side of the wall dispersed. Lindsay grabbed her mug and returned to her office. Along the way she passed Hunt, who stunned her by pasting a warm smile on his face as he murmured, "Good morning."

She glared, telling him to go to hell with a frosty gaze. He looked puzzled at first. Then his eyes narrowed as he looked past her to the coffee station.

"Lindsay," he began.

She swept past him and firmly closed her door, hoping to lose herself in her work. It usually worked. However, as she sat typing, Lindsay couldn't help reliving old hurts, mostly dealing with past slander and innuendo. The proverbial blue-eyed blonde, Lindsay knew she looked more like a California beach bunny than the *summa cum laude* graduate who'd worked her ass off to put herself through school. In college, her forays through the job market, and now here at Tron Corp...well, unfortunately, people remained the same. There were always at least one or two men who didn't sit well with rejection, and at least a handful of jealous women with catty snipes and hateful glares.

A friendly but aloof attitude provided a measure of self-preservation when dealing with these people, but frankly, Lindsay was tired of constantly having to defend herself. Her looks had nothing to do with her character, and everything to do with her parents. She didn't date much, if at all, kept her nose clean at work, and stayed away from the gossip mill. Why, then, did she continue to find herself in the midst of nasty rumors?

Enough was enough already. After leaving two previous jobs due to her supervisors' inability to accept the word "no," Lindsay refused to be treated like a victim again. She'd been working at Tron Corp for two years now, and everyone knew she kept her business life professional. Bad enough Maclearn and Simmons made crass comments. She thought she'd dealt with them effectively by ignoring them.

But Jared Hunt had gained popularity here in his short tenure. Who the hell was *he* to make up stories about *her?* Stories that people she worked with every day might believe. She could envision her hard-won reputation and career starting to crumble. Lindsay saw red. She refused to leave this job because Hunt couldn't deal with rejection.

"Lindsay," Janice, her assistant and friend, called through the door. "Do you have a minute?"

"Come on in."

Janice closed the door behind her and stood uncomfortably in front of Lindsay's desk. Even dressed conservatively in tan slacks and a pink, short-sleeved sweater, Janice shouted "different" with her tattoos and nose ring. A free spirit, she was a genius when it came to Tron Corp's logistics software and a great friend when the chips were down.

"What's up?"

"I, ah, shoot. There's no easy way to say this. I just heard Ken Simmons talking about you to Dale Maclearn. And what they were saying was X-rated to the extreme." Janice swallowed audibly. "Could there be any truth to the rumor that you and Jared Hunt were caught in a compromising position and captured on film?"

"Not unless I have an evil twin." Lindsay grimaced. "I overheard the idiot twins and Hunt earlier. But I hadn't realized they'd started spreading rumors through the office." *Already.* She fumed.

"Well, I overheard Ken and Dale whispering about it. Jared was nowhere near. So maybe it's just the idiot twins."

Lindsay chewed her lip in thought. "Janice, there's no way Hunt could have a picture of me doing anything like…that. And speaking of 'that,' I have a question for you. Do you know what a 'money shot' is?"

"Huh?"

"I overheard Hunt telling the others he had a picture of me, and it was a money shot."

Janice looked confused, and then blushed scarlet and met Lindsay's eyes in horror. "Good Lord. My old boyfriend used to be really into porn." Janice glanced around, as if anyone outside the office could hear them, and lowered her voice. She leaned closer. "The money shot is when the man, um, ejaculates into the woman's mouth."

Lindsay knocked her coffee to the floor. *"Shit."*

"Yeah. Not a picture you'd want circulated around the office." Janice looked sympathetic.

"You don't understand. I didn't do that, any of it." *Though I'd fantasized about it with Hunt once or twice. Now I'd rather strangle him than swallow him, good looks or not.*

"Then maybe Hunt has a hell of a graphics program. Heck, you can make anything nowadays. My brother Photoshopped his picture next to Pamela Anderson in a *Baywatch* ad as a gag. I guess anything's possible."

Lindsay was horrified. Though she hadn't been in a compromising position with Hunt, she had been a little tipsy at the last company party. What if he'd pieced together some damning photographs out of context? Pasted her alongside him in some embarrassing position? God, just what she didn't need after all she'd done to project a professional image. "I need to get my hands on Hunt's picture."

Janice shook her head. "No, you need to put your hands on his computer. If he has a picture of you, it's probably on his hard drive. And from there...well, it could be in Peru in two seconds with one touch of a button."

Lindsay stared blindly down at the documents on her desk.

"Like I said, Lindsay, sorry to spread the bad news."

"Yeah, thanks, Janice."

Janice paused at the door. "You know, I heard Hunt has a date Friday night with Sara in accounting." Lindsay looked up. "They're going to dinner and a movie. Be gone for hours." Janice smiled innocently. "Just thought you'd want to know."

Lindsay stared after her friend, not quite putting the dots together. Money shot? Home computers? And what was this about Hunt going out on a date?

Her eyes widened when she noticed the memorandum on her desk. George Hower, Tron Corp's CEO, would be making the rounds next week. *Shit.* If he heard a hint of the rumors about her, all her hard work the past few years would be out the window. Hower was a stickler for professionalism and ran a tight ship. She *had* to get her hands on that picture or, at the least, confirm that there wasn't one, and find something to keep Hunt and the idiot twins quiet.

Janice was right. Lindsay had to find out what Hunt had on his computer. Maybe through him, since the idiot twins seemed to hang on his every word, she could blackmail them all into silence. Because lately, when Hunt said "jump," Maclearn and Simmons leaped for the sky.

The more she thought about it, the more she liked the idea. No way would she let Hunt, the new guy, steal her thunder and ruin her in the office. She'd made a place for herself here, and refused to be the one to leave...*again.*

Lindsay was through being nice, tired of always trying to turn the other cheek. No longer would the chauvinist males in her world hold the power. She visualized Jared Hunt in her mind's eye and smiled—an evil grin that would have unnerved him had he seen it. A plan formed, slowly, methodically, as she pledged to be no one's fool ever again.

* * *

Lindsay used the next two days to organize the details of her Friday night mission. As the daughter and sister of three Marines, she knew well how to prepare for battle. She'd sketched out a plan of attack at home following work Wednesday, and with Janice's help, had used Thursday to gather more information from Sara. After a full day's work and a hasty dinner, tonight—Friday night—was go-time.

She knew where Hunt lived, his habits—heck, she'd even peeked at a copy of his recent physical, courtesy of her buddy in the insurance department—and tonight's agenda, thanks to Sara and Hunt's chatty secretary, a woman old enough to be his mother, yet sincerely in lust with him. Lindsay grinned. She had no problem with Ruth dating Hunt, a much younger man, but she doubted Ruth's husband and grandchildren would feel the same.

Chuckling at her odd turn of thought, Lindsay gathered her tools and tucked them into a discreet black backpack. Pulling on a ball cap and tucking her blonde hair underneath as best she could, she resolved to keep to the shadows, grateful for the clouds and waning moon.

Fifteen minutes after leaving her place, she arrived at Hunt's home in an upscale section of town, a modest cottage on the Hill. She parked several houses down and glanced around, noting his black GTO was conspicuously absent.

Breathing a sigh of relief, Lindsay exited her car and locked it. She walked toward his home as if she were expected and tried to remain cool. The moon's ambient light was nearly nonexistent, but she wanted no chance of being noticed. Hopefully, his neighbors were used to seeing women coming and going at all hours of the night. And it was Friday, when normal people with a life were out dating and dancing.

Lindsay frowned at the thought and walked up his drive. How the hell could she expect to have a life when no one treated her seriously? Most men wanted to date her for sex and little else, and in the past, those few she'd been passably interested in had listened to the rumors about her and believed them.

Her anger returned in full force, and she hurried toward Hunt's back door, out of sight of any passersby. Studying the exterior of his home, she noted the lack of motion detectors as well as security signs anywhere along the drive. Sara'd been right. Hunt hadn't had the time to install security yet. Lindsay reached for the knob to the backdoor and was surprised when it turned easily.

"So sure of yourself, hmm? No one would dare steal from the great Jared Hunt," she murmured, her voice heavy with sarcasm.

Letting herself in, Lindsay performed a quick survey of the premises using her handy little Maglite with a red lens. A galley kitchen overlooking a family room connected to a hallway, to which a bathroom and two bedrooms were joined. The décor was masculine but plain.

Ignoring the family room and kitchen, she darted toward the bedrooms, where she'd most likely find something worthy of blackmail.

A man like Hunt would have something he wanted to hide; she could *feel* it. A man who lied to gain admiration from bozos like Maclearn and Simmons had skeletons in his closet. She just needed to find that closet.

Her search showed her a disturbingly organized man. In his bedroom, his dirty clothes actually lay in a hamper, and his shirts and pants hung divided in his closet. His shoes were all carefully grouped together, and his ties were hung to prevent wrinkles. For a moment she wondered if Hunt were perhaps gay.

Lindsay brightened at the thought. He would hate a secret like that exposed. After searching for evidence to corroborate his sexual preference and finding none, she left to search the next room. In the spare bedroom, one he clearly used as a study, she sighed with frustration when she came across a few porn sites on his computer. Porn sites— *money shots,* she thought dryly—but no pictures of her.

The sites emphasized large breasts and man-on-woman action. Good lord, but how did a man expect a normal woman to enjoy sex with her legs thrown over her own shoulders? She peered closer at the screen and froze when the sudden roar of a car sounded.

Chapter Two

Damn it. Lindsay glanced at her watch and noted more time had passed than she'd thought. An hour and a half of searching, and she'd found nothing. And what the hell was he doing home so early? Thankfully, she'd taken pains to leave everything as she'd found it. She gasped. With the exception of his computer. She quickly closed the file and turned off the monitor, then shut off her flashlight and slid behind the bedroom door, praying the darkness held.

She could barely see her hand in front of her face and hoped his night vision was as poor. The cloud cover nonexistent moonlight certainly helped her cause.

Lindsay held her breath as the front door opened. It slammed, and a moment later footsteps sounded in what she thought was the kitchen. Another door opened, and a soda top popped. The refrigerator. Crap. It was nearly midnight. Would Hunt putter around the house? And...oh, shit! Was he alone?

Straining, she thought she made out only one set of footsteps. He tread along the oak wood hallway with a measured stride and to her relief, passed by the spare room alone.

Lindsay exhaled slowly and waited while he moved around in his bedroom. He hummed under his breath, his deep voice making her itch to…well, to do something she'd regret.

For the first time in a long time her libido responded to a man, and said man turned out to be as bad as the idiot twins. Just her luck. Her stretch of celibacy was growing not only tedious, but frustrating as well. Why else would she still hunger for a creep like Hunt when she knew he was no good?

The sound of running water jerked her out of her reverie, and Lindsay decided to make her move. She stepped out from behind the door and cursed under her breath when the shower suddenly stopped. The hall light flicked on and gave the spare room dim illumination. Glancing around in alarm, she raced for the only hiding spot in the room, the slatted closet doors across from the spare room's doorway.

Thankfully, the hinges made no noise, and the only neighbors she had in the roomy closet were a leather jacket and a trench coat that would see little wear here in the South.

Just in time, too. Through the slats she could see the vague outline of a darker shadow in the doorway. Lindsay froze like a deer in the headlights, more than grateful when he headed toward his computer instead of the closet. The desk the computer sat on was perpendicular to the closet, and she faced the side of the monitor. Thankfully, it was a high definition flat screen, so she could see what was on it from her angle. From her vantage, she'd be able to see Jared's profile and the material he viewed. Lindsay shivered, both from nerves and excitement. What the *hell* would she have said if he'd opened the closet door and found her there? *Hi?* Her adrenaline surged, and she wiped her hands together. Perhaps tonight wouldn't be a total waste after all.

He flicked on his desk light and computer monitor, and her mouth dropped open.

Jared Hunt stood before his desk without a stitch of clothing on that beautiful, streamlined frame. Corded muscles clenched and released as he bent low, his delineated abdomen making her mouth go dry. His arms were tight and larger than she'd thought, his biceps making her think he must lift weights, regularly. He turned away slightly, bringing attention to his thighs... Lindsay couldn't breathe. Long and muscular, he looked like a runner or cycler. That ass looked as if it could bounce a quarter.

Jared shifted, and she couldn't blink. Holy hell! Jared Hunt had a penis both long and thick, and he was more than aroused. She should have taken her camera out of her bag and snapped a few digital pics, if for no other reason than to capture the memory of perfection. But she stood transfixed, unable to look away from such male beauty.

He finally sat, legs splayed, as he reached between his thighs and began stroking himself.

She couldn't believe it. A man like Jared Hunt jacked off by himself in the privacy of his house on a Friday night? Apparently, his date with Sara hadn't gone over well. But she knew a dozen women at work who would have taken Jared with open arms. Half as many had candidly propositioned him. So why was he here, now? Lindsay's breathing hitched, and she watched as he clicked through several files with one hand while he continued pleasuring himself with the other.

Despite the strangeness of the situation, she felt an answering need within her. Watching Hunt touch himself excited her, almost unbearably. Her nipples pressed against the cotton of her thin T-shirt, and she felt uncomfortably wet watching his hand sweep over his erection. And, God, what an erection it was. He was so thick. She could only imagine what he'd feel like inside her.

Stop it! Had she forgotten what she was doing here in the first place? And it would be beyond bad if he found her hiding in his closet.

"Lindsay," he murmured, and her gaze shot to the monitor. To her amazement, his hand increased its movement over his penis, rubbing faster as he stared at images of—*her.* She leaned closer to the closet door, amazed at the pictures on his computer screen.

Lindsay in a plum-colored cocktail dress she'd worn a month ago to a company function. Another picture of her in office casual, a slim skirt and matching top. Another shot of her coming out of the bank. *The bank.*

She could only stare, not only amazed, but confused. Hunt had made up lies about her at work, and he was apparently spying on her. She should have been completely turned off, not to mention scared. But she wasn't. Hunt, the man who'd figured prominently in her fantasies since she'd first laid eyes on him, fantasized about *her.*

To her dismay, his desire spiked hers.

I must be freaking nuts.

Needing to leave his place before Hunt found her, Lindsay held her breath and prayed for him to finish quickly. She felt flushed and tried to look away as he pumped into his hand, but his obvious enjoyment turned her on, incredibly so. And like a Peeping Tom, she watched in horrified fascination as he came, groaning her name.

He cleaned himself with a towel she hadn't seen before. That's Jared—always prepared, she thought peevishly, excited and frustrated because of *him*. Dammit. This whole mess was his fault in the first place.

Scowling, Lindsay saw him sigh and stand. He stared at the monitor as he shut it off. Rolling his neck, he stretched before turning off the desk light, apparently relaxed enough to leave the room and go to sleep—she hoped.

After what felt like half an hour had passed with no further movement, Lindsay snuck out of the closet and glanced at the dark monitor. After tonight, she knew she had to return. She needed to download what she'd found and dig deeper into his computer. If he had just plain, ordinary pictures of her, odds were he might have a doctored photo or two as well.

That he had any photos of her at all was, well, just a little too unsettling for her peace of mind.

After checking the hallway, she left the room and walked quickly toward the back exit. Just as she reached the tiled kitchen floor, a battering ram knocked into her back, taking her down.

Grunting, Lindsay rolled instinctively. The lifelong lessons of self-defense drilled into her courtesy of her father and brothers kicked in, and she had her assailant clutching his groin and gagging in seconds.

"Fuck you," Hunt whispered, groaning as he tried to roll to his feet. He slipped on a loose dishtowel on the floor and fell hard, hitting his head on the cold tile. When he made no more sudden moves, Lindsay carefully reached toward him, her heart pounding so hard it threatened to leap from her chest.

"Hell," she muttered, completely unnerved. Hunt was out of it. No blood that she could see, but then maybe he was bleeding inside his brain. The lack of lighting was a real problem, but even more so was the fact he might really be hurt.

Making a snap decision, Lindsay reached down and gently felt his head for possible injury. She was no doctor, but aside from the lump on his head, and his subsequent unconsciousness, he seemed to suffer from no further injuries. Pleased when he moaned and began reaching for her, she grabbed his hands. "Come on, let's get you to the bedroom," she murmured, pulling with all her might. *Thank you, Dad, for the weightlifting lessons.*

With what little help Jared provided, she dragged him down the hallway into his bedroom. He groaned twice, and she knew she had to act quickly. Relieved he was regaining consciousness, she nevertheless was running out of luck in dealing with her "attacker."

Urging him to help her, Lindsay managed to get him flat on his back on the bed. She found the secure ties she'd brought with her—just in case—and zipped his wrists and ankles to the head- and footboard, careful not to make them too tight that they'd cut off his circulation. Naked, spread-eagle, and helpless on his bed, Jared Hunt lay vulnerable before her.

Mentally, she added assault to the breaking-and-entering charge sure to come her way.

Dammit, she needed a minute to think... After this stunt, he'd no doubt up his security. She highly doubted she'd be able to sneak back into his place without the cops waiting for her. Glaring down at him, she realized she couldn't, in good conscience, leave him here alone. And when he woke up, then what? She'd be toast.

Lindsay scowled, refusing to end up the victim in Hunt's petty little battle. Despite her hostility, her eyes roved over his delectably naked body with a will of their own. So, he liked looking at her, hmm? Enough to relieve his sexual frustration, apparently. Maybe she could use that to her advantage.

I'm over the edge. This is absolutely insane. I should leave before it's too late.

But the sight of Hunt naked, and thoughts of him besting her again, pushed Lindsay into a choice she had a bad feeling she'd regret later.

Fuming at the mess *he'd* made of this, she refused to consider civilized rules anymore. Oh, she'd make sure he recovered from his head injury, but after that, he was going to do some apologizing. Lindsay reached for a thick bandana from her backpack and rolled it into a length of blindfold, then stowed the bag next to the bed.

His apology had better be one heck of an "I'm sorry." Because if she didn't like it—and she had a feeling she wouldn't—he was in for a real treat.

* * *

Jared groaned. His head felt like it was splitting in two, and the annoying voice that refused to let him sleep through the night was two seconds away from a fist in the mouth.

"Oh, good, you're awake."

He frowned, the voice eluding him. It was gruff yet husky, but the throbbing in his temple made it hard to focus on anything. And there was the fact he couldn't see. "What the hell is over my eyes?"

He blinked beneath a blindfold of some sort, and when he tried to remove it, found he couldn't move his hands. Or his feet.

"You're going to be just fine, Hunt." The voice was taunting, and he swore it sounded…odd. He inhaled, but the subtle fragrance in the air eluded him.

Gritting his teeth, he tugged again at his wrists. *Shit.* Had Maclearn or Simmons learned something he hadn't anticipated?

"Now, now, you don't want to chafe that pretty skin. It's tight enough that you're not going to escape without a knife. And the one in your nightstand is right here."

Jared sucked in his breath when he felt something sharp and cool dragged over his stomach.

"Don't worry, Hunt. I'm not going to hurt you…much."

That voice. His head swam, and he unwillingly flinched when a hand lifted his head off his pillow.

"Take this."

He refused to open his mouth and heard a sigh.

"It's Motrin from your bathroom cabinet. Eight hundred milligrams has been working for you all night. I'm not planning on killing you now, hotshot."

So he hadn't imagined someone caring for him for several hours. He began to calm down as his brain processed what he knew. Swallowing the pill and an accompanying mouthful of water, Jared smelled a hint of lemon and lavender soap from the person aiding him. The voice was husky but feminine. Add to that the soft, somewhat small hand on his neck, and...

Oh, hell. Lindsay Riordan. It had to be. But what the *hell* was she doing in his house? And why was he tied to his bed? The last thing he remembered was drifting to sleep when a feeling of wrongness hit him. Listening to his instincts, he'd found a dark shape prowling in his kitchen and attacked.

Pain, the likes of which he never wanted to experience again, followed by a blow to the head. Then...this.

"Why am I tied up?" he asked, after she slowly set his head back on the pillow. For a woman bent on harming him, she was acting decidedly gentle about it.

"Let's just say I have a few things on my mind we need to discuss if you want to see the light of day again."

She kept her voice on the low side, and the blindfold told him she didn't want to be recognized. Realizing it was her, and not whom he'd at first suspected, Jared allowed himself to fully relax. He'd play her game, for a while, until he found out what he needed to know. He'd always imagined having her the other way around—with her tied up, naked, and under him—but it intrigued him to see what she would do.

As the silence thickened, a sudden thought hit him.

"I'm naked, aren't I?" Nothing. "And you were here since last night?" He felt himself flush but could do nothing about it. Damn. That meant the odd feeling he'd had in his study had been on the money. He would just bet she'd seen his "performance" and had a ton of questions as to why he'd been beating off to pictures of *her*.

This had to be the most embarrassing moment of his life. But he'd be damned if he'd let her see that. He was actually thankful the blindfold was in place.

"You have interesting taste in porn, I'll say that," she said after a moment, her voice amused.

Of all the instances he'd imagined when confronting Lindsay Riordan, this had never entered his mind.

The first time he'd seen her, his first day of work at Tron Corp, he'd fallen in immediate lust. But ever the consummate professional, he'd ignored his desire and focused on his job. After several weeks had passed and he'd earned the same rejections she'd given everyone else, he'd turned to the rumor mill. Funny thing, that. Gossip had turned his investigation in a completely new direction.

A hand trailed up his thigh, and he sucked in his breath, stunned. Wearing the blindfold enhanced his other senses, and her hand felt like a satin whip that beat at his need. His cock hardened in an instant, and he wondered what she thought about him.

"Well, well. Apparently last night didn't get it out of your system after all." He heard what sounded like a snick, and alarm replaced his desire.

"Shit. Tell me that's not a camera."

"It's not a camera."

She was lying. He knew it. She *had* overheard him with Maclearn and Simmons on Wednesday. He'd tried to talk to her about it, but she'd refused to speak to him. Considering she usually put him off, Jared had hoped she'd just been angry for some other reason not related to his talk with "the boys." But if she'd heard him, she was no doubt pissed as hell. Maybe he'd do better to tell her the truth and let her...

"Ah," he moaned, arching into the fist that now held his cock with ecstatic tightness.

"I believe you like this. At least, you did last night."

Incredibly, she began priming him, pumping his cock with her small fingers. He couldn't help moving with her, aroused beyond measure that Lindsay Riordan had her hand around his shaft and was stroking him to oblivion.

"More," he couldn't help saying. "Harder."

She complied, and he lost all reason.

"You like a firm hand, don't you?" He moaned and thrust up, and she stopped. "Don't you?"

"Yes," he gasped, grateful when she started again. Hell, she was setting him on fire. He felt so hard he wanted to burst. Fluid leaked from his tip, making her hand slide over his shaft with wonderful friction. Her touch was like nothing Jared had ever felt before and being tied up and helpless while being pleasured was a huge turn-on he would never have expected.

"You want to come, don't you?"

"Yes."

"Your balls are tight, your cock impossibly hard. Like steel, velvet steel," Lindsay murmured, and he could hear the arousal in her voice.

She pumped him harder, making him pant.

"Yeah, baby, make me come," he urged, thrusting into her hand. He was so hard, so wet and ready. God, he needed it. He was so close...

She stopped.

"Don't worry, stud. We'll get back to that real soon. I've got a few things to do in the meantime." She chuckled. "Don't go anywhere."

Chapter Three

Lindsay leaned her head back against the wall outside Jared's bedroom, grinning at the curses pouring from his mouth. Oddly enough, he said nothing directed at her in particular. Just foul worlds describing his immense frustration.

She squirmed, so wet she felt as if she'd come herself. Lindsay fanned herself and closed her eyes. Jared Hunt was an Adonis, and touching him had been an exercise in pleasure. But watching him reach toward fulfillment, seeing his muscles strain for relief, had been as much an act of erotic art as having sex with him would have been.

"Yeah, right," she mumbled. She'd wanted nothing more than to strip naked and sink over that rock-hard erection. Between her contraceptive NuvaRing and the glimpse she'd had at his medical form at work showing him to be as clean as a whistle, she had no fears of any sexual repercussions. And hell, she'd been in a dry spell for what felt like forever. She wanted an orgasm so badly she could taste it. But that might mean giving Hunt pleasure, something she didn't intend to do for some time. If at all.

Lindsay pulled away from the wall and smiled. Though physically tired from the strain of his attack—her hip was bruised—and the adrenaline rush from breaking into his home and fighting with the big guy, she felt more alive than she had in years. She could only thank her lucky stars she'd nailed him in the groin last night, or he would have mopped the floor with her.

Having studied him sprawled out on the bed, she couldn't help but dwell on his perfect build. Six-feet-four inches of prime male flesh and not an ounce of fat on him, which explained the difficulty involved in dragging him to his bedroom last night. She'd never have landed him on the bed without his help.

But once again prior planning had saved the day. Bringing those secure ties had been genius. One never knew when they'd come in handy, as her older brothers were fond of saying. Of course, she highly doubted Derrick and Andy had intended for their little sister to use them on a naked man in his own house.

"Hey, out there!" Hunt shouted.

She frowned. Maybe she should gag him. She didn't want the neighbors getting curious. Entering the room, she couldn't help staring at him.

"Yes?"

"I have to go to the bathroom."

She smiled. In the wee hours of the night she'd thought about that. "Okay. I'm going to cut two of your ties, which should allow you to roll onto your side. Then you can hold this bucket and go."

He sputtered, and she chuckled, masking her laughter with a cough. If he hadn't guessed her identity by now, he wouldn't as long as she kept talking to a minimum and in a deep voice.

"I'm not pissing while you watch."

She snorted. "You masturbated while I watched. What's the difference?"

The color rose high on his cheeks, and she wanted to run her fingers over his whiskered jaw. What damned fine genes.

Jared clenched his jaw tight. "I said—"

"Relax, *Mary,*" she drawled the common taunt her brothers used on one another. "I have no desire to watch you. I'll cut two of your restraints. Just yell for me when you're done. But I'm not coming in unless your blindfold is on and you lay back on the bed, hands and legs apart."

He grimaced and after a minute nodded. "Can I at least have some clothes?"

"No." Shoot. Her voice sounded a lot huskier than she liked. She was going for a disguised sound, not an aroused one.

Hunt said nothing, waiting.

She carefully cut his left ankle and wrist restraints, leaving the bucket on the bed within reach. "You have two minutes."

Leaving the room, she knew he'd take off the blindfold to see what he might learn about her. Fortunately, she'd taken pains to remain anonymous. Using blankets, she'd darkened the room to a heavy shade. She could still see him under the muted light of the bathroom, which she'd left on for him to see by, but when she returned she'd turn it off again. And once he was safely tied again and blindfolded, Lindsay would remove the blankets. *The better to see you, my dear.* She laughed.

Lindsay entered the bedroom after several minutes and noted his stiff posture on the bed. The small bucket she'd found under his kitchen sink sat on the nightstand.

She dumped the bucket in the bathroom and then paused. This would be the tricky part.

"Put your blindfold back on. And not one move, genius, or I hit the "send" key on your computer, sharing your wonderfully naked and bound image to everyone in your mailbox."

He put the cloth back over his eyes and remained motionless, tense, but she could see her bluff worked like a charm. And was she ever glad for those restraints. Quickly grabbing two more secure ties from her bag, she refastened his wrist and ankle, conscious not to hurt him by making the restraints too tight, and grabbed a nearby chair to sit on. Stripping off her ball cap, she ran her hands through her hair.

"Now what, Lindsay?" he asked quietly.

She froze, and then shrugged with a sigh. With a man as intelligent as Hunt, the odds were he would have figured it out sooner or later. She dropped her disguised voice but refused to remove his blindfold. His lack of sight gave her an odd sense of power, and she planned on keeping him under her control.

"Who's Lindsay?" she teased. "I'm just a helpful neighbor who was passing by."

He snorted. "Give me a break. I know what this is about. And I tried apologizing to you the other day—"

"I don't know what you're talking about."

He sighed, his throat so tempting, so strong. "I need to tell you something, Lindsay. I'm not who—"

She interrupted him by leaning in to nip at his throat. He tasted salty, so essentially male. She lingered over his pulse, sucking hard enough to leave a mark.

"Oh, shit," he groaned and arched toward her. "You're going to torture me over those stupid remarks, aren't you?"

She grinned. If he only knew. She was so sick of always being good, and always getting the brunt of everything. Breaking the rules, not to mention the law, felt so very, very satisfying. And she was far from done. "'Stupid remarks'? Why don't you remind me about what you said?"

"Come on, Lindsay. I was just trying to win Maclearn and Simmons to my side. And I'm sorry to say, you're one hot topic of conversation with those two assholes."

His tone gave her pause. But seeing him at her mercy made her doubt his sincerity. Were their positions reversed, she might say anything for a shot at freedom.

"What did you tell them, Jared?" she fairly purred. As he recounted Wednesday's conversation with the idiot twins, she left to grab a washcloth, bar of soap, and small pan of water from the bathroom and returned to his side. "So you think my breasts are real, hmm?"

She ran a soapy washcloth over his erection, satisfied when it grew stiffer, and he groaned under her touch. She cleaned him thoroughly, all over, wanting him perfect for her play.

After several minutes, his raspy breathing broke the silence. "What are you going to do?"

She stared at him, pleased at his telling response. The man really did want her. Despite his stalker-like tendencies, the thought of Jared Hunt wanting *her* made her feel warm inside. Vanity be damned. She planned on taking something from *him* this time. A bit of pleasure, just for her.

Lindsay leaned close to his mouth and watched him lick his lips. Stifling a groan, she breathed into his mouth, "I'm going to take...a shower."

Jared sucked in a breath. His balls ached, he wanted to come so bad. And she decided to take time out for a shower? *Fuck. Payback was more than a bitch.* Groaning at the cruel punishment he knew *Jared Hunt* deserved, he wished he'd decided to confront Lindsay about the odd happenings at Tron Corp when it first appeared she was innocent of any wrongdoing.

He lay still, taking deep breaths as he tried to ignore her lingering perfume. No longer there, yet just the scent of her made it impossible for him to relax. Hell, he felt as if he'd taken ten helpings of Viagra. If he could just get one hand free he could ease his suffering...

Sighing, he eased on the wrist restraints and concentrated on the mess at work—namely Simmons and Maclearn—two shitheads certain to take his mind off sex. Doing his best to ignore the shower and the gloriously naked woman in it, Jared brought the technology specialists to mind.

Both men were in their late twenties, typical metrosexuals who believed well-groomed cuticles and overpriced suits would get them laid, provided a woman was stupid enough to overlook their massive egos and pathetic social lives. In Jared's opinion, any guy who had to brag about sex wasn't getting any. And Simmons and Maclearn were hands-down the unluckiest bastards he'd ever met.

Of course, there was that vibe he kept feeling that the two meant more to each other than they let on. Which put a whole new twist on why they seemed so pissed off about Lindsay's constant rejections. He rubbed his throbbing head against the pillow, glad the ache had dulled. But thinking about the puzzle of Maclearn and Simmons brought on an all new headache he didn't want just now.

Jared's venture into Augusta, Georgia, was more a favor than a regular job. H&R Security had a solid reputation and was growing by leaps and bounds, thanks to his and his partner, Ethan Reaper's, many successes. Ethan was currently on another case for the government—top priority with H&R. But Ethan's cousin had married Tron Corp's CEO, George Hower, three years ago, which explained why Jared had turned a celebrity protection detail over to one of his best men and taken this task on himself.

He yanked at his wrist and swore. What should have been an easy assignment had turned out anything but. Contrary leads kept turning up everywhere he looked. At first, Jared had been convinced someone in the Tech department was responsible for leaking vital contract bid information. Then he'd found evidence to implicate a twenty-year Tron veteran in Yields and Assessments. That hadn't panned out. But then he'd hit pay dirt.

Lindsay Riordan, the beautiful ice queen who reigned supreme over all things logistical, had a trail of dirty money. Her savings account had suddenly skyrocketed. He'd found confidential documents she had no business possessing on her computer and in her office. And during his not-exactly-legal venture into her home a few weeks ago, Jared had found an unopened envelope detailing information exchanged with one of Tron Corp's biggest competitors.

So why did he now believe in her innocence? His body heated as he recalled the tasty blouses that hugged her breasts, the knee-length skirts that showcased her ass, and the waterfall of blonde hair she always wore pulled up in a twist that made him want to see it unbound and hanging over her shoulders—her preferably naked shoulders.

Shaking his head, Jared knew her innocence had nothing to do with his fierce attraction, thank God, and everything to do with his instincts. The evidence surrounding Lindsay's guilt was too pat, too easy. It was almost insulting that whoever was framing her kept shoving clues in his face. Lindsay had always struck Jared as intelligent, so why would she leave such incriminating evidence showing her guilt *in plain sight?*

Simply put, she wouldn't. And the fact that someone wanted her implicated sent up warning signals. His last two leads had been confusing and almost too obvious, as if the guilty party needed practice in how to point out someone culpable of traitorous intent. The more Jared pondered the matter, the more he looked to the technology specialists. Most of the evidence had been electronically doctored, so who better to compile the information than the experts so familiar with the company?

And Maclearn and Simmons weren't exactly being subtle. They talked about Lindsay constantly, their immature lust grating and growing more annoying daily. Everything Jared had done prior to Wednesday's crude conversation to bring the two dickheads into his confidence had failed. Lindsay had been the key that turned them.

Now the assholes thought he was "the man" because he'd supposedly bagged their sexual fantasy. Not that he necessarily disagreed with their choice of desire. Shit. His cock stiffened again, and when he heard the shower stop, it grew harder.

Lindsay Riordan was any man's wet dream come to life. And he should know. He'd had enough of them since meeting her two months ago. Tall, leggy, blonde Lindsay possessed clear, sky-blue eyes, sexy, pouty lips, and breasts that made his mouth water. The fact that she possessed intelligence and a sense of humor to go along with her physical assets was incredible, including the fact she was still single. After learning about her many rejections, and the fact she'd turned *him* down, Jared had wondered if she might be gay. A woman didn't look like Lindsay and not have at least one man on the side.

He still had a hard time figuring her out. She was *normally* very nice, pleasant to everyone, even the creeps who kept coming on to her at work—not including himself in the creeps category, of course—and she followed the rules to the letter, making her supposed decision to turn traitor to the company baffling. Even before the recent hefty deposits into her savings account she'd been financially well-off.

"Missed me, did you?" her sultry voice interrupted his musings.

"I don't get you. I would never have pegged you as a woman to do this." He jerked his hands and feet.

She chuckled. "There's a lot about me you don't know, Jared Hunt." The bed dipped, and he caught his breath. "For instance, did you know how angry I was hearing you lie about me to those jerks, Maclearn and Simmons?"

"Lindsay, I have to tell you why—"

"And did you know I planned this whole thing out? Down to every detail," she murmured. Jared could feel heat alongside him, and barely contained a primitive growl at the erotic sensation of having her body so near. Then she rubbed her skin against his, and he groaned when he realized she was naked, too.

"That's right, Jared. I'm not wearing a stitch of clothing."

Sweat popped out over his brow. He knew she was still pissed at him and was deliberately making him suffer. Already he burned to fuck her. Soft hands trailed over his thighs, up his cock, and rested on his abdomen.

"What do you want?" he groaned. "I'll apologize. I'm sorry. Very, very sorry. If you'd just let me explain," he rasped, as she took him in her hands and began stroking the underside of his shaft.

"Why, Jared? Why would you be here on a Friday night when you could be out screwing any woman you want? You have to know how attractive you are. Why would you sit alone at a computer, looking at pictures of me as you come over your hands?"

Her words were killing him, making him shudder at the need overtaking reason.

"God, Lindsay. You know I want you. Stop torturing me, and let me go. I swear I'll make things right."

"Yes, you will." She leaned closer to whisper in his ear. "I'm tired of the lies, of the rumors." Her breasts touched his chest, and he leaned into her, brushing against her taut nipples. "So you're going to apologize, and you're going to mean it."

He nodded. "Whatever you want, Lindsay." She began rubbing herself over him, her nipples scoring his chest with heat, her thigh grazing his cock, sliding in the fluid that leaked from his tip. Then Lindsay opened her legs and sat astride one thigh, riding him and coating his leg with moisture.

"Shit," he growled. "Lindsay, baby, I promise I'll explain everything to those assholes at work. I'll tell everyone I lied. Just please, stop this, and take me inside you." Jared couldn't believe he was begging, but she had him so hot, so lost to truly *feel* her.

"I have a better idea," she purred. Crawling over him, Lindsay straddled his neck so that her scent, the sultry essence of woman and sex, drew him close. "Make *me* come. You owe me," she breathed.

"Oh, yeah," he sighed, nuzzling her curls as he reached for her sweet pussy with his lips. "I'll make you come, Lindsay. I'll make you scream."

He nestled between her folds, spreading her with his tongue as he coated his mouth with her essence. God, she was so hot, so wet. And her aggressiveness only spiked his already aroused state. Needing to taste her, Jared greedily nuzzled her flesh, searching and finding her clit easily.

"Oh, ah," she groaned, pressing into his mouth.

He was in heaven.

Her clit was full, near to bursting as he eagerly lapped and sucked on the swollen nub. Jared drank in her aroused cries as hungrily as he devoured her cream. Harder he stroked, trying to penetrate her with his tongue, but he couldn't get as deep as he wanted at this angle.

As if reading his mind, she shifted, and he drew her clit deep, nipping and pressing until she writhed over him like a woman in the throes of orgasm.

"Jared, more." She rode his mouth, her clit impossibly tight. "Please, Jared, more."

He grinned and complied, edging his teeth over her flesh and swallowing the gush of honey that jetted from her pussy. Fuck, but he wanted inside her as she spasmed, wanted to feel her body clasping his as she came.

"Jared," she cried and shook, coming over his lips, exploding like a nova, as he lapped up every drop.

On and on she shuddered, her grip on the bed's headboard rapping the wood against the wall. Moments later, Lindsay eased up from him, making him miss the sultry evidence of her passion.

"Oh, Jared," she breathed in his ear. "That was incredible."

He trembled from the effort not to thrust into *something*. Christ, but the sweet taste of her made him harder than stone. He'd been close to coming just from that alone. But he had to admit even this torturous frustration had been more than worth it.

"You're still aching, aren't you?" she whispered, kissing her way down his face to his lips. "Mmm, I taste me on your mouth." She sighed and deepened the kiss, making him crazy.

Her mouth pulled and pushed, teasing and dragging on his tongue until he was sure he would come, and without any more help from her.

"Jared, baby, you deserve a reward," she promised. And as her mouth moved steadily south down his body, desperation threatened to break his silence about how close to the end he was. One touch of her mouth and he'd erupt.

But his conscience suddenly demanded he warn her. *Stupid principles.* "No, Lindsay," he said thickly. "If you put your mouth anywhere near my cock, I'm going to come. I'm so close as it is..."

Her breath whispered past his chest down his navel, until he could feel the heat from her mouth over his shaft. "I know."

She took him inside her mouth so suddenly he swore, and then she sucked him so hard he saw stars. Unable to stop himself, he thrust once, twice, and then came powerfully, shaking with his release. The act was liberating, but the image in his mind, of her taking him deep in her throat, prolonged his orgasm.

He continued to pulse, filling her luscious mouth with his cum. He was in what felt like a frozen arch, his shaft still firm even as she milked him dry. She lifted her mouth off him in a slow, shivery movement.

"You taste good, Jared. Like warm, sticky candy."

He groaned, clutching hard at the bedrail. "Lindsay," he uttered in a hoarse voice, still not recovered from her heavenly touch. "I can't... That was..."

"I can tell. But that's only the beginning. I think you owe me more than one climax, don't you?" He heard the grin in her voice, knew she'd want more, and thanked Ethan a million times over for the opportunity to help Tron Corp.

"Yeah, baby. I figure I owe you plenty more," he growled.

Chapter Four

Lindsay stared at him, licking her lips as she studied his naked body. She'd shifted the heavy curtains over his windows and could now see the hard body lying calmly beside her.

Resting her gaze on his penis, she had to admit to being impressed. Seeing him last night had been erotic, but she'd never considered going down on *him*. Taking her to heaven should have been its own reward, but she hadn't counted on hungering for him. Taking him in her mouth, swallowing him, had been emotionally intimate, binding her to him in a way she hadn't expected. Of course, his fantastic tongue and skillful mouth didn't hurt any.

Desire for more had hit her hard, amazing considering how intensely her climax hit her. Gazing at his lips, Lindsay ran a finger over the full, red flesh and shivered as she recalled the bliss he'd taken her to so unselfishly, so completely. And he'd been turned on by it, she knew, as evidenced by how hard he'd been. The few forays she'd had into oral sex had been nowhere near as mind-blowing as her experience with Jared.

Touching his cock made her hot, but tasting him had rekindled her fire. Knowing she made him that hard was as much an aphrodisiac as taking him in her mouth. Mmm, just thinking about sucking him made her squirm.

Hell, she desired him again, but she wanted more than his mouth. Should she take him inside her? Ride him? The thought teased her imagination, but she found she needed more than a captive body beneath her. Yet, what if she let him go, and he turned on her?

As if reading her mind, Jared smiled and suggested, "Why don't you release my ankles? Or my wrists? If you're worried about me being pissed, don't be. I feel boneless right now. The only thing I want to do is taste you all over again."

His shaft stirred, and she stared at it with hunger.

"Come on, Lindsay. At least remove the blindfold."

She hesitated, suddenly unsure. It was one thing to hold the power, to have done the incredible and tied up a dominant man like Jared to use for her pleasure. But to have him see her, to know he watched her helpless desire, would put her in a position of vulnerability she didn't feel comfortable showing him. Sure they'd had sex, but it had been at her whim. *Just a game,* she reminded herself. The fact that she had to work so hard to convince herself to keep things light worried her. It made no sense, but there it was.

"I don't think so," she said slowly.

Before the sex, Jared had been a weakness. Now, he was more, an intimate part of her she felt surprisingly loath to let go. And how stupid was that? One stint of sex and she was seeing happily ever after? She knew better than that and blamed her unruly hormones, ignoring the clamor of her heart that said differently.

If she hadn't been so confused, and so damned hungry for his body, Lindsay would have demanded an explanation for his behavior Wednesday. But oddly enough, she realized she didn't want to know. She liked this Jared much better than the lying braggart. And it made her pause to reconcile the many similarities between this guy and the salesman everyone at work continually praised, the man she thought she'd known.

She shook her head. Reality was an ugly heartbeat away. Now, however, for the first time in her life, she indulged in a fantasy, one that had her tying up her lover and driving him insane with lust.

This Lindsay Riordan didn't step aside when she'd been wronged, and she loved the sense of strength pouring through her veins.

Smiling, she felt so pleased with herself she ignored the small sense of disquiet that she'd forgotten something important.

* * *

Needing time to clear her mind, Lindsay distanced herself from the temptation tied up in the bedroom and fixed herself and Jared some lunch. She had yet to put on any clothes, liking the hedonism of being naked in his house, and in front of him, no less. That he knew she flaunted herself gave her a sense of command that pleased as much as it aroused.

Humming under her breath, she finished the sandwiches and grabbed two sodas, balancing everything carefully as she returned to the bedroom. Along the way she noticed what had bothered her last night during her brief surveillance.

Jared's home looked comfortable but not lived in. His walls were bare. No family pictures decorated the space, and even the furniture seemed too neutral, as if it had come with the house. And maybe it had. She shrugged and continued to the bedroom. Though Jared was a marketing genius at work, he didn't necessarily have to be a domestic perfectionist as well.

Entering the room, she noted his calm, even breathing. Disappointed, she nevertheless knew he needed the rest. He'd had a rough go last night, not to mention the subsequent bondage and sexual frustration she'd put him through today.

"Poor guy." Lindsay smirked and left his food on the nightstand. She nibbled hungrily at hers, studying him and wondering exactly what it was about him that had heated her blood from the first minute she'd laid eyes on him.

Okay, so he had height. She was a sucker for tall men, being close to five-eleven herself. And he had muscle. Dear Lord, he had muscle. A broad chest tapered into a lean waist. Taut abs, thick arms, and ropy forearms complemented his strong thighs and toned calves. The man could have modeled for *Muscle and Fitness,* and she couldn't stop staring as she ate.

All her life Lindsay had been told she was pretty, but she had never understood precisely why men found her fascinating. She had blonde hair and blue eyes, big deal. So did a million other women, women more attractive than her. And so what that she'd been cursed with large breasts? Nowadays, anyone could fit into a C-cup with the right doctor. Good genes were responsible for her trim frame— that and her fair share of maintenance aerobics.

Yet since puberty, boys, then men, refused to leave her alone. To her consternation, she'd felt little attraction for the opposite sex. Maybe it was the false praise, the inability to trust another to see past the surface into the woman within. Looking at Jared brought her issues into perspective. Lindsay had seen more attractive men, but Jared packed an unmistakable wallop that made him nearly irresistible to anyone in a skirt. And she wondered if he knew of his hold on women—on her—or if he felt as unsure as she did. After all, if Jared had been that vain about his looks, he sure as hell wouldn't have been pleasuring *himself* when he could have been enjoying any one of the available women from work.

She felt overly warm and drank her soda. The memory of him staring at her image on the computer when he'd touched himself kept resurfacing in her mind. He'd been so beautiful reaching climax, so incredibly hot while staring at pictures of *her.*

Lindsay squirmed. She wanted him again, as if she hadn't experienced an earth-shattering orgasm a short while ago. The small niggle of guilt that crept up when she stared too hard at his restraints left her. A small grin graced Lindsay's lips. This whole mess was his fault, in a twisted kind of way, and this was her fantasy, damn it, her right to extract a bit of revenge for being treated like an object. She might be taking sexual advantage, but he'd found as much pleasure, if not more, at her hands—or rather—Lindsay licked her lips, her mouth.

She grinned wider, pleased with her rationalizations. Jared was hers for another thirty-six hours, and she intended to use that time to her satisfaction. She walked to his side and knelt close, placing her lips on the pulse at his neck. She kissed him slowly, sucking and teasing, until she felt an increase in the flutter of his heartbeat.

Inhaling the subtle scent that was Jared, the raw blanket of sex that clung to him like a second skin, she continued over his neck to his chest, focusing on his nipples that, as she licked, tightened into small knots. She kissed him, laving the taut flesh until he awakened, groaning her name, arching into her touch. His muscles rippled as he fought the restraints, but he didn't argue, merely urged her for more with his body.

Gratified she could so enhance his desire, Lindsay whispered all the things she wanted to do to him as she reached down and stroked his turgid erection. His breathing increased until he was panting, pressing hard into her palm.

"You're so hot, Jared," she said, nipping his earlobe and making him beg for more. "So thick." Her hand slid over him easily, rubbing his silken flesh.

"I need to move, to touch you," he groaned. "Please, Lindsay. Cut me free."

Glancing at his feet, she decided to meet him halfway. Cutting the bonds off his ankles, she tossed his knife to the floor. "That's as free as you're going to get for a while. Now ease back and relax," she said, her voice throaty. She wanted to taste him again. Moving down his body, Lindsay breathed over his penis and made him writhe.

Taking him fully, she began sliding him in and out of her mouth, stroking with her tongue and raking her teeth ever so lightly under his crown. He shouted and pushed deeper, making her groan. She felt as desperate as Jared acted and decided to fix their problem with undue haste.

Releasing him, Lindsay straddled his groin and waited, sliding over his arousal without allowing penetration, her body completely wet and needy. "I'm going to ride you, baby. Long and hard," she promised, taking the tip of him inside her. "And you're going to come inside me."

"Lindsay," he groaned, his voice harsh. "Fucking do it!"

She rocked, taking him inside, little by little. Helpless to do more than thrust as high as he could, Jared trembled, ordering, asking, and then pleading with her to take all of him. Sensing he'd reached the end of his endurance and perilously close to coming herself, Lindsay sank over him. Up and down she pressed, slamming onto him and grinding her clit into his pelvis.

"So good," she breathed, as she quickened her pace, noting his encouraging motions, his jerking hips and clenched buttocks. "Oh, Jared."

She needed... So close to the edge... Reaching down, Lindsay rubbed her clit and swore she felt him swell inside her. Coming, she cried out and clenched him tightly, dimly aware of his shout as she continued to ride him.

Finally stilling, she stared at him through half-closed eyes. His nipples were tight, and his chest flexed as he panted, as if he'd just run a marathon.

"Shit, Lindsay," he rasped. "You're going to give me a heart attack." Jared groaned, and she smiled. "Now, please, take these things off." He shook his hands. "I need to touch you."

"Not a chance. I'm having too much fun with you at my mercy. Come on, Jared, admit you've thought about being tied up and seduced."

"Actually, I have. But in my fantasies, I'm the one doing the tying, and you're helpless under me," he rumbled. "I'm not going to ask you again, Lindsay."

Something in his tone made her sober, and she glanced at his ties with alarm. Seeing them intact, she relaxed and kissed him firmly on the lips. Feeling him inside her, she squeezed him tighter and warned, "Don't ask again. My answer is still no. You'll be freed before Monday so you can go back to work. And our time will be over." She paused, not wanting to, but needing to make sure he understood.

If only she knew which Jared she clung to, the hard-working man she respected or the mouthy rumor mill trying to impress his juvenile associates. Recalling too easily his chatter with the idiot twins, she frowned. "Jared, don't even think about mentioning this time together to anyone. I'll not only deny it, but everyone at work will get a glimpse of the great Jared Hunt naked and stiff as the day is long."

He stilled, his body tense, but he said nothing. She squelched the small measure of guilt for threatening him after the pleasure they'd just shared, but *he'd* been the one chatting it up with Maclearn and Simmons. He'd been the one who insinuated that he had a naughty picture of *her.*

"Just so we understand each other. Now, lie back and relax." Petting his chest, she relaxed when he took a deep breath and settled into the bed. Yawning, Lindsay eased off him and moved next to him. "Just give me an hour or so, and I'll show you a few things that will set your hair on fire."

Chuckling, she snuggled closer to his heat and threw an arm around his chest. Lindsay hugged him tight, wishing he was as perfect as he felt inside her. She sighed. Would that he were.

The minute Lindsay's breathing evened into sleep, Jared tugged his hands free from the restraints he'd been working loose for the past hour, ripped off his blindfold, and carefully substituted a pillow in place of his body for her to hug. He eased out of the bed, stifling a groan at the pain in his stiff arms. Working the blood flow back into them, Jared flexed and released his muscles as he stared, for the first time, at Lindsay Riordan in the flesh.

His mouth dried as his gaze caressed her the way he soon planned to, with hands that itched for erotic revenge. In retrospect, it was probably a good thing he'd been blindfolded. Had he seen her like that, those full lips, rosy breasts, and long, sleek thighs, he'd no doubt have broken out of his bonds earlier. As it was, it had been all he could do to remain in her control, succumbing to her teasing. Her sexual torture had made him desperate while she'd ridden him.

Christ, he'd never come so hard before, or for so long. He couldn't believe she made him so crazy. But looking at her, he could readily imagine their next time. And what a next time it would be.

His eyes narrowed as he traipsed carefully out of the bedroom and down the hall to the second bathroom. After seeing to his needs and taking a quick shower, Jared cleared his bedroom of the stale sandwich and returned to the kitchen, suddenly ravenous. He grabbed a bite to eat and made a few phone calls. He should have checked in with Ethan last night, so he hoped his buddy wouldn't think anything was amiss by his silence.

As luck would have it, Ethan had been too busy on his current project to bother with him. A call to their secretary assured Jared he hadn't missed much, and he returned what messages he could before leaving his office behind, far behind, in his new list of priorities.

Returning to his bedroom, he saw Lindsay was still curled around his pillow. She murmured his name and hugged it tighter, causing his heart to stutter.

What the hell was that?

He felt a moment's panic that he'd fallen in way over his head on what had started out as a small job. Hell, the woman didn't even know his true reason for being here. Or his real name.

Jared's toe nudged something cold on the floor, and he felt a measure of relief, his attention thankfully distracted by the small knife and black backpack sitting near the bed. After several moments spent perusing the pack's contents, he smiled a slow, satisfied grin as he withdrew four more secure ties. Noting the time, he decided to give her a few hours of uninterrupted sleep before awakening her to a "new day," with newer rules.

He'd hoped she would release him, that she'd allow him to show her he could be trusted. But no, not his Lindsay.

His Lindsay. Mulling the words, he found to his surprise that he liked the sound of them.

His Lindsay was a stubborn sex goddess with little room in her heart for forgiveness, apparently. She'd taken him to heaven but refused to let him stay there. Damn, but the images she'd stoked in his brain as he'd wondered what she'd do next had nearly killed him.

But now...Jared gave a wicked smile. Now Lindsay would have plenty of time to regret her actions. And he'd make her listen to the truth if he had to gag her. His cock stiffened, and he rubbed the well-used member, amazed he was still so hungry for the stubborn woman. As long as he'd come, as perfect as it had felt to be inside her, Jared wanted her yet again, right now, but had to content himself with waiting.

No matter, he told himself, and sat down in a chair to study her while he killed time. Jared tapped the secure ties against his knee. Soon he would have Lindsay at his mercy. He hadn't been lying earlier when he'd admitted his fantasy of tying her up. And now that she was nearly in it, he wondered how many times he could make her come while she sighed his name. He studied the contented look on her sleeping face, affection tugging his heart. How was he going to prove to her that Monday was just another day, but their relationship... Oh, hell. Why not be honest with himself? Their *relationship* had progressed to a whole new level, one she would soon be powerless to refuse.

Chapter Five

Lindsay woke on her back with her arms stretched above her head. It took her a moment to regain her bearings, and when she did, she panicked.

"Shit."

"Shit is right." Jared Hunt towered over her, his jutting penis stiff and eager, his lips curled with humor, and his eyes glowing with satisfaction. "I told you I wasn't going to ask again."

"Jared," she cajoled, as she twisted her wrists, only to find them tied with her own equipment. Damn. That had been sloppy of her. She *knew* she should have tied him tighter, but she'd been determined not to cause him any undue pain. *Idiot.* "You know you deserved a bit of harmless payback for what you said about me to Frick and Frack at the office. Admit it."

"I do," he said easily, rubbing his flesh as he stared down at her.

Look away, please. Unable to break eye contact, she was completely ensnared by his hungry gaze. Blindfolded, he'd been more a fantasy than a person, just as he'd made her out to be in his discussion with Maclearn and Simmons. But now she couldn't help seeing the real him. Her heart hammered with more than worry at his nearness. She was deeply in lust, and scarily growing more and more drawn to the handsome devil, despite her inner plea to remember his callous words.

Damn her conscience. It refused to shut up. *But everyone at the office really likes him. And he never had one bad word to say about anyone until you overheard him on Wednesday. He even took your rejections in stride.* Lindsay's heart beat faster.

"Do you know what I was thinking about when I was touching myself last night?" he asked, his voice throaty.

Lindsay licked her lips and cleared her throat before she could answer. "Wh-what?"

"I was thinking how gratifying it would be to come inside your slick heat. About how hard I could push into your wet pussy, how long I could make you come around me."

Lindsay bit her lip to hold back a groan. Why did he have to be so sexy and so damned hot when he talked frankly like that? Her attention settled on the large hand covering his shaft, and she had an unquenchable urge to swallow him again.

"That's right, baby. You want this in your mouth, don't you?"

She said nothing, a little embarrassed to be so obvious. And she knew she and Jared had gone far beyond "embarrassed" hours ago.

"Tell me, Lindsay. Tell me you want to suck my cock, to swallow my cum. All of it."

She shifted in sexual frustration, feeling deliciously wet and strangely uninhibited under his gaze. "I want you, Jared." She stared into his light green eyes. "I want to feel you shudder when you come, to taste you as you slide down my throat, so creamy and sweet."

He increased the friction on his penis, and she wondered if he meant to mark her with his cum. The thought aroused her further.

"I'm going to do to you what you've been doing to me since I met you," he answered silkily, showing another side to the charming, affable Jared Hunt. This man seemed dangerous, controlling, and he thrilled her to the quick. "But first I need a measure of control, one you're going to provide."

He knelt on the bed, moving up her body to straddle her neck, his cock imposing and large before her. "Lick me," he growled. "Suck my balls, my cock. Make me want to fuck that pretty mouth until I come."

Lindsay was on fire. She'd always wanted to try being dominated, not the heavy stuff, but a little play like this. Now she couldn't believe what she'd been missing. She felt so aroused. His mere words and nearness made her want to come. Had he felt the same, when she'd had him tied up and at her mercy?

Staring up at his lust-glazed expression, Lindsay opened her mouth and stroked him with her tongue. He moved with her, and she shivered at the touch of his balls on her cheek and began licking and sucking the velvety sac with a generosity that made him moan out loud. Jared tilted his pelvis and put the tip of himself in her mouth, as if waiting to see what she would do.

She smiled, then sobered as she stared at his beautiful shaft. Licking her lips, she opened wider. He pushed forward, cursing when she began urging him deeper. Clutching the headboard with an iron grip, Jared began thrusting inside her mouth, slowly but surely, his girth growing until she had no thought for anything other than his shaft.

Thick, hot flesh filled her, made her breathless with desire. She tasted salty sweetness and knew his climax neared.

"Fuck, Lindsay. You're so good." He groaned, pumping faster. "I'm coming."

He shot into her mouth, and she greedily swallowed him, squirming on the bed for the release she desperately needed. Watching him come was a heady stimulant, and one that stoked her desire to feel the same, free of any constraint.

"Don't worry, baby." Jared withdrew and lay over her, blanketing her with his body. His penis was still semi-hard, moisture beading at the tip as he rubbed it over her middle. "I'm going to give you exactly what you've given me. Pleasure until you want to die from it."

He smiled then, his expression one that made her nervous. "Now, now," he teased and lightly grazed his chest against her breasts. Sparks of pleasure feathered throughout her body. "We have plenty of time to make love, Lindsay. The question is, how soon after I put my mouth on you will you come? And how many ways can I take you before you finally stop being so stubborn and listen to what I have to say?"

Three orgasms later, Lindsay still couldn't catch her breath. With his hands and mouth, Jared had taken her to heaven again and again. But he refused to put himself inside her. Frustration at the lack of joining made her climaxes pleasurable, but not quite enough. She needed his complete penetration for full satisfaction.

"Lindsay, honey, I have never seen anything more beautiful than you in climax," Jared murmured, as he pressed kisses along her neck. "You are so open, so incredibly sexy. And you taste so good."

She blushed, amazed she could feel self-conscious after the things he'd done to her—and she to him. His quiet question surprised her.

"Why did you turn me down so many times before?"

"Office romances never last. And they make work an awkward place to be."

When he spoke again, his words were casual, but she could feel him tense beside her. "So you had an office romance that went bad? Some guy broke your heart?"

"No." She saw Jared's jaw relax and frowned. "Why should you care?"

"It matters," he said thickly, running his hands through her hair. His large, blunt fingers stroked with a gentleness that soothed, making her want to curl into him, and she closed her eyes, relaxed. "So why aren't you in a relationship now? It's not like any guy with half a brain is going to turn you down."

She frowned, opening her eyes to see his light green ones full of curiosity. "Who says I'm not in a relationship now?" At his knowing look, she huffed. "Oh, that's right. You've been stalking me. Obviously, you know I don't date."

"But why not?" He looked baffled. "You're smart, you're funny, and you're obviously gorgeous."

Lindsay stared, her mouth dry. Good lord. Yesterday she'd wanted to brain him. A bit of flattery, and she melted. He thought she was smart and *funny?* "You think so?"

He nodded.

"Most men don't see past the blonde hair and breasts," she said wryly.

"You forgot the baby-blue eyes."

She narrowed her gaze. "When I get free from here—"

"I'm just teasing." He chuckled. "But I can't complain about having you at my mercy. Christ, this is a dream come true. A naked Lindsay Riordan tied up in my bed." He shook his head. "Are you sure I'm not dreaming?"

"Untie me, and I'll pinch you."

"Ha, ha. I'll untie you when you let me apologize for the other day."

She stared at him, aware the intimacy between them had strengthened, and it was more than just sex. Warmed, yet still wary of where this might take her, Lindsay nodded.

"You have to promise to keep this secret, just between us. I'm trusting you with vital information that could hurt Tron Corp if it becomes known in the company."

She frowned. "I promise. Tell me already."

"My name isn't really Jared Hunt."

That, she hadn't been expecting.

At her silence, he continued. "It's Zachary Jared Hunter, a mouthful, I know. I co-own a security firm in Seattle. H&R Security."

"I don't understand."

"The head honchos at Tron Corp suspect a traitor in their midst. Someone within the company has been leaking bid information to its competitors. And with this new government bid on the table, we, H&R, were called in to stop the leak, *quietly.*"

"You're kidding me."

"I wish I was. But I have to admit I'm glad Tron Corp's having problems. If I hadn't taken this assignment, I never would have met you." Jared trailed his fingers over her neck to her breasts, teasing the nipples into taut peaks. "Baby, you have no idea how happy I was to put you in the clear."

"What?"

He sighed at the obvious shock in her gaze. "I had to assume everyone at Tron Corp, with the exception of the CEO, was a suspect. After a month, I had mostly narrowed down the field of potential traitors to a dozen. And then some surprising leads turned up."

"Leads?" Lindsay had a bad feeling she knew where he was headed.

"Two suspects didn't stand up under further investigation, and I found myself pointed in your direction, despite my desire to see you innocent. Someone at Tron Corp is setting you up to take a huge fall, Lindsay. And unless I can find out who that is, you're going to be in some serious trouble."

"This is insane." Lindsay flexed her arms and glared at her restraints. "Do you think I can lose these now?"

He shook his head. "I'm not crazy. Until I explain this, I'm not letting you free to knee me." Jared winced. "Or do anything else detrimental to my health. Sorry, baby, but you're going to lie there and listen to what I have to say." His eyes were hard, his jaw clenched, and he looked every inch a dangerous man—one that made her heart race.

Sighing, she tried to ignore the fact they were naked as they discussed her future. Could her life get any more bizarre? "Go on."

He relaxed and had the nerve to smirk. "I knew you'd see it my way. I followed the trail set for me and found you to be a very sloppy criminal, a trait completely at odds with the woman I've come to know. You're too smart to leave a paper trail, or an electronic one, for that matter, in your office."

"What are you talking about?"

"And the mail in your home was blatantly planted."

"What mail?"

"The evidence addressed to you from Marker National, a hefty payoff for bid information on Project Runway for Uncle Sam."

"Please tell me this is a joke."

"I wish I could. I have the letter in my briefcase under the bed, if you want to see it. Bottom line, I began to grow suspicious at your apparent laziness. I couldn't see any personal vendetta against Tron Corp, which meant your motive had to be financial. Yet from what I saw in your bank accounts, you don't need the money."

"No, I don't." Lindsay struggled with her wrists, incredibly angered at the thought of someone besmirching her good name. What? It wasn't enough to label her the office "blonde" anymore, now she had to be a corporate spy and thief?

"Fifty thousand hit your savings account a week ago."

The blood drained from her head, and she stilled. "Fifty thousand?"

Jared nodded and stroked her tense abdomen. "And the collective evidence against you is pretty damning."

"Then why haven't you done something about it before now?" Was he possibly toying with her? But how could he be after today, when he could have treated her much, much harsher instead of gifting her with mindless pleasure?

"I told you, Lindsay. I believe in your innocence, and I don't like being made a fool of any more than you do." His tight lips and dark scowl told her he meant what he said. And despite the situation, joy took root, the knowledge that he believed in her liberating.

"So, do you have any idea where to look for these traitors?"

"Remember my obnoxious conversation on Wednesday?" He shook his head with disgust. "Maclearn and Simmons don't like you much. Or I should say, they're pissed you won't give them the time of day. Of course, the minute you do they'd be all over you. Simmons gets a hard-on anytime he mentions your name."

"That's gross."

"Tell me about it." Jared caressed her skin. His callused hands and the friction of his palms circling her abdomen made her shiver. "The thought of either one of them seeing you like this makes me want to break every bone in their pathetic bodies."

She sucked in her breath as his fingers threaded through the tight curls of her sex. "So you were lying to trick them into your confidence?"

He stared at her through hooded eyes and toyed with her cleft, his fingers sliding through her wet arousal and grazing her clit. "I was telling them what I've imagined for two months. Since that first meeting at Tron Corp when I was introduced to your section, I've dreamed of sliding deep within you. For weeks I've come in my hand, surrounded by memories and pictures of you."

His fingers parted her nether lips and plunged into her tight sheath, making her moan and arch into his touch. "I want you all the time. And this is one particular fantasy I'm obsessed with, the one where I have you tied up and at my mercy." His voice roughened, and he began thrusting his fingers faster, harder. "In my fantasy, I control all of you. I suck your breasts, your pussy, and lick your clit until you want to scream. And when you're helpless and begging me to finish, I fuck you hard, repeatedly, coming inside you until there's no more you and me, only us."

She groaned and thrashed her head, desperately seeking relief from his too-skilled digits. "Jared, please."

"Not yet." He slowed his fingers and leaned over her breast, taking one nipple in his mouth. The heat and pull of his mouth set her on fire. Tugging at her nipple, he sucked until she wanted to beg for mercy. He then turned his attention to her other breast and treated it to the same erotic torture.

"Oh, my God."

"You are so wet," he rasped, slowing the glide of his fingers in and out of her, teasing the sensitive nub between her legs. "And your tits are so big, so perfect." He sucked one, then the other, laving her breasts with sensual, almost painful attention. She felt so sensitive, so needy, and yet her pleasure hovered just out of reach.

"I need—"

"Beg me." He thrust violently against her leg, his shaft hot and thick. "Tell me how much you want me. Tell me you'll do anything I want." His voice shook and deepened, and she could tell he was as caught in his fantasy as she was.

"Please, Jared," she gasped. "I'll do anything you want. Just fuck me." Lindsay saw his eyes go dark with desire.

He kissed her with so much passion she couldn't think. Leaning into her, he placed himself at her wet entrance but waited while he teased her with his tongue, engaging in brutally pleasurable thrusts to her mouth that mimicked what his body would soon be doing.

"I need you so much," she managed, before he gave her what she craved.

Jared sank to the hilt inside her, making her clench him tight as he began pounding. She cried out at the exquisite sensations, her nerves taut as he increased his pace.

"Oh, yeah, baby, take me deep," he groaned and pushed harder. Pistoning his hips, he gave no quarter as he promised her ecstasy. "Your pussy is so good, so tight. Ah, Lindsay, I want to feel you come around me. Fuck, this is so right."

He didn't stop his rocking, and soon ripples of pleasure shook her as he seemed to thicken even more. Filled with

Jared, with his essential maleness, she felt feminine, desired and needed.

"I'm going to come, Lindsay." He stared down into her eyes. "And you're coming with me."

He shifted his angle of penetration so that his pelvis rocked her clit.

"Jared."

"Fucking you is sheer heaven." He took her harder and groaned. "And you're so hot and wet. Come, Lindsay, with me."

She was helpless to deny his and her body's needs and shook at the force of her orgasm. Moaning his name, she clenched him tight and heard his hoarse shout. Astonishingly, her orgasm multiplied, and her bliss flowed as if forever, until she felt as if she'd died and gone to heaven.

Jared shook over her, his body fully planted within hers.

"Hell, Lindsay. That was better than anything I could have imagined." He wiped his forehead and leaned weakly over her. "I don't have the energy to think beyond 'wow.'"

Lindsay laughed, a throaty sound that was all she could manage. "Me neither."

Chuckling, he lowered himself to lean on his elbows. "I know I have to cut you loose, but give me a minute to revel in my macho fantasy. After all, you had your time with my helpless little body."

"Jared, as I'm sure you know, there's nothing little about you."

"Ah, a woman after my own heart. One who can't lie."

She rolled her eyes but didn't have the energy to tease him. All seemed right with the world, and she wished, for just a moment, this day would never end.

"We have a long way to go, Lindsay." Jared stared, his expression inscrutable. "And don't think a little thing like Monday is going to stop *us*. I have an investigation to solve, one now circling around you." The hope inside her shriveled, but before it could die, he added, "And I'm not through with you yet, not by a long shot.

"You, Lindsay Riordan, are mine."

Chapter Six

Breakfast, then lunch, came and went Sunday, and Jared sat with Lindsay on the couch. Relaxed, they watched a movie like a normal couple.

She'd brought in a stash of clothes and shower gear she said she normally kept inside her car for gym workouts. And now some of her toiletries sat next to his in the bathroom, looking like they belonged there. The contentment inside him continued to grow, as did the warm feeling in his heart when she leaned closer to him.

Never in his life had he been as happy as he now was with Lindsay, and he could only pray things between them deepened. A woman like Lindsay didn't do casual sex, and despite the fact she'd explained she was on birth control, he surprised himself by realizing he didn't care if she got pregnant. His entire adult, sexual life, he'd been a stickler for protection; he was not an irresponsible man by any means. Yet with Lindsay, all thoughts but those about her faded in importance. Hell, he almost wanted a child with her so they'd be tied together forever...

Wanted a child? Jared froze at the thought, forcing himself to smile and nod at the movie when she glanced at him. Kids? He wasn't ready for kids yet, was he? Though his mother constantly prodded her oldest child to marry and reproduce, he'd always thought of himself as too young. But hell, he'd reached his thirty-fourth birthday last month.

Jared glanced at Lindsay and wondered what their kids would be like. No doubt beautiful, with her light hair and bright blue eyes, intelligent, and introspective. Or maybe they'd be dark-haired, like him? A blond boy with his green eyes. A dark-haired girl with her mother's baby-blue gaze.

Fantasies began to build around a life in Seattle, two kids, a blonde bombshell for a wife, a successful career, maybe a dog...

"Hello? Earth to Jared?" Lindsay frowned. "Or should I call you Zachary?"

He made a face. "It's Jared. Only my mother calls me Zachary, and that's when she's ticked at something I did."

Lindsay grinned, a full-mouthed smile that made his heart flip. "You know a lot about me, but I know nothing about you. Tell me about yourself."

"What do you want to know?"

"Don't be deliberately dense, *Zachary.* Tell me about your family, your job. No girlfriends, I take it?" she asked lightly, though he heard an underlying vulnerability.

"Lindsay, how can you ask me that after yesterday? Dumb question," he said bluntly, frowning. "I'm a single, *unattached* thirty-four-year-old with a mother, father, and three sisters—all three of whom spell 'trouble' with a capital 'T'—on the West Coast."

"So you live where?"

"Currently in Seattle, where Ethan, my partner, and I base our business, though I'm originally from Spokane. Ethan and I met in the Marine Corps and have known each other for years."

"Marine Corps?" Lindsay's eyes grew wide, and he recalled, from the files he'd read on her, that her father and brothers had all served. Pleased they had that in common, he nodded with pride.

"I was Force Recon and left the Corps after ten years." If only he could have stayed a naïve young corporal forever... But with promotion came the distasteful political posturing, and he was old school. In Jared's opinion, getting the job done was more important than kissing some officer's ass. Unfortunately, he and his last commanding officer hadn't seen eye to eye. "Don't get me wrong, I'll always love the Corps, but I needed to get out when I did."

She nodded, her eyes bright as she watched him, and stroked his arm gently.

Damn, but that felt good.

"So you and Ethan decided to open a business yourselves?"

"Actually, Ethan had gotten out a few years before me and worked for a security firm for a while. He knew he could do a better job, so when I left the Corps he brought the idea to me. We both invested money and time, and before we knew it, we had a working, successful firm. Of course, neither of us suffer fools or bullsh—ah, BS, so we take what clients we want and refer the others."

"And Tron Corp? How did two guys from the West Coast get interested in a logistics firm on the East Coast?" She bit her lip in thought.

Jared could almost see the wheels in her mind turning, and his cock swelled. Smart and sexy, a killer combination. He silently groaned and shifted next to her.

"Not that Tron Corp isn't great," she continued, "but it's just one of many logistics firms, and we're not that big."

"Ethan's cousin married your CEO a few years back. This is more a favor than a true business venture."

"Ah." She toyed with the neckline of his T-shirt, and his body reacted. Every nerve in his cock jumped to attention. "So it's for your friend's family that you're trying to help Tron Corp."

"Yeah." His voice sounded gritty, but damn it, she made him hard with very little effort. How did she do it? He'd been trying not to think about sex and just be with her, to enjoy their time together. But his body didn't want to forget hers—not when he'd just found her, so to speak.

"You're a very loyal man, aren't you, Jared?"

Her hand trailed lightly over his chest, ran over his sensitive nipples, and down the thin, soft cotton of his T-shirt to his belly. Christ, but she was killing him. Trying hard to be good was never so...*hard.*

"I try to be."

"And you say you're going to help me, because you believe in me."

"I do." He swallowed and couldn't help staring at her breasts straining against her thin, cotton shirt. She wore it over a pair of panties. That she hadn't donned a bra made him a very, very happy man.

"Then I should be able to tell you something in confidence and know you'd never share it with anyone aside from us."

He frowned. This sounded serious, but her constant petting distracted him. "Lindsay?"

She leaned up on her knees to whisper in his ear. "I've spent the last half hour staring at the television, wondering why anyone would want to frame me. And the entire time, visions of you naked kept interfering. The way your body tenses right before you come. I love the way you taste, Jared."

Her hand fell to his lap and unsnapped his jeans. Working her fingers under the denim, she clasped his cock and stroked him.

His eyes crossed, and he leaned back against the couch, grateful when she finally unzipped him, giving her better access.

"I should be too tired to make love with you again." She licked her lips, as though unsure of herself, an odd contradiction considering she had her hand wrapped around his shaft. "But I can't stop wanting you. And you're so big, so hard," she marveled, making him even harder.

"You little tease," he growled, utterly aroused. After a few moments tolerating her petting, he knew he couldn't take much more before he exploded.

Pinning her to the couch, he kissed her, licking at her lips and tongue until she gave him what he wanted. Angling a hand between them, he ran his fingers under the large shirt she wore and delved into her panties. Sweet, slick need covered his fingers as he stroked her clit.

Moaning, Lindsay reached for him, but he shook his head.

"On the floor, on your hands and knees."

Excitement flared in her eyes as she quickly positioned herself. Not taking the time to undress, Jared quickly joined her and stripped her underwear from her legs. Pushing his jeans off his hips, he lifted the shirt she wore to bare her ass, palming the soft, white flesh.

"Lindsay, baby," he groaned, fixated on her pale cheeks. "You are so hot."

Nudging her knees apart, he fitted himself between her legs and positioned his cock at her folds. Pressing slowly, he held her hips and watched with satisfaction as she pushed back, urging him deeper.

"That's it, take all of me." He rubbed her ass as he thrust further, wanting to take her in ways that would most likely shock her. "I want you, Lindsay," he rasped, loving the feel of possession that consumed him as he took her from behind.

"Jared, more."

She rubbed against him, and he pulled out, only to thrust harder into her.

"Oh, yeah." He squeezed her ass cheeks, groaning at the tight feel of her pussy gripping him. Over and over he pounded, as if to mark her as his own. Lust consumed him as he noted how wet she was, how much she wanted him.

"Jared," she groaned, arching back. "Harder."

He gave her what she wanted, dimly aware of a sudden banging at the door. But he was on fire, unable to stop, and even as he heard the knob twisting, he plunged deep and came, filling her as she milked him dry.

Sated but aware she had yet to come, he reached around for her clit.

"Jared, someone's at the door," she whispered, pressing back against his fingers.

"They can wait." He had locked the doors and closed all the drapes this morning, wanting his privacy with Lindsay before the real world intruded. "Now be very quiet when you come, or they'll know what we're doing."

Still bent over, she held him inside her, and his touch on her clit made her walls clench him tight. Shuddering, he withdrew, pleased at the semen running down her legs. He loved that he was all over her—in her womb, on her skin.

Turning her onto her back, Jared lifted the hem of her shirt to expose her groin. Her golden curls were wet with her desire and his, and he found the sight unbearably arousing.

"Come for me, baby," he murmured and eased her folds apart with his fingers. He loved looking at her, loved seeing her this way, naked and vulnerable *to him.* Playing with her clit, he increased the pressure of his strokes, loving the way she gasped his name.

She moaned quietly, gripping at the carpet as if to hold on before she flew apart.

Unable to resist, Jared lowered his mouth to her sweet pussy and thrust two fingers deep, covering her clit while he pumped her vagina. She tasted so sexy, so right. And the thought of taking her ass, as he'd wanted to do earlier, stirred him. He continued thrusting his fingers and sucking at her taut flesh. And when he added just the tip of his pinky to her tight little anus, she flew apart. Screaming his name, she came hard, coating his tongue with cum.

Lapping it up, he continued to pump, shoving his pinky in further until she begged him to stop.

"Oh, God, oh, Jared. Stop, I—" She drew a deep breath. "Too sensitive. But—oh, my God!"

He grinned, thrilled with her response. Hell, he wanted to fuck her again. His cock was actually beginning to get sore from so much use, yet he still wanted her.

The banging on the door came again, this time followed by a voice.

"Hunt? You in there? Sounds like some real good pussy being had." Maclearn's muffled chuckle froze Jared and Lindsay at once.

"Shit! Lindsay, go back to my bedroom and wait until I can get rid of him, and probably Simmons, too. Don't come out no matter what you hear," Jared urged quietly.

She looked nervous. "But Jared—"

"No buts. Maclearn and Simmons are assholes, and there's no way I'll let them drag you into their twisted games, let alone see you like this." *Not to mention they could be dangerous.* Where Maclearn went, Simmons was sure to follow. They'd never before visited him at home, and he wondered what had brought them here today.

She glanced down at herself and blushed.

"Yeah," he whispered with satisfaction, "that's me all over you."

As they stood, she couldn't help staring at his erection. "Better cover that up, or the idiot twins might think that's for them."

"Very funny. The thought they might be gay crossed my mind, but they're too much into women for that. Not to mention what they told me they want to do to you."

"You never know." She gave him a cryptic look before clutching her panties and hurrying into his bedroom.

Wondering what she knew that he didn't, Jared grimaced and tucked himself back into his jeans. Looking around him, he saw nothing to indicate Lindsay's presence. Unfortunately, it smelled of sex in the room, something he would have found arousing but for the arrival of Maclearn and Simmons.

Taking a deep breath, Jared strode to the door and opened it. Sure enough, Dale Maclearn and Ken Simmons stood waiting, trying to stare over him to see who might be behind him.

"Damn, Hunt. I heard a woman screaming your name. Guess you weren't lying about Riordan, hmm?" Maclearn chuckled and shoved past him into the living room. "Oh, yeah, definitely smells like pussy to me."

Simmons joined him, and Jared closed the door behind them with a sigh. So much for the real world not intruding until Monday.

Turning to the idiot twins—he loved that name—Jared shrugged. "Who said it was Riordan?"

Maclearn and Simmons looked at each other, and then back at him.

"No shit?" Simmons glanced casually around him. His mean brown eyes settled on Jared, and Jared felt a small tingle of discomfort. Something about the man seemed off. "So who were you banging if not her?"

Maclearn looked puzzled by his friend's less-than-friendly behavior, but when he opened his mouth, Simmons shook his head. Surprised by the apparent role reversal, Jared stared at the two, realizing there was more to Simmons than he'd first thought.

Ken Simmons had a slight build. Obviously no weightlifter, the twenty-nine-year-old had a wiry toughness to him that only added to the incongruity of his geeky, yet arrogant, persona. From his initial meeting with the two, Jared had seen Dale Maclearn take charge time and time again, yet if Jared were honest with himself, he'd always felt something not quite right between Maclearn and Simmons. Something in their relationship felt odd, a small detail in the way they looked at each other, despite their seeming fascination with the opposite sex, and with Lindsay in particular.

"You never know," Lindsay had said about the idiot twins' sexuality. As he stared at them, Jared suddenly realized he'd missed a vital clue to understanding Ken Simmons, and his unease grew as he sensed he'd greatly underestimated the pair. Whether gay, straight, or bisexual, Ken Simmons was the leader, not the follower he'd appeared to be.

"Who was I banging?" Jared repeated, deliberately looking confused. "What does it matter? One woman's as good as the next, right?"

Maclearn grinned, his mouth tight and his watery blue eyes...nervous?

Simmons merely stared. "Women are all the same, to a degree." He shifted and stepped closer to Jared, who forced himself to remain at ease. Simmons eyeballed Jared up and down, disturbingly resting his gaze on Jared's crotch. "You said you wanted to hang out with us sometime. Well, sometime is now. Why don't you go find the bitch you've got stashed in your quaint little home? I bet she'd love to play with us." Simmons sneered and grabbed his own dick, taking Jared aback at the total about-face in his personality.

Jared's instincts told him Simmons had discovered his real identity and the reason why he'd been sent to Tron Corp. Always before the quiet, seemingly submissive one in the Maclearn-Simmons pairing, Simmons now projected an arrogant challenge.

Suddenly, Maclearn shifted, and his jacket opened. And Jared glimpsed the handle of a small pistol.

The stakes had just been raised.

The idiot twins apparently knew all about him. And the one person they wanted most out of the way was in his back room.

Lindsay.

Chapter Seven

Lindsay stood with her ear pressed to the door. She could hear the three talking and wished Jared hadn't insisted she remain holed up in his bedroom. After spending so much time with him and learning about him, she had decided to hell with the rumors at work. Lindsay *wanted* to be linked to Jared, and who better to spread the gossip than Dale Maclearn and Ken Simmons?

Maybe finally getting even with Jared had pushed that ' sense of empowerment always lacking in her before. But she no longer intended to play the "victim." She'd previously left two jobs she really liked in order to avoid confrontation and an unpleasant work environment. But she refused to leave this job. More importantly, she refused to leave Jared alone to deal with a problem she should have fixed long ago.

Simmons and Maclearn were assholes. Plain and simple. Yet, they were also the men Jared believed behind the scheme to send her to jail. And all because they couldn't have her? That didn't make sense. She'd never before told anyone this, but she'd once caught Simmons and Maclearn in a liplock at work. Though she knew the two men would have sex with her in a heartbeat, they also seemed to have no problems satisfying each other—and at work, no less.

Lindsay still had a hard time visualizing Maclearn and Simmons in a passionate embrace, and she frowned away the image. *That* she had not needed to remember. Lindsay had been surprised, however, that even after she'd caught them kissing, Maclearn and Simmons had continued to pursue her. Lindsay was grateful they didn't know she'd seen them together. She could only imagine how obnoxious, and even threatening, they might have become.

She couldn't have cared less if they were gay or even bi. But to "real men" like Maclearn and Simmons, apparently being labeled anything other than heterosexual was a bad thing.

"Bring her in here so she can watch the show." Simmons's loud voice dripped with menace.

Lindsay grew worried. He didn't sound right, and Jared was out there alone. Granted, physically he could probably take on both Maclearn and Simmons, but men like the idiot twins didn't play fair. And if they really were leaking information on government bids, they might be dangerous.

"What show?" Jared asked after a moment.

Damn, she wished she could see their expressions. Oh, to hell with this. Surely she could ride to his rescue. After all, she'd broken into Jared's home, tied him to his bed, and had her way with him. Just thinking about what she'd done made Lindsay grin. She wasn't about to let the idiot twins screw up her perfect weekend.

Besides, Jared had bragged to them about sleeping with her, so it wouldn't be out of place for her to be in his house, let alone his bedroom.

Going braless and showing a bit of leg wouldn't hurt for a distraction, but she drew the line at more than that. After a quick cleanup in the bathroom, she threw on her underwear. Flushing the toilet, as if that was the explanation for her delay in showing up, she sauntered out of the bedroom and down the hall.

She pasted a stunned expression on her face as she met Jared and his "friends" in the living room. "Jared? I didn't realize you and the id—ah, Maclearn and Simmons, were friends."

To her relief, both Simmons and Maclearn looked completely surprised. Simmons couldn't stop staring, his eyes flickering from her breasts to her bare legs.

Maclearn whistled. "The mother lode." He angled for a closer look.

Jared gave her a brief glare, one that told her he was more than irritated that she'd ignored his instructions. Lindsay watched her lover change, ever so subtly, as he crossed to her.

"I told you... " he murmured and kissed her hard on the mouth, reaching up to cup her right breast. Not understanding why he would do such a thing after he'd told her he wouldn't parade her in front of them, Lindsay struggled to be free.

Jared laughed and squeezed her harder, and then pushed her from him with a disgusted look on his face. "You're good, Lindsay. But a fuck isn't worth the hassle. Get dressed, and get out. I've things to do with my friends, and you're in the way."

Stumbling to find her balance, she tried to reason out his cold words as Maclearn moved to steady her. His jacket opened slightly, and she saw the handle of what looked like a pistol tucked in the side of his trousers. *Oh, shit.*

Her nerves gathered as she and Jared stared at one another; she understood what he was trying to do. Summoning some fake tears, Lindsay let them fall, adding to the dramatic scene he'd created. She needed to get out of there and summon help. Her defense moves worked well when taking an unarmed person unaware. But against someone with a gun?

Jared watched her with a scowl. A sudden pounding in her heart told her what she'd refused to acknowledge for some time. She simply couldn't imagine Jared getting hurt, even killed. Not when she'd just found him. Anger rose to the surface as she stared at Maclearn, then Simmons. A plan formed.

Sighing heavily, she let Maclearn hold more of her weight and leaned into him, pressing her breasts against his chest. Fluttering her eyelashes, she dropped a few more tears.

"Don't cry, Lindsay." He wiped clumsily at her cheeks.

"Please don't tell me you're falling for the helpless-female routine." Jared crossed brawny arms over his chest, his eyes frosty.

Maclearn glared, suddenly "Mr. Supportive" as he hugged Lindsay. She could feel his erection prodding her thigh. Lust made a wonderful weapon, almost as good as a gun. "Shut up, Hunt. You don't want her? Fine. She's through with you anyway, aren't you, honey?"

Lindsay blinked and nodded, curling closer him.

Simmons, however, stared at her suspiciously. "Funny, but for a woman who never gave us the time of day, she's awfully chummy with you now, Dale." He took a step in her direction, his gaze shifting from her drawn face to Jared's bored expression.

"Maybe that's because you've always been so rude to me at work." She saw Maclearn watching Simmons, waiting for some word on what to do. Lindsay pursed her lips as she stared at Simmons, realizing who was truly in charge of the situation. Maclearn might have the gun, but Simmons called the shots.

"Rude?" Simmons looked surprised. "I've been honest, a lot more than you've been, you and your prick boyfriend." He nodded at Jared.

"I don't know what you're talking about. I've tried to be nice, but you're always leering, always saying things." Lindsay bit her lip, noting Maclearn's breathing beginning to rasp as he pressed harder against her thigh. *Ignore the disgust.* "At least Dale is gentleman enough to see what a creep Jared turned out to be."

"A creep, hmm? Is that why you were crying out his name just minutes ago?"

She couldn't help the blush that stole over her cheeks.

"She made a mistake," Maclearn defended. "She wants to fix things, right, Lindsay?"

"Right." Shooting a glare at Jared, she prayed he'd follow along. Maclearn's jacket flared again, and she urged Jared with her eyes to look down at his waist. But she needn't have bothered. Simmons suddenly palmed a pistol, aiming it dead center on Jared's chest.

"Fine. You want to make things okay? Tell me what you know about Hunter here. The real man behind the scenes. And while you're at it, strip out of those clothes. I figure we've got nothing but time...to kill."

Jared felt his rage begin to spiral out of control and knew he needed to relax. Dammit, why hadn't she listened when he'd told her to stay in his room? Now he not only had to deal with two guns, he had to worry about Lindsay being hurt.

Her eyes looked impossibly blue as she stared at Simmons in distress. "You want me to strip naked?" Lindsay looked at Maclearn, then back to Simmons in disbelief. "With you here?" Her gaze fell to Simmons's hand. "And where did you get a gun?"

"Why not?" Simmons shrugged, ignoring her question and waving his gun. "Hunt's already seen what you've got, and it's only a matter of time before you do it with Dale." Lindsay's eyes grew impossibly big. "We share everything."

Jared had had enough. "Look, Simmons—"

"Now, now, Hunt. Don't feel all left out." Simmons crossed to Jared and grinned lazily at his body. "I'm sure we can work something out for you, too."

Jared's skin crawled, but he said nothing, keeping his expression blank. All he needed was a moment, a temporary distraction, to disarm Simmons. Once he had Simmons, Maclearn would fall in line. He hoped.

"I don't understand," Lindsay said, her feigned innocence surprisingly convincing. "What did I ever do to you, Ken? Why are you treating me like this?" She stared pointedly at his weapon. "And why do you have a gun?"

Simmons narrowed his gaze. "Don't play me for a fool. You know Hunt isn't who he says he is. Please, Lindsay. Dale and I work in Tech Services. We know all of his files have been doctored. The question is, who is he really working for, and how much does he already know?"

"Working for? He's working for Tron Corp." Lindsay looked to Maclearn, nodding as if to engage his agreement.

Simmons glared. "Bullshit. You know he's not really an employee."

"What?" Lindsay turned to Jared, looking shocked. "Is what he says true?"

Jared shrugged, playing along. Maybe he could at least put her in the clear. "So what if it is? You never really wanted the real me. You just wanted to score what every other woman at Tron Corp is after. My dick."

She stared at him, her mouth agape, and more tears fell. Shit, even though he'd explained his reason for being at Tron Corp he hoped she wasn't really buying it. But apparently Maclearn and even Simmons were beginning to.

"So you didn't know about him, Lindsay?" Simmons asked, lowering the gun a fraction as he studied her.

"I don't get it." She angrily swiped tears from her face. "What are you doing at Tron Corp if you don't really work there? Hell, you brought in two new clients just last month!"

Simmons nodded. "Yes, *Jared*. Do tell us what you're really after."

"Fine. But take her out of here. I'm sick of the clinginess, and the tears are really beginning to irritate me."

Simmons grinned, but Maclearn refused to let go of Lindsay.

"She wants to stay with me."

"Oh?" Simmons glanced at Lindsay. "What does she have to say?"

"I'm disgusted with Jared-whoever-the-hell-you-are." Her eyes shone with angry tears. "You're lucky I'm not the one holding the gun. And yes, Dale, I'd love to go home with you. Can we leave this tired place and the asshole who owns it? Quite frankly, I don't care who he is as long as I don't have to see him again."

Dale Maclearn grinned and rubbed his hand over Lindsay's abdomen. Not quite as stupid as Jared might have wished, Maclearn narrowed his gaze and lifted his hand higher, cupping Lindsay's breast as if testing her. Lindsay, bless her, blushed and whispered something in Dale's ear that had him grinning. At a subtle nod from Simmons, Maclearn released her arm and walked back with her to the bedroom, while Jared and Simmons watched her leave the room.

A moment later, Maclearn returned with Lindsay. She was clad in jeans and a fresh T-shirt, her backpack in hand. Turning up her nose at Jared, she smiled at Dale. "Let's get out of here."

She paused at the door. *What the hell was she doing?* "Ken? You're not really going to shoot him or anything, are you?"

Simmons shook his head. "I'm going to hold him here until I can get Tron security and the police involved. I have a bad feeling Jared here is a corporate spy."

Her eyes widened. "Oh. Well, then, Dale and I can get help. Come on, Dale. I helped handle security for a while a few months ago, and I still have the head of security's number on my cell. It's in my car."

So close... Jared knew Simmons watched him, waiting for some sign Lindsay wasn't as innocent about the situation as she seemed. He huffed in disgust. "Traitor, my ass. Good riddance, Riordan, and my compliments on the blowjob. Maclearn, you're a lucky man."

Lindsay gasped and practically dragged Maclearn out the door with her.

Finally. Now he only had Simmons to contend with.

Chapter Eight

Lindsay tolerated Dale Maclearn's fondling until they reached her car. "Hold this for me, will you, Dale?"

He grabbed her backpack, and she quickly unlocked her car. "My cell phone is just in the glove compartment," she mumbled, bending over the driver's side seat to reach the compartment. She gritted her teeth as she felt his hands on her butt. For the love of...

Finding what she needed, she squirmed back out of the car and turned with a can of Mace in her hand. Surprising Maclearn, Lindsay sprayed him in the face. She watched with satisfaction as he dropped to the ground, writhing and howling in pain. Recalling his more than grabby hands, she kicked him in the balls and watched with relish as his shouts turned into mewling pleas. Reaching into her backpack, she grabbed her last secure tie and tied his left hand to the driver's side door handle inside the car.

One down.

And then she heard a gunshot; it nearly scared her witless. Grabbing her cell phone from the floor of her car, Lindsay quickly dialed 9-1-1 and apprised the police of the situation. Another gunshot sounded. Not willing to listen to the dispatcher's demand that she stay clear of the house, Lindsay raced toward the back door with her pepper spray in hand. She stopped and listened.

Nothing. Her nerves were erratic, but tension and fear for Jared propelled her forward. She quietly jiggled the door handle, cursing when it refused to open. *Shit.* Racing around to the front door, she listened again. *Nothing.* Taking a deep breath, Lindsay opened the door.

Jared knelt on the ground beside Simmons. He bled from a gunshot wound to his arm, and he pressed one hand into Simmons's red-stained belly. He aimed a gun at her with his other hand.

"Oh, my God! Jared, are you okay?"

Lowering the gun, he swore and turned back to Simmons. "I'm fine, but next time you might want to announce yourself. I almost shot you, thinking you were Maclearn."

"Police are on the way."

"Good, I was getting ready to call them. Simmons has lost a lot of blood, and a gut shot is never good."

They heard sirens, and Lindsay started shaking, trembling with relief and a hearty dose of receding adrenaline.

"Are you okay?"

She nodded. "Fine. But Dale's not doing so well. I pepper sprayed him."

Jared stared over his shoulder at her with a grin on his lips. "That's my girl." His grin faded into an angry slash. "Why the hell didn't you listen when I told you to stay out of sight? Damn it, you scared the life out of me—"

"Drop the gun! Hands in the air!"

The police had arrived. Lindsay let out the breath she'd been holding, glad they could wrap up this mess. Now only one question remained—where did she and Jared go from here?

* * *

Jared rotated his shoulder and swore at the stinging pain.

"Did you not hear me say to take it easy for the next few weeks?" The doctor sighed with exasperation and tugged on the bandage circling Jared's upper arm. "You're lucky the bullet passed through the fleshy part. But no heroics for a while, okay?"

He nodded, and the doctor left. Jared looked for his shirt and saw it in tatters on the floor. Oh, well. If a little pain and a torn shirt were all he had to suffer from this ordeal, he'd say he came out on top. *And thank God Lindsay hadn't been harmed.* As if his thoughts conjured her up, she appeared in the doorway.

"There you are. The detective told me to remind you about your statement. I already made mine."

"It's going to have to wait. I want a shirt, and I want a nap. What a day."

Lindsay remained in the entryway, solemnly watching him. "Are you in a lot of pain?"

"It's not too bad. They gave me some painkillers and a prescription for more. And the bullet managed to avoid bone."

She nodded, her eyes focused on his bandage.

"Lindsay?" Why wasn't she saying anything?

She glanced up at him, and he panicked. Tears filled her eyes.

"I was so worried!" Lindsay began crying and approached him slowly. She gently put her arms around him, careful not to jostle his bandage. "The thought you might be hurt just about scared the life out of me. And then to *see* you hurt…" She squeezed his waist and pressed her face to his chest. Warmth filled him, a curling emotion of love, worry, and tenderness.

"Don't cry, baby." Jared leaned down and kissed her forehead, her cheeks, the tip of her nose. When he reached her mouth, his lips glided over hers with a tender possession that had her sighing his name. "We're both all right. Let's say we get out of here, okay? How about your place?"

She nodded. As they turned to walk out of the room, the detective in charge of the case entered after a brief knock.

"The doc told me you should be out of here shortly. And I have to say, you're looking a lot better, Hunter." The detective nodded to Lindsay. "Ms. Riordan." The detective focused again on Jared. "Sorry to interrupt, but I'm taking off, and we still have a few things to resolve."

"Detective Schroeder, can I meet you down at the station in a few hours for the formal statement? I need a change of clothes."

"And a little time to decompress." The short woman nodded. "Tron Corp's George Hower verified your story, as did your partner in Seattle. With what Ms. Riordan and Dale Maclearn have already told us, Ken Simmons won't be too happy when he recovers. Both he and his partner will be facing major prison time for attempted murder for starters, not to mention fraud and embezzlement."

Jared frowned, his arm throbbing, and recapped for Lindsay what he'd told the detective. "From what I pieced together, Maclearn and Simmons were obsessed with you. They'd been stealing from the company for almost six months, but when they read through Hower's messages and found his decision to use my company to investigate the suspected fraud, the idiot twins decided to pin the blame on someone else fast. That is to say, get revenge on you, the woman who refused them."

Detective Schroeder nodded. "That's the story Maclearn tells, too. He and Simmons weren't satisfied with their lot in life. And with access to everything in the IT department, they figured to make it big on the company's dime. In fact, they'd amassed close to seven hundred thousand dollars before Hunter arrived on the scene. But a month and a half ago, when they learned of Hower's internal investigation, they panicked."

"And started planting so many false leads."

"Yeah. Good thing your cover was so tight, Hunter. Maclearn told me they immediately looked at you as the undercover security, but you seemed too much a company man, not to mention your background was as solid as a drum. And then, of course, there was Ms. Riordan."

"How did I figure into this, exactly?"

The detective shook her head. "Call it bad luck, Ms. Riordan. Both Maclearn and Simmons had a real thing for you. Despite their attachment to one another, the two planned one big happy lovefest for all three of you. Believe it or not, Maclearn thinks Simmons had issues with his own sexuality, and thought the right attention from you would make him more a 'man.'"

Detective Schroeder scowled. "From what Maclearn admitted, once they took in over a million, they planned on ditching the company and taking you with them, whether you wanted to go or not. They intended to blame you for the embezzlement, using staged evidence of your supposed 'guilt' to blackmail you into running with them. Maclearn mentioned South America a few times. Good thing Hunter stepped in."

"Yeah, lucky me." Lindsay smiled at Jared.

The detective smiled at them in turn. "Cops are great believers in luck." She glanced from Lindsay to Jared. "Now if you two don't mind, I have some paperwork to start. And it'll be a while before I put the final details to rest."

Jared nodded. "I'll see you tomorrow morning, then, if that's okay."

"That's fine." She waved and left, and they exited the room soon after the nurse handed Jared his discharge papers.

Leaving the hospital after a quick stop at the pharmacy, Jared dozed in the car while Lindsay drove to her place. He didn't recall much of their conversation. The next thing he knew she was nudging him awake.

"Jared? Time to get up."

Stumbling into her house and then her bedroom, he fell into her bed and sighed at the soothing feeling of her thick, down comforter and fluffy pillows. The bed smelled like her, soft and feminine, and he settled into a deep sleep.

When he next awoke, it was to see Lindsay hovering over him, staring down at him with a loving look on her face. She stroked his cheek, and he turned into the caress, kissing her palm.

She smiled and stepped away, as if to let him fall back asleep.

"No, don't go."

He couldn't explain his driving need to hold her, to feel her in his arms. The scare he'd suffered earlier—when Lindsay had rejoined him in his living room where there'd been two armed crazies just itching for an excuse to pull the trigger—had showed Jared how much he truly cared for her. The months of him wishing they could be together, of fantasizing about her, only to realize reality was far better than the fantasy, suddenly came to a head.

Reaching toward her, Jared cursed at his lack of mobility. The painkillers had not only numbed his injury, but his situational awareness as well.

"Easy, Jared. Move slowly." Lindsay sat next to him on the bed, soothing his strain by gently running her fingers through his hair, over his face, and down across his collarbone, her touch feather light and sensuous.

He wrapped his left hand behind her neck and pulled her close for a kiss, groaning at how good she felt. Telling her without words how much she meant to him, Jared teased her lips and tongue, licked at the warm recesses of her mouth with loving strokes. Despite the throbbing in his arm, he wanted—no, needed—to be inside her.

"Make love to me, Lindsay."

She cupped his face in her hands and tenderly returned his kiss. Discarding her clothes and then his, she joined him on the bed. Instead of returning to his mouth, however, she kissed her way down his neck, running her hands over his chest. Pinching his nipples, she elicited a groan out of him. And when she pressed her breasts against his chest, he arched into her, desperate to join her.

"I have to have you," he panted, urging her over him.

He reached a hand between her thighs and sighed as he felt the evidence of her desire. Hot and wet, she sank down, their union sheer perfection. She clearly felt it as well, for she murmured words of love in his ear as she leaned close, rocking over him and pushing down hard.

When she straightened, he fondled her breasts with his left hand, frustrated he couldn't touch more of her the way he wanted to.

"Don't worry, Jared. You just lie back, and let me do all the work."

So beautiful, so caring. He would never forget the courage she'd shown today, or her unflinching loyalty when she'd come back to try to "save" him. If he hadn't already loved her, today would surely have pushed him over the edge.

She rocked faster over him, and he moaned. Heat flowed through him, centered at his cock, and traveled throughout his body. An ache burned in his loins, and the need to come loomed precariously near as he watched the most beautiful woman in his life ride him, magnificent in her desire.

"Jared," she panted, clutching his chest. "I need you so much."

"Not as much as I need you."

He gasped as she shifted ever so slightly; he couldn't hold back any longer. Shuddering, he shot into her, aware she came along with him. Clenching him tightly, she enhanced his orgasm as she milked him of everything he had to give.

Utterly spent, he lay beneath her, his pain all but gone as his body throbbed with pleasure, with love.

She let him slip from her body and rolled next to him, her breathing harsh, but said nothing. He grabbed her hand, clutching her smaller palm tightly in his. Jared wanted so badly to tell her how he really felt. He wasn't one to hold back, had very little patience in fact, but he didn't want to screw this up.

In a few more days he would have to return to Seattle, to his partner and their business. But for the life of him, Jared couldn't imagine living without Lindsay. He now understood that *she* was the reason he'd waited so long to marry. What he didn't know was how Lindsay felt.

Sure, she didn't do casual sex. But nothing about this weekend had been casual, or typical. Her strength and notion of payback appealed to his "eye for an eye" mindset. Lindsay Riordan had looks, brains, and better yet, she was no one's doormat.

And she absolutely loved her job.

Could he ask her to move out West with him? Would she think him completely insane? They'd known each other for two months, but it was only this weekend that she had really come to *know* him. And there was so much more they both needed to learn about one another. Making love with her six ways from Sunday didn't guarantee him a say in her future, much as he might want it to.

"A penny for your thoughts," she said, her husky voice stirring him again.

He sighed. "Trying not to think about leaving this bed." He turned carefully, watching her reaction. "I'll have to return to Seattle soon."

"Yeah."

Yeah? What did "yeah" mean? "What about you?"

Her eyes widened. "Me?"

"Have you ever been to Seattle?" he asked casually.

"Uh, no. I haven't."

"It's a beautiful place. A little rainy, but that just makes everything greener. The climate's cool. I noticed at work you drink a lot of coffee. In Seattle, there's a coffee shop on just about every corner."

She blinked at him before a slow grin settled over her lips. "Sounds like you're trying to sell me on Seattle."

"And they have some really fine men out there."

"Oh? Do tell."

He scissored a thigh over hers, trapping her effectively under his weight as he scooted closer. "You know, I have contacts at Tron Corp. A few days ago a certain CEO was mentioning how much he'd like to expand his business, into, say, the West Coast. Seattle's prime for a Tron Corp handhold."

"Hmm."

He ran his hand along her waist and up to cup a breast. "Yeah. And you know, Tron Corp isn't the only company out there needing good logistics folks."

"Just good?" Her hands closed over his growing erection, and he groaned.

"I meant great, incredibly talented logisticians." Almost purring, Jared couldn't help thrusting into her able hands.

"Then maybe I should think about moving out there. Or at least scoping out the possibilities."

"The possibilities are endless. And I'm sure you could find a guy in no time who wouldn't mind your average looks and so-so body," he teased, cursing under his breath when she cupped his balls, enflaming his desire. "Hell, I'm sure the minute you land in the airport some good-looking guy will snap you up and offer you a marriage proposal, and all from gazing into those gorgeous baby blues."

Her hands stilled, and she stared at him.

"Hell, Lindsay, don't stop. Just say yes and put me out of my misery."

"Say yes?" Her eyes narrowed. "To what, exactly?"

The teasing suddenly turned very serious, and he blew out a harsh breath. "To hell with it. I know it sounds crazy, but I can't imagine returning to Seattle without you. You are so much better than my fantasies, Lindsay. So much more than I ever thought I'd find. I've been waiting my whole life for you." She said nothing, and he panicked.

"Shit. Look, I don't want to rush you. But you could at least come out to visit for a while, see if you like it there. And don't do it for me, do it for you. Expand your horizons. A woman as smart and sexy as you can have her pick of jobs. Did I mention they pay better in Seattle?" He was growing desperate.

After a tense moment, a grin slowly lit up her face. "So you've been waiting your whole life for me? That was beautiful. Did you mean it?"

"Did I mean it?" Annoyance took root. "Why the hell else would I have let you tie me up and take advantage of me? Not to mention not running your tight little ass in for questioning the moment I found all that planted evidence against you? And the months spent dreaming about you, trying to charm you when I could have had you in bed from day one..."

She rolled her eyes. "And I used to think you were charming."

He didn't laugh; the topic was too near to his heart.

Lindsay pursed her lips in thought, dragging out his nervous anticipation. "I could be persuaded to move to Seattle. But I'd need two things first."

Anything. As long as she'd be his. "What?"

"First, I'll need some time to see where this leads. As much as I might think I love you, I need to be sure. And if it turns out you're as good as you look," she teased, "I'll expect—hell, I'll demand—that proposal."

He immediately relaxed, his body on fire with joy. *She loved him.* "The second?"

"I want a ready supply of secure ties—and the right to use them whenever I feel the need." Her eyes twinkled with naughty intent.

"Like I said before, Riordan." He tasted the promise of tomorrow in her kiss. "You're hell on wheels."

REAPER'S REWARD

Chapter One

Seattle, Washington

Maybe the handcuffs had been too much. That, or the orders to please him, to do whatever he said, when he said it. Ethan Reaper sighed and stared at the empty space on the bed next to him. He'd really thought Miranda would be able to handle his demands. Or, as she'd called them before fleeing from his place, his "perversions" in the bedroom. Hell, it wasn't as if he had some freaky fetish. He didn't want to suck her toes, and he wasn't into whips and chains.

The thought made him pause. Well, maybe soft whips, and chains only to secure his sexual slave, who'd come to him on her hands and knees, all willing and eager. His dick spiked, and the erection that had once impressed Miranda rose again.

Frustrated, Ethan groaned and lay back in bed, wishing he'd at least fucked her before opening up about the cuffs. Hell, the woman was a screamer in the sack, and she'd hinted she might want to try it up the ass. The word "might" should have told him all he needed to know.

Miranda had beauty and brains but not enough of a backbone to suit him. She was no one's doormat, but still, she didn't offer much of an opinion when he wanted to do anything. Unless, apparently, it included some "perversions" that bruised her fragile sensibilities.

Ethan snorted. "Another two months of dating down the drain. Women are a fucking headache."

He fisted his hand around his cock and imagined what tonight might have been like with the right woman by his side.

On her hands and knees, she'd crawl to him, licking her lips with a skilled pink tongue. Her body would be slender, curved in all the right places but toned, strong so that she wouldn't break from rough handling.

"Whatever you want, Master."

"I want you to suck me."

She wouldn't question him, wouldn't weep or argue. She'd crawl until she found his cock with her mouth, and she'd suck him straight to heaven. With ripe lips, she'd take him deep, her tongue firm as she licked his shaft, stroking beneath the crown in that most sensitive spot. Her hands would rub his balls, sliding her fingers along the seam of his ass, teasing his anus while she pleasured him.

Her tits would fit in his hands, and she'd beg him to fill her in any and every way. Long hair would cover her face, making her look demure even as she blew him.

As he stared down at her, ownership, pure possession, would fill him; he'd know he'd found the woman meant for him and him alone.

She'd pleasure him as fast and as far as he'd order, and she'd be wet, dripping with arousal from sucking him off, a woman to match his desires.

"Make me come," he'd command harshly, tangling his hands in her soft, silken hair, fucking her mouth with groans of ecstasy.

As she sucked him harder, she'd rim his asshole with her finger, until he reached that precipice. She'd know exactly when and how much force to use, and she'd shoot him into orgasm with the pull of her mouth and a finger shoved tightly into his ass...

"Fuck." Ethan shot over his belly, his orgasm both powerful and empty. He lay there for a moment, his breathing loud in the darkness, until finally, the pleasure drained.

Maybe if his dreams weren't so damned perfect, he'd be able to find a woman to satisfy him. But he couldn't seem to stop himself from ruining his relationships. After a few bouts of sex with a woman, Ethan grew dissatisfied. And his need to fulfill his fantasies would inevitably scare the woman away.

"Maybe I'm going after the wrong types."

Lindsay, his partner Jared's wife, had said as much. Ethan liked Lindsay, but she had a tendency to say whatever the hell she thought, regardless of Ethan's blunt reminders to keep her thoughts to herself.

"You go for the demure women, professionals with so much femininity it makes me want to scream. Women don't have to be frilly to be women, Ethan," she liked to nag.

Jared would only smile and say nothing. And the bastard should keep quiet. Lindsay looked like a centerfold—blonde hair, large breasts, and long, long legs. Sure, a woman didn't have to be frilly when she looked like a sex goddess, but in Ethan's experience, even the goddesses were lacking. Most of them fucked like rabbits and could barely remember their names.

He'd run into women who loved the submissive shit, so much so that they freaked *him* out. He didn't want a woman under his control all the time. That would drive him nuts. Then there were the missish, missionary-only types. Women like Miranda. He sighed. They either wanted too much or not enough, and he had yet to find a happy middle ground.

Wishing just once he could have fantasy sex with a woman and not by himself, Ethan forced himself out of bed to clean up. So much for a pleasant weekend filled with sex, beer, and more sex. He'd visit the office tomorrow to take his mind off his problems. When all else failed, he could always count on his baby, H&R Securities, to keep him happy.

The next morning, Ethan rode to work in a much more cheerful mood. Free as a bird, no women or problem clients to mar the perfection of his Saturday, he parked behind his office downtown on Pine and grabbed a coffee from the nearest Starbucks. Black and strong, it sated his need for normalcy, and with a sigh of pleasure at the coffee and the clear blue May sky, Ethan entered H&R.

"Marcy."

She nodded back, her graying hair framing a pixie-like face streaked with wrinkles and laugh lines. "You look like shit."

He grinned. Nothing like a woman who reminded him of his grandmother and swore like a sailor to start the morning. "Don't sugarcoat it, sweetness. Tell it like you see it."

"Don't I always?" She nodded toward the hallway. "Think you might have a problem in room three."

He sobered quickly. "Situation?"

"Mike and Steve finally collared the guy stalking Ms. Finley, and he's an asshole, let me tell you. He's also taller than you, with an attitude bigger than King Kong."

"Oh?" he said softly.

Her eyes gleamed. "Threatening to sue us, that he'll kick our collective asses, blah, blah, blah. I was just getting ready to call in Jared since it's *supposed* to be your weekend off." She eyed him knowingly. "Gave Miranda the boot, eh? Good. I never liked the uppity—"

"Yeah, yeah. I know. I dumped her because I knew you couldn't stand her. And don't call Jared. I'll take care of this."

Could his day get any better? Whistling, Ethan downed the rest of his coffee and neared room three. Loud voices carried. Mike sounded angry, Steve calm, and the other guy roared like an animal. Ethan tossed his coffee cup into the nearby trashcan and rubbed his hands together. He hoped the asshole would prove difficult.

Throwing open the door, he saw that Marcy hadn't been exaggerating. The creep stalking Amy Finley had to be six-six and weigh close to two-fifty. Though his eyes looked hard, he didn't stand like an experienced fighter. He put the weight on the back of his heels instead of the balls of his feet. Taking him down would be easy, and not nearly as fun as he'd hoped.

"So you're the asshole I've heard so much about," Ethan said, smiling. "Mike, Steve, want to tell me what's going on?"

"I'll tell you what's going on, shithead."

"And you are?"

"Leo Tolstoy," Mike deadpanned. "I swear to you, that's his name."

"And why the fuck is that so funny?" Leo demanded, his fists clenched, his eyes mean.

Steve smirked but kept silent and stood casually against a wall. Ethan had seen the tension ease out of him as soon as Ethan had entered the room.

Closing the door behind him, Ethan turned again to face Leo. "Why are you stalking Amy Finley?" he asked bluntly.

"Where is she?" Tolstoy took a step toward him. "What did you do with her? She's my wife, dammit. I want her back, now."

"She *was* your wife. The divorce was final three months ago. Leo, you need to move on." Ethan knew his calm, even tone would irritate Tolstoy all the more. And he was pleased when the big man moved right up into his face.

"Look, you fucker. That woman is mine. She belongs to—"

Having seen the bruises on Amy's poor face, Ethan did what he'd been dying to do when he'd first taken the case. Feinting close, he startled Tolstoy into swinging first.

Grinning with pleasure, Ethan plowed his fist into Tolstoy's nose, breaking it with a snap. Blood spurted, and Tolstoy cried out in shock, but Ethan wanted to press his point. Using the training he'd received courtesy of Uncle Sam and the United States Marine Corps, he grabbed Tolstoy in a wrist lock, pinned his arm behind his back, and swept his legs out from under him.

The big man's head cracked against the tile floor as he landed on his back, and Tolstoy blubbered as he tried to defend himself. The pitiful arm he raised to spare his face did no good.

Ethan cuffed him, hard, across the cheek with an open hand. "Look, shit for brains, the cops will be here in ten minutes."

Mike muttered under his breath and grabbed the nearby phone to call them, and Ethan continued. "I'm pressing charges for assault, and Amy's doing the same. She still has a limp from where you broke her ankle two months ago before you ran like a coward. So, guess what? Now that we have you, your sorry ass is getting locked away for a long time."

"You can't do that," Tolstoy choked through the blood pooling in his throat. "You attacked *me.*"

"Oh?" Ethan glanced back at Steve, who shrugged.

"That's not the way I saw it." Steve smiled, and Mike nodded.

"But, but—"

"But nothing." Ethan grabbed Tolstoy by the throat, squeezing hard. "You step one foot near Amy again, and I'll kill you. Pure and simple; it'll be self-defense. My witnesses will stand by me," he said through his teeth. "And did I mention I have friends on the force?" Namely, his brothers Hale and Trevor.

Tolstoy's eyes bulged, and his face turned beet red. He sputtered and weakly tugged at the arm holding him to the floor.

"Uh, Ethan? You might want to let up before you crush his larynx." Mike's eyes danced, laughter in their depths, as he hung up the phone.

"Whatever." Ethan stood up and faced his men. "Make your statements to the cops, about how Leo attacked Steve, and we were forced to defend him."

Mike chuckled, and Steve frowned. Between the two of them, Steve was the obvious victim. Dark skinned with menacing brown eyes, Mike stood six-three and was a former linebacker for the Seattle Seahawks. He'd retired on medical leave after only one season due to a bad knee. Steve, on the other hand, had skin so pale he looked as if he'd never seen the sun. He was slim, barely reached Mike's shoulder, and looked like he could be blown over by a stiff wind.

"What?" Ethan asked, his lips curled.

"Nothing. I'll talk to the cops," Steve muttered and stalked out of the room.

"You okay with handling him?" Ethan asked Mike, glancing down at the shaky form of Tolstoy on the floor.

Mike grinned. "Sure. And if he pisses me off, we'll add that he tried attacking me, too. Maybe Hale could turn this into a hate crime, like this fucker hates blacks or some shit."

"Good thinking. I like your creativity, Mike." Ethan pounded Mike on the shoulder.

As he left, Mike called out, "Sorry about Miranda, Ethan. But you know, I think you're better off."

"How did you—"

"It's your day off. You always come to work when you lose the ladies. But I made fifty off this one. Miranda lasted a hell of a lot longer than the others thought she would."

Grumbling, Ethan slammed the door on Mike's laughter and stalked to his office.

The phone rang, distracting him—which was to Mike's benefit. Ethan wouldn't have to go back and pound the shit out of him—and after several minutes of conversation, Ethan sat down and began taking notes. This looked like the perfect case. A hefty fee, intrigue, and a definite need for H&R's services. A case where Ethan could dirty his hands and escape from this blasted city for a while.

* * *

Two weeks later

Julia Marciella knocked tentatively on her uncle's door. "You wanted to see me?" *Please don't let this be about the pearl necklace. I returned it before it was missed, didn't I?*

"Jewel, there you are. I was looking for you." Uncle Tommy seemed way too upbeat for a Monday. Normally storming around the office like a hurricane, he actually looked pleasant. Which meant one of two things—he'd found luck with the ladies this weekend, or luck with the dice in Atlantic City.

"I won fifty thousand at the tables," he said with a smile. "And found a new client in the process."

Jewel sat down in the chair in front of his desk, intrigued.

"Sophie Ayers, wife to business tycoon Timothy Ayers, joined me for a few rounds of poker Saturday night at the Borgata. But it wasn't as chance a meeting as it first seemed." He grinned, and Jewel wondered if Sophie Ayers had sought out her uncle for help or for some fun between the sheets. A handsome man, Uncle Tommy never hurt for companionship and was far less concerned about married women than he ought to be.

"Please tell me you didn't sleep with her."

Tommy's brows rose. "Jewel, I'm surprised at you. Sophie's a married woman." At her look, he laughed. "Besides, I like her husband. Tim and I golf together on occasion."

"So..."

"So, Sophie and I indulged in some high-stakes poker, and both of us came out winners. Unfortunately, that doesn't help her much. It's a common but sorry tale. And I want you handling this one."

She nodded, wanting to know just what she needed to find. Since working for her uncle the past six years, Jewel had recovered items ranging from stolen jewelry to vintage cars and even a thoroughbred horse. Dreemer's, Inc.—the best retrieval business on the East Coast—provided discreet services to those who could afford them.

"Apparently, Sophie was suckered by great sex and a snake charmer by the name of Joshua Denton. They met in

Atlantic City while he was on vacation, and after a few heated, naked exchanges, Denton returned to his job at Satyr's Myst, an exclusive resort on a privately owned island in the Caribbean."

"Blackmail, right?"

"You guessed it. Sophie was taken by her younger lover and followed him to the resort. There they played in a variety of *games,*" he dangled the word, and Jewel could only imagine what Sophie and the man had done. "Denton took her to his room, where he kept a hidden video camera. He's now asking for one hundred thousand dollars in exchange for the film."

"Which of course he won't give her until he's bled her dry."

"Exactly what Sophie fears. Bottom line, we need to retrieve not only that camera, but any copies of the film he may have made. In this digital world, nothing's safe any more. And that's why you're the best one for the job."

Jewel preened but knew he spoke the truth. When it came to computers, she had yet to be beaten by any hacker, security system, or program. A little worm like Denton shouldn't prove too hard a challenge.

"A tropical paradise, hmm? I guess I'm going in as a vacationer then?"

Uncle Tommy paused, a strange look on his face. "Actually, no. I did a little research and found they're in need of a waitress. You're going in undercover to get close to Denton, and then find what you need. You only have two weeks, because Sophie has until June first to come up with the money. She's to hand it over in person on the island."

"Okay. But wouldn't it make more sense for me to go in as a potential victim? Take advantage of him instead?"

"No. Definitely not. Jewel, I feel awkward enough asking you to do this, but we need your skills to help Sophie, and none of the others are as good as you are when it comes to computers. The resort, Satyr's Myst, caters to a…different sort of crowd."

Suspicious, she watched the odd look on her uncle's face turn instantly uncomfortable the moment they locked gazes. Jewel sensed there was a lot more he wasn't telling her. "Oh?"

"Hell. I'll stop dancing around it. You're a grown woman, for God's sake," he muttered. "Just don't tell your mother about this, or she'll skin me alive. Satyr's Myst is a sexual fantasy resort, where anything and everything goes. From what Sophie told me, clothing isn't required, and sex happens just about everywhere."

Jewel blinked. "Are you serious?" Curiosity and a strange interest took hold. God, it had been forever since she'd last had sex, and just as long since she'd had any interest in it.

"Yes, quite. The guests almost never dress. But as a waitress, the worst you'll have to do is dress in a skimpy outfit." He looked her over and sighed. "Not that your nunnish lifestyle couldn't do with some livening up. I'm probably going to hell for this, but I already sent your résumé and a picture, and they've accepted you."

"Hit me with my cover."

"Your name is Jewel Riser, age twenty-seven, from Cape May, New Jersey. I've kept it as close to the truth as possible, only blurring a few key components of your identity. You're desperate to find a job away from home since your fiancé recently dumped you. Which at least gives you the hint of a love life."

"Gee, thanks."

"I thought it was a good cover, myself. This way you're unattached, far from home, and probably desperate for some fun. Sophie discreetly gave you a reference, and the owner, Rick Hastings, will meet you on Wednesday for the final part of your sit-down interview. You pass with him and you'll start work immediately after."

"And if I don't pass?"

"You'll pass, or I'll tell your mother you blew off another of her arranged dates by blackmailing your sister to take your place."

"Hey, Danielle wanted to go out with that schmuck. And I have no urge to give Mom grandchildren any time soon. Let Danielle or Nick do it."

"You're a lot more like me than you like to think," her uncle said with a laugh. "Okay. I'll book your flight for tomorrow afternoon. Oh, and Jewel? Pack light. As I mentioned, they're not big on clothes at the resort." He grimaced and handed her a file. "I'll expect you to check in regularly. Aside from the resort, this is a standard grab and go."

She nodded. "I'll be fine. And I'm *not* taking off my clothes for anyone. I can waitress in a bikini, for cripes' sake."

"Good girl." He kissed her on the cheek and shoved her toward the door. "I'll smooth things over with the family.

Now get out of here before Nick comes in wanting to know what you're up to."

She quickly left, knowing her "little" brother, whom she'd once stuffed into her closet, would pester her until she told him all the details. The giant man and his twin Danielle were a year younger than Jewel, and both were pests. One or the other was constantly getting her in trouble with her mother. Dad, God rest him, had normally run interference, but having been dead and buried for three years now, John Marciella was picking pockets in heaven, or cooking up trouble at the very least.

Jewel shook her head and grinned, relishing the chance to break away from home for a while. She loved her family but needed some space. Her mother constantly badgered her to marry, but frankly, Jewel liked being single. She had no man to worry about unless she wanted one. Though the lack of sex frustrated her at times, she stayed busy with exciting cases. Sex had never been that fulfilling to begin with, and to Jewel, flirting with danger was a hell of a lot more fun than flirting with a potential lover.

"When my biological clock starts ticking, I'll find a guy. But, hell, not yet," she mumbled, skirting her brother's glance as he rounded the corner by dodging into the elevator. *Good, let Uncle Tommy deal with Nick, that "giant" pain in my ass.* Jewel grinned good-naturedly.

She reached her new Crossfire in record time and drove home feeling cool and sophisticated.

In two days she'd be half-naked in the sun, undercover, and steaming it up among the rich and sex-starved. The element of danger, of subterfuge, and unknown adventure thrilled her, and Jewel smiled as she drove. Not even her mother's car sitting in her driveway took away her excitement.

Chapter Two

Wednesday afternoon

An expansive ceiling, bright coral paint, and potted palms surrounded the large room in which she sat. Teak chairs accented with incredibly comfortable cushions in tropical prints complemented the décor in Rick Hastings's office. The rich mahogany of his desk hinted at a professional, and the organization of his work space further illustrated that she was looking at a very intelligent, savvy businessman. And a very young one.

Jewel hadn't expected a man with as much money as Hastings to be in his thirties. He'd either inherited his wealth or had made his fortune playing the market. But she admitted to being impressed by his finances, his style, and his looks.

Hastings was *GQ* handsome, with sharp blue eyes, white-blond cropped hair, and a charming grin. She could see why both women and men flocked to this place. Rumor had it Hastings wasn't too choosy about the sex of his bed partners. The thought that provoked made her belly flutter, and she glanced at the large man standing by the wall. All too easily, images of sex dotted her brain...sex with Hastings or the huge security guard behind him. Both men were sexy as sin. *Damn, a few minutes in this sexual fortress and I'm turning into a nymphomaniac.* Shaking free of that unnerving thought and ignoring the attraction to her future boss, Jewel focused on the here and now.

Hastings had yet to take his eyes off her in the five minutes she'd been sitting across from him at his desk, and his intense perusal was beginning to unnerve her. To say nothing of the glare the behemoth standing by the wall imposed. She'd caught a glimpse of him before quickly turning her gaze back to Hastings. And despite Hastings's obvious male beauty, she had a hard time keeping her eyes on him. Her gaze kept straying to the guy holding up the wall.

Holy crap, but the giant stood several inches over six feet. The tan trousers and light orange shirt he wore only emphasized the muscles under his clothes, yet Jewel noted his paler skin next to Hastings's. Either the guy was new or he did most of his work indoors.

Whereas Hastings was handsome, his guard looked tough, full of corded strength, with an attitude to back up the threat of his appearance. She couldn't classify him as handsome, but his raw masculinity captivated all the same.

"Your paperwork appears in order." Hastings finally glanced away from her face to look down at the folder in front of him. "I have your application, résumé, and current physical results. Like everyone else on the resort, you're free of disease and appropriately protected from unwanted pregnancy. An implanted contraceptive, is that correct?"

"Yes."

He frowned and looked up. "How do you feel about sex, Jewel?"

She blinked. "What?"

"Sex. What are your thoughts on the topic? You do know what type of resort this is, don't you?"

Get it together, idiot. Stop focusing on the muscle by the wall and jump into character. She gave Hastings a wry grin. "Yes, I do. I applied out of a sense of curiosity, I admit. And because your salary is amazing." She paused, gnawing on her lip, and noted both Hastings's and his guard's keen attention on her mouth. "I don't have any hang-ups, if that's what you're asking. Homosexual or heterosexual, as long as it's consensual, I'm okay with it."

"And bisexual?" Hastings murmured, his gaze still on her mouth.

She couldn't help flushing. Not that she was a prude, but she didn't normally discuss sexuality with strangers. *Concentrate on the job.* "Like I said, as long as it's consensual, and legal, I don't care who's doing what to whom."

"Hmm." He glanced over his shoulder at the giant, who said nothing. Hastings turned back to her. "And nudity. How do you feel about that?"

"Hey, you want to get naked, I'm not going to complain." She continued after his laughter settled. "Myself, I'm more modest. I'd assumed I'd be required to dress rather scantily for the weather, and because it's a fantasy resort. But

I don't think I'd be comfortable doing my job naked." She made sure to emphasize the last. Uncle Tommy might have given her a pathetic background, but Jewel had standards. Besides, her trademark smart-ass attitude had always stood her well in the past.

"A lot of my employees felt the same way when they first started, but now I have to remind them to wear clothes when they leave the resort." He grinned, but the guard by the wall remained stoic.

Geesh, what would it take to get a rise out of him...literally? She flushed at the thought. *Why the hell do I care?*

"I like you, Jewel," Hastings said. "You're incredibly beautiful, but that's obvious, isn't it? It's your sense of humor, that smile, and the buoyancy that survived a wrecked engagement and sought out a job here, in a fantasy surrounded by paradise. We'll start you out on a trial basis, let you get a feel for the job.

"You're required to wear the resort uniform. There are three different uniforms, depending upon the occasion. They'll be provided to you later this evening. Size what, six?"

She swallowed, aware the guard was listening intently. The man said nothing, but his eyes remained focused on her, traveling over her body assessingly. "Eight, actually."

"A very nice eight, I might add." Hastings chuckled and nodded to his man behind him. "This is Ethan Reaper, one of my special security guards. Ethan will join us on the tour in a few minutes, and you'll receive orientation this evening from Jaz. You met him when you first entered the resort. He'll bring you to dinner at seven, so be ready."

Hastings stood, and she rose as well. He held out a hand, and she placed hers in it without thinking. He offered a firm handshake and ended it with a caress as he slowly released her palm. Unable to help herself, Jewel shivered and saw satisfaction flare in his gaze before it vanished as if it had never been.

"Give me a few minutes with Ethan, if you would, Jewel. You can wait outside in the receiving room."

She nodded, conscious of their stares burning into her back as she left. The minute Jewel closed the door behind her, she took a deep breath. Too much testosterone to deal with after a long-ass flight. Spotting two rattan chairs and a couch with a great view of the ocean, she sat carefully on the plump, mint-green settee and stared at the scene that begged for description.

A clear blue sky overlooked white sand and a calm, blue-green ocean. From this vantage on the main floor, she stared through palm trees and the occasional bush and caught the sweet scent of honeysuckle off the bright pink bougainvillea scaling the outside of the hotel. The red amaryllis and orange bird of paradise stood out against the immaculately kept lawn surrounding the main building, and she couldn't help but wonder about the resort's water bill.

Practical, as always, Jewel thought with a grin, which faded as she stared down at her short, blue, *fanciful* sundress. In keeping with her sexy, desperate persona—*thanks so much, Uncle Tommy*—she'd worn a cornflower blue sundress covered in purple, green, and yellow flowers. The cursed thing had spaghetti straps, which showed the thin blue straps of her bra, allowed too much cleavage, and was way too short. It came to the middle of her damned thighs.

Fidgeting, she practiced sitting ladylike on the settee, reminding herself not to spread her legs in comfort unless she wanted to go for the sexual side of employment here. Jewel snorted, imaging her uncle's expression should he learn she'd gone native in a sex resort.

"Serve him right," she muttered as she leaned toward the open window, unable to take her gaze away from the beauty of paradise.

"Serve who right?"

She had to look up, way up, to match the face with the gravelly voice. This close, she could see the dark brown color of the guard's—Ethan's—thickly lashed eyes. Hot damn, but he fairly oozed sex appeal, and Jewel was taken aback at her awareness of it. In Hastings's office, Ethan had been intriguing in a standoffish, don't-screw-with-me kind of way. But now, he looked as if he wanted to dance the horizontal mambo...*with her.* And her heart wouldn't stop racing.

Swallowing loudly, she glanced beyond him. "Is Mr. Hastings finished with your meeting?"

"He has a few things to take care of or he'd join us." He leaned down and took her hand in his, dwarfing her with his size. Electricity zinged through her at the contact.

This is so not normal.

Helping her to her feet, he caught her by the small of her back and walked her down the hallway. Plush green carpet softened their steps. A chair rail along the corridor separated the pale mango upper wall from the white wainscoted lower wall. Beautiful and classy when combined with the island prints framed in dark walnut on the walls. But the décor still wasn't enough to blot out her consciousness of her hunky escort, who stood way too close for comfort.

"Um, so this is the tour?" Jewel wanted to slap herself for the obvious comment, especially when his brows rose as if questioning her intelligence.

"Part of it at least. You'll notice there aren't too many people in the hallways. Most of the action today is outside, in the private cabanas and in the central courtyard out back. But I think we'll start by taking you through the hotel to your room. You look scared already, and the scene poolside takes some getting used to."

She immediately bristled at his tone. "Look, I applied for this job. I may be new, but I don't need to be handled with kid gloves."

His hand shifted on her dress, and Jewel squelched an insane urge to increase the contact.

"Well then, Miss Assertive, let's go outside, shall we?"

Though his voice hadn't changed much, she could tell she'd pricked his temper. Good. Jewel needed a handle on those around her, and Ethan was like a locked vault. Apparently, chatting up security with a wide grin and a hint of boobs wasn't going to work. Although... She glanced at Ethan from the corner of her eye, recalling the heated look he'd given her earlier.

Best to smooth over his annoyance. Smiling up at him, Jewel breathed deeply, throwing out her chest as she did so, and earned his attention. "So are the employees' rooms grouped together?"

He studied her, but not with the sex-crazed expression she'd hoped for. "Yeah, on the fifth floor. Depending on your duties, you'll either stay up there or transfer to the main floor."

"Depending on my duties? I thought I'd been hired to waitress."

He grinned suddenly, and the sight of his smile transformed him from arrogant tough guy to sex personified. "Baby, no one here is paid to fuck. We have food staff, housekeepers, landscapers, and more. You're here to wait on the guests, food-wise, but Satyr's Myst is all about service. Like the others, you'll be trained to please the guests in *every* way. But that's a side benefit of the job." His grin faded at her look of shock, and his eyes narrowed. "That *is* why you're here, isn't it?"

Jewel sputtered, then found herself outside under the shaded canopy of the hotel, overlooking group sex by the pool. *Holy shit.*

Ethan took her to the side, still under the shade and in full view of anyone looking, then lowered his head to murmur in her ear, "I told you it takes some getting used to. But since you're here to participate, why not start your training now?"

"I'm not..."

"Not what?" he asked softly, positioning himself firmly behind her. She felt his erection brushing above her ass, but was distracted when his hands circled her front to cup her breasts. "Not here to service the guests, Jewel? But that's what you applied for, after all. You told me not to handle you with kid gloves, remember?"

Tell him to get the hell off. To back away. But she said neither. Anticipation made her light-headed. He pinched her nipples, and she moaned, amazed at the flood of need pooling between her thighs. She had never been this turned on in her life, and by a stranger no less. The erotic tableau before her only spiked her arousal higher.

"Look at the water, Jewel. The play there is only the beginning."

She helplessly glanced up, her body no longer hers to control as he played with her breasts and circled her belly with one large, hot hand.

Several naked people in the pool—she had yet to see a guest wearing clothes—were having sex with each other and masturbating. One man sat on the ledge, gripping his cock with desperation as a petite redhead watched. He cried out and came, and the redhead quickly bent to catch his cum in her mouth. As she bent over, a dark-skinned man with a huge cock buried himself in her ass even as she swallowed her other lover's orgasm.

Jewel stared so hard her eyes hurt. She'd seen a few pornos before but nothing so decadent as this. And Ethan's hands on her only increased her stimulation. To her shock, Jewel felt on the verge of orgasm.

"Hmm, a closet hedonist, eh, Jewel?" Ethan chuckled and continued to play with her breasts, while his other hand traveled lower, inching up the hem of her skirt. "But what have we here?"

His finger inched past the silk of her thong, delving into her wet heat.

"Ethan," she gasped, jolted out of her daze by the intrusion. What the hell was wrong with her that she allowed a stranger to fondle her in public? *You're undercover. Go with it.* The devil within her prodded her to cooperate. *Besides, you need this.*

"That's it, honey. Damn, you're wet." He rubbed his cock against her backside, his excitement making her wetter. "Feels to me like you're over the bastard who dumped you." He chuckled and shoved another finger deep inside her. "Shit, baby, you need this as much as I do."

He began priming her.

"That feels so good." Was that her shuddering under a stranger's touch, in full view of anyone happening by? *Undercover my ass.* The sane part of her took charge, and Jewel squirmed, trying to free herself from Ethan. But the movement only put her clit in direct contact with his knuckles, and she moaned his name in a throaty voice, needing more.

"That's it, baby. Come. Drench my hand with your cream."

She didn't need it. Jewel didn't need sex, didn't need some bossy, bodybuilder type telling her what to—

"Oh, my God." She blew apart, between one breath and the next, exploding into the biggest orgasm she'd ever had in her life. She shuddered and moaned while Ethan's fingers plunged in and out of her with greater speed.

She was dimly aware of the sound of a zipper lowering and then felt another shock, this one fatter and thicker against her ass.

"Bend over," he growled and turned her to face the wall. Before she could comply, he had her bent at the waist, her legs spread apart.

"Ethan, wait," she protested before he thrust deep. The feel of him took her breath away. He was huge, hot, and incredibly arousing. He fucked her with long, hard thrusts, his breath raspy as he pushed inside her. Arousal spiked, and she felt the beginning of another climax when he stilled and groaned.

"Fuck me," he rasped, pulling out only to slam back into her. When his hand came around to stroke her clit, she felt his touch before she shattered again, clenching him tight.

"Baby, you're killing me." He groaned and repeatedly thrust, coming inside her with such force that cum starting dripping down her legs.

When they both finally stopped, Jewel realized what she'd done, and with whom. She'd just had sex, in public, with a man she'd met only minutes ago. Talk about going native…

Ethan pulled out and straightened his clothes, then reached into his back pocket and retrieved a handkerchief. Without a word, he squatted down to clean her legs, then pressed the cloth between her thighs.

Too sated to feel embarrassed, she stared at him. She couldn't believe her nonchalance at what they'd just done. But Jewel had always been adaptable, and she resolved to feel no guilt for the amazing sex she'd experienced. No one around them seemed to care, engrossed in their own sexuality. And hell, it had been a year since her last sexual encounter. Why not break her cold streak with a no-strings-attached, one-shot deal?

Glancing down into his eyes, she murmured, "Always prepared, hmm?"

"Not always." Ethan's gaze probed deep. He rose and stroked her cheek, taking her lips in a breath-stealing kiss. "Now for the rest of the tour."

* * *

Ethan had a hard time concentrating as he showed Jewel the rest of the resort. They passed several outdoor class sessions that were focused on mutual and independent pleasure, a foray into bondage—which he would have dearly loved to stay for—and more group sex that covered everything from oral to anal and several positions he couldn't imagine being comfortable in.

Through it all, Jewel remained cool and composed, interested but in a detached manner. Yet the shocked look on her face when he'd shown her the pool wouldn't leave his mind. The woman had applied for the job, but she'd acted completely astonished by the description of her duties and by what she'd seen. He should have felt better about their shared bliss, that she really was here to pleasure both herself and the guests. Yet something about the encounter told him she'd surprised herself with her lack of inhibitions.

For a woman who'd been dumped by her fiancée because she had particular needs in the bedroom, she shouldn't have been so hesitant about having sex with him by the hotel. He was a stranger, yes, but supposedly she liked sex with strangers so long as she had an audience. Ethan had been scanning all the applicants' resumes for the past couple of weeks and had found little to titillate him. He'd been surprised by Jewel's application, however, and more than intrigued by her accompanying photo.

Ethan's cock rose again, despite his heart-shaking climax just moments ago. Jewel had been so tight, so incredibly hot, that he wanted to experience her again, to relive the moment and prove to himself it had just been a fluke. Already thoughts of restraints and dominance intertwined with images of Jewel, and he had to force himself to focus on his reason for being there.

Two weeks ago he'd shown up on Rick's door, both curious and eager to wrap up the case. With five new employees and a host of guests at the resort, Ethan had his hands full investigating potential thieves. This newest employee, however, prodded his instincts to delve deeper. Unfortunately, he wasn't sure if said instincts were hormonal or suspicious in nature.

Someone was stealing artifacts from the Bacchus Club, Rick's highbrow secret society, where Bacchus, the Roman god of wine and pleasure, was the central figure and which consisted of members—millionaires, professional athletes, and actors—who shared a desire for guiltless pleasure. Several of the club members were missing paintings, urns, and sculptures, all stolen within the last year. And one unfortunate member had actually been murdered during the course of a robbery. Very big news in the swanky circles of Rick's private world.

The phone call warning Rick he was to be the next one robbed had spurred Rick to contact H&R Securities; that and the fact he was friends with George Howell, a former and very satisfied client of H&R's. Hired to guard Rick's priceless chalice, the Mirvolo Cup, as well as beef up security for Rick himself, Ethan put everyone and everything under the magnifying glass. But in Jewel Riser's case, the view was more than pleasant.

Good Christ, but he'd never been so hard for a woman in his life, and just from the look of her. Tall and lean, Jewel had surprisingly full breasts, a flat belly, and long, muscular legs. Her arms were toned, and she possessed a clear, olive complexion that spoke of Mediterranean ancestry. Her long black hair curled at the ends, and he could all too easily imagine wrapping the strands around his hands as he guided her cherry-red lips toward his cock.

The feel of her had seared him, left an aching need in its wake.

Again, he suddenly sported a massive hard-on, a condition Ethan had been learning to live with since his arrival. Hell, he was only human, and he'd seen more kinky sex in the last two weeks than he'd seen in his lifetime. He wiped his forehead, aware he couldn't use the handkerchief stuffed in his pocket because it was filled with his and Jewel's cum. Damn, but his time on this island was proving a real trial. Absently, he wondered if Jewel would welcome another bout of mind-blowing sex, and just as readily dismissed the idea.

The sex was already clouding his senses, and he glanced at her walking so quietly next to him, wondering why. She seemed off somehow, but not dangerous. And that kind of snap judgment would only lead to a mistake he couldn't afford to make, not for himself, or for Rick. Even relieved of his frustration, Ethan still felt tense. Maybe he should take Rick up on the offer of some regular, therapeutic sex to clear his mind. Then again, Ethan had a feeling Rick had been volunteering his own personal services.

Clearing his throat, Ethan guided Jewel toward the hotel doors and finished taking her through the building. "The place is full, all twenty rooms completely booked. Most guests stay a week and leave, but a few have special packages and are here a bit longer. You new employees are grouped here before Rick begins your training."

The hunted look in her eyes reappeared, and Ethan continued as if he hadn't noticed.

"Jaz will meet you tonight and introduce you to a few fellow employees. He'll get you situated with everything you need as far as amenities and your uniforms." Ethan gazed into her whiskey-brown eyes and felt something within him clench. Irritated at the foreign feeling, he backed away, needing to remain in control. "Oh, and Rick will be by later to check on you."

The thought of Rick touching her made Ethan want to pound something, and he had to restrain himself from taking hold of her and dragging her to his room to stake a claim.

"Thanks." Jewel coughed and opened the door, then turned back to him, her face red. "What happened earlier... Thanks for that, too." She spoke so fast he'd barely understood what she'd said before she closed the door in his face.

He stared, full of suspicion and a helpless sense of satisfaction. Composing himself, Ethan trekked back to Rick's office, wondering why this woman, of all the gorgeous women on the island, fascinated him. For a suspect who ought to have been easy to read, she was a puzzle, an intriguing mix of seductress and wary female.

He found Rick waiting, pacing the floor.

"Well, how was she?"

So fucking sexy I'm ready to come again... "She's fine and checked in to her room. Good idea, letting me show her around, giving me a feel for her. I gave her the tour—"

"And a bit more." Rick grinned, his eyes fixed on Ethan's groin. "I hear you're just as impressive as I'd thought."

Ethan flushed; he couldn't help it, and scowled at Rick's chuckle. "I was checking her out, and one thing led to another."

"Well?"

"She's hot. Really, really damned good. But I don't think she's who she says she is."

Rick's grin faded.

"She doesn't seem comfortable sexing it up in front of others, and as much as the play in the courtyard aroused her, I think it also intimidated her."

"So our exhibitionist only acted out because she was infatuated with you?"

"That's not what I'm saying."

"But that's what I'm saying. Her eyes barely left you the entire time she was in here. Oh, she looked at me and smiled when I spoke, but I know when a woman's interested and when she's not. Pity, I really like the look of her."

Rick's disappointment eased Ethan's tension. But Rick's next words startled him.

"I want you to handle her, Ethan."

"Handle her? Rick, I have my hands full with your antique chalice and making sure Elise rides herd on you when you refuse to listen to reason."

"You'll train her."

"I'm no expert on sexual games, and I'm not into fetishes." *Except for the bondage fantasies I can't shake.* "Hell, I'm a detective, not a sexual instructor."

"But she's someone you need to focus on. A suspect, right? You've already cleared the other four new people, as well as most of my guests. And you yourself said she felt 'off.' Trust your instincts. I do. After all, the cup spoke to you, didn't it?"

Ethan inwardly flinched at the memory. Even though he was working undercover for Rick, Rick treated him like family. He'd ordered Ethan to sip from the Mirvolo Cup, from Bacchus's own supposed chalice, a treat reserved for those closest to him. And damned if Ethan hadn't tingled throughout his entire body after just one sip of wine. Lust and love had swirled through him, the promise of tomorrow's passion just within reach—none of which made any sense.

"The Mirvolo Cup only speaks to those Bacchus favors. Pleasure of the flesh, of love and life, will soon be yours. Face it, Ethan. You were fated to be here." Rick grinned. "Once you're finished with this job, you're more than invited to join the Club." Rick looked a little too interested for Ethan's peace of mind.

"Thanks. I'll have to think on it."

"You do that. And while you're at it, here are the last of the reports your partner faxed while you were gone."

Ethan took the folder, glad of the reprieve. As much as he towered over Rick and could easily outmuscle the smaller, though by no means small, man, there was something about Rick Hastings that threatened. Ethan had never been attracted to men, not in his entire life. But here, surrounded by sex, and after sipping wine from that damned cup, he felt almost...tempted...by Rick Hastings. The man packed an incredible amount of charisma and power inside that frame of blond-haired, blue-eyed charm. *And what the hell am I thinking about?*

Ethan thought of Jewel and the questions she presented. He reaffirmed his focus. "I need to look these over. You're going to be with Elise and the others until midnight, right?"

"Yes. She's been with me for five years, but who knew? That minx of a bodyguard is proving as entertaining as she is infuriating. I'll be fine, Ethan. Go do whatever it is you've been doing." Rick flashed him a knowing smile. "I'll make sure to mention you to Jewel when I see her. Oh, and Ethan? I wasn't kidding. You *will* oversee Jewel's training as soon as she's settled in."

"I'm not here for pussy," Ethan said bluntly. "I'm here to keep your ass safe."

"As much as I love hearing you talk about my ass, the bottom line is that I'm in charge, as we agreed."

Fuck. Ethan normally took charge of every investigation. But this one was different, and Rick had been insistent that he have the last word on everything. Since "training" Jewel wouldn't necessarily put Rick in danger, Ethan couldn't exactly refuse. And the truth of the matter was, he didn't want to.

"Fine. But if I'm training her, no one else handles her. Not even you." Expecting a refusal, Ethan was taken by surprise when Rick grinned.

"Outstanding. I'll see you tomorrow, then." He paused by the door. "Ethan? I've left a DVD in your room outlining how to train our girl. Nothing too rough, just some light bondage I'm sure you'll easily manage." He glanced down at Ethan's growing erection. "Pleasant dreams."

Chapter Three

Three days later, Jewel glanced down at her "uniform" in mortified disgust. "Hell, I might as well be naked."

She'd had to shave *everything* south of her navel in order to look trim and smooth in the bikini. And damn if she didn't feel naughty having done it.

Why she should feel so dismayed by the skimpy two-piece she didn't know…considering she'd had sweaty out-of-your-mind sex in freaking public. Two nights of thinking had brought her to some uncomfortable realizations.

One, she liked sex more now than she ever had, and she feared it had more to do with Ethan Reaper than the act itself. Two, she still wasn't as embarrassed as she should have been after orgasming in public, making her wonder if she wasn't a closet exhibitionist. And three, if she thought half as much about her case as she did about her hulking lover, she might already have found and secured Sophie Ayers's sex video.

If only Jewel had her equipment, but she'd anticipated
having her things systematically searched before she'd be
allowed to step foot on the resort and had left her kit at
home. If only the doors to each employee's rooms weren't
electronically scrambled and coded. If only Joshua Denton
were still on the damned island. Who the hell needed a
vacation from a place like this?

Sighing, Jewel tugged at the green thong biting into her
hip and rolled her shoulders, wishing the thin bikini top
covered more than just her nipples. She wasn't huge, but had
enough on top to want herself covered. Cripes, but outdoors
sex with Ethan had been easy next to walking around nearly
naked. She'd received more leers, grins, and suggestions than
she knew what to do with.

"Jewel, honey, your order's up."

She nodded at Jaz, a tall, mouthwateringly sexy
employee and the epitome of the Latin lover. He worked
with the waitstaff and had been assigned to help her adjust to
her domestic duties. When Rick had met with her two nights
ago, he'd been specific about listening to Jaz and her
expected performance when it came to serving drinks and
dinner. Unfortunately, Rick had been vague about her *other*
expected duties.

Hefting the tray of drinks poolside, Jewel mentally
cringed every time she bent over to hand off an order.

After meeting the other newbies Wednesday night, Jaz
had introduced her to the senior staff. Friendly, sexy, and
undeniably charming, Jaz had led her throughout the resort
with a running commentary on everything from favorite
fetishes to the cleanup routine after dinner. The actual
waitress tasks were easy for a woman who'd waitressed

through college. But the sexual aspect of the job kept getting weirder and weirder.

Near midnight, Jaz had left her with Rick, no sign of Ethan anywhere to be found. And to her dismay, she'd been looking. Then Rick had presented her with the Mirvolo Cup...

"Thanks, sugar." The voice and wandering hands of a middle-aged man brought her out of her musings.

"Anytime," she murmured, keeping a smile on her face. *Think of Denton. Remember your real purpose for being here.* In just four more days, the little jerk would return from his vacation from paradise, and she'd finally get a shot at taking him down. If Jewel could survive the wait.

Because ever since she'd sipped from that oddly shaped chalice—that damned cup—her mind had been decidedly screwy, in a sexual kind of way.

Granted, Satyr's Myst was inundated with sexual fantasy, but Jewel would have thought the excessive sex might grow old after a while. Unfortunately, seeing so much raw carnality made her hunger for more...with Ethan.

And where was he, anyway? Jewel had been working her tail off to understand the schedules and memorize names and routines. Thankfully, though she'd only seen Rick twice more since her first night here, he hadn't mentioned that whole sexual side of her job. The sexual side Ethan had gladly introduced her to. She swore softly, aware she missed the big lug and couldn't ask anyone about him without revealing her interest. Instead she focused on the job.

Jewel watched and listened, and added her observations to what Jaz had told her about the sexual proclivities of the staff and guests, her nerves strung as tight as piano wire.

And speaking of Jaz... Glancing to her left, Jewel spotted him outside, under the bright sun, naked, and in the middle of two busty women. Her breath caught at the sight. She took her tray back to the outdoor bar to grab some empty glasses and, along with several other people, watched, helplessly caught, as her co-worker and the women enjoyed one another.

Jaz glistened as if he'd been slathered with oil, his body hard and muscular, the women slithering over him, naked as well. One woman sat on his face, the other over his cock. And damn it to hell, Jewel felt her own desire rise.

But in her mind, she became Jaz, and Rick and Ethan pleasured *her.*

"I'm seriously losing it," she mumbled to herself and turning around, headed back inside in an effort to cool her libido. Rick and Ethan... As if. She'd just come off a year-long celibate streak. Apparently, Ethan had broken the dam on her sexual reserve, because she felt in perpetual heat. Jewel winced at the slickness between her thighs, wishing she had on a decent pair of underwear and shorts.

"Jewel, just the person I've been looking for."

Jewel wanted to groan, Rick's voice coming way too soon on the heels of her lecherous fantasies. She turned slowly and forced a smile. "Rick, how nice to see you."

"Everything okay?"

"Just fine. Jaz has been great, a real help..." She paused when said help moaned and bucked under the woman sitting astride his pelvis. She cleared her throat. "He's been wonderful in introducing me to the resort. I'm almost convinced I can work the dinner shift without assistance."

Rick's eyes glittered with humor as he followed her gaze to Jaz and the women. "Good. You know, even if you hadn't listed it on your résumé, I'd know you'd waitressed before. And you're very good with our guests."

"Thanks."

"If Tyrone can spare you for a moment, I have a few more items to discuss with you."

Tyrone, the man behind the bar, smiled and nodded. "We'll make do, though she's quickly becoming a guest favorite."

Great, just what she didn't need, more attention from the sexual dynamos getting it on poolside. She had a hard enough time believing her impromptu sex with Ethan had been real. Jewel hadn't been kidding when she'd told Rick she was modest. Imagining an orgy with any of the guests turned her way off.

"Come with me, Jewel."

Jewel hesitated a second before putting her hand in Rick's, and he noticed, if the small frown he gave her was any indication. They walked inside and back into his private wing, where she'd had her interview. Instead of sitting behind his desk, Rick led her to an intimate loveseat and sat down next to her.

His gaze wandered lazily over her barely covered breasts and flat belly to the small triangle covering her groin. "You look beautiful. An erotic temptress. Eve sitting in Eden."

Her nipples hardened, and she flushed, wondering what the hell was wrong with her. "Thanks, I think. I don't know that I like being compared to Eve, though. She was Adam's downfall."

"Then how about a likeness to Venus?"

"I don't think so. She had a habit of screwing with any woman whose beauty was compared to hers."

Rick's lips twitched. "You're a hard one to please, Jewel. And you know we're all about pleasure here."

He ran a hand over her shoulder, and she froze, both aroused and nervous about it. If Rick would just give her some space...

"So tense. See, this just won't do."

"What?"

"I know it's only been a few days, but you're not losing those inhibitions as fast as I'd hoped."

"I'm practically nude. I'd say that's losing some inhibitions." Jewel felt grouchy, knowing he was both right and wrong. She didn't like being almost naked among strangers, and she didn't want anyone groping her...unless that "anyone" happened to be Ethan.

"You're an interesting character, Jewel. You're a natural at putting others at ease, until they move too close." He cut the small space between them on the couch. His breath fanned her face, he sat so close. "Then you tense up, like one of Diana's maidens at a man's approach."

What was it with Rick's Roman references?

"I don't know what to say." Shit, he wasn't going to fire her, was he? But she just couldn't make herself sleep around the resort to finish this job. Ethan was the exception, and one she still didn't understand. No, she'd find Denton's blackmail material another way.

Rick glanced behind her and pressed a button on the intercom fixed to the side table. "Come on in. She's here."

Jewel sucked in a breath when Ethan entered. Wearing a security uniform, the orange polo and tan slacks he'd worn when they'd first met, he radiated power. He stopped before them, his arms crossed, his biceps bulging with unconcealed strength. The unfamiliar gleam in his dark brown eyes snared her, and she stared, unable to look away.

"Hello, Jewel."

His voice made her shiver, and before she knew it, Rick had hoisted her into Ethan's arms. Ethan's forearms locked under her breasts and held her tight.

"You, Jewel, are going to be in Ethan's hands for the next few days." Rick looked to Ethan. "I assume you'll be with the cup at all times?"

Ethan nodded.

"I'll be with Elise and several of my closest friends while Jewel undergoes training. Jewel, don't panic." He smiled, but his grin looked too satisfied for comfort. "I'm sensing you have unexplored talents that I think Ethan can help you discover."

Ethan's grip tightened on her arm when she tried to extricate herself, and a frisson of unexpected desire unnerved her into speaking without thinking.

"But, Rick, what the heck can Ethan do? I'm doing well with the waitressing stuff. I don't need Ethan. Just give me time, and I'll eventually be able to, ah, help pleasure the guests." *Yeah, with enough time I'll be out of this sex circus and home with Sophie Ayers's video in my hands.*

Rick shook his head. "But I need you ready to please now, Jewel. Every one of my staff revels in their sensuality. It's that gift that separates my employees from every other 'specialized' resort. And despite what you may think, you do need Ethan. He's just the man to bring all that untapped sensuality to the surface. After all, you didn't seem to mind his attentions after our meeting Wednesday."

Jewel blushed, her embarrassment choosing that moment to make itself known.

"What a pretty color, Jewel." Rick glanced slyly at Ethan. "Now just imagine that fiery shade of red on her ass after a spanking, when she's coming around your cock."

Ethan's erection was impossible to miss against her bare back. "I'll take her, and I'll 'train' her for you. But if I get one phone call from Elise, you know where I'll be."

Rick grinned, his eyes shining with mirth. "Do tell, Ethan. Where will you be?"

"So far up your ass you'll—Dammit, Rick. This isn't a joke."

Rick laughed, and she glanced behind her to see Ethan scowl—not so expressionless now.

Jewel didn't quite understand the byplay, still reeling from the fact she'd be with Ethan for the next few days. *"Coming around your cock,"* Rick had said. Good Lord, the man had no problem speaking his mind. And yet when he spoke with Ethan... There was more between Ethan and Rick than employer and employee, though the relationship didn't seem sexual, at least on Ethan's part. Rick, however, eyed the other man like a dog salivating over a bone.

Though curious, she couldn't think past the opportunity heading her way. She had four more days before Denton returned. Four days to plan how to engage the man, and how to make sure she had a shot at his computer. Letting him invite her inside his room would be the easiest way to find what she needed—she'd take note of his security code and enter his room later, when she knew he was busy. Then she'd be able to find Sophie Ayers's pictures. But if he returned to the resort and played hard to get, she'd have to tap into the main security system, a mean feat considering Mr. Dominant by her side.

"Come on, Jewel. Appears we have some work to do."

Fire raced through her blood, and she left with Ethan, not willing to argue the point with Rick watching. A glance back at her new boss showed a smug grin that alarmed her, but when he gave her a questioning look, she merely smiled and waved good-bye.

What the hell was all this about? Ethan, from what she'd ferreted out from the staff, had only arrived on the island a few weeks before she had. He headed a specific security for Rick. For the Mirvolo Cup. Jewel shivered. Ah, yes. She recalled every detail about the blasted thing.

It was some kind of a test, Jewel had learned, a ritual Rick used to induct his new people, having them drink from the cup. And that strange tingle…she wasn't quite sure what to make of that. She admitted the cup had impressed her when Rick had placed it in her hands. Pure gold, its base encrusted with rubies and sapphires, it had to be worth a fortune. And the intricate carvings of the men and women engaged in sex had fit in with Satyr's Myst all too well. Jewel understood the antique's allure. Similar to the temptation the pearl necklace owned by the president of a rival company had held for Jewel, the cup would attract anyone with an interest in the unique and expensive.

Thinking about the pearl necklace she'd stolen from Serena gave Jewel a thrill, as had the danger in returning the item without getting caught. The rush from that theft had been more than satisfying, and a sudden, unbidden thought grabbed her. How hard would it be to steal the cup, and out from under Ethan's very nose? Sexual excitement mixed with the anticipation of a heist, and Jewel had to remind herself to focus on her job. All she needed was to be caught stealing from Rick. Then she'd never find Denton's pictures.

"Where are you, Jewel?" Ethan whispered as he tucked her against his side. "You're awfully quiet. Scared?"

His voice taunted, and she played into his hand even knowing she shouldn't. "Of you?" She snorted. "Not quite."

"Then I must not be doing my job." He said the words in a low growl in her ear, and her womb clenched with need at the feel of his breath in the sensitive canal. He nipped at her earlobe, and she couldn't help the gasp that escaped.

Before she could say anything else, they neared the end of the corridor, where a secured door stood. Ethan stepped in front of her, putting his broad back between her and the sensors, and punched in a code. The door hissed open, and they entered into a hedonist's utopia.

Plump cushions in dark purple and gold littered the cream-colored carpet, reminding her of a sultan's chambers. Through the thinly veiled windows the clear blue water of the ocean rushed onto the soft, white sand of the nearby beach. The scent of honeysuckle and saltwater breezed through the room, and the circulating air stirred the grounded sensuality in the room, teasing with soft touches and sultry scents.

A wooden border surrounded the floor, in patterns of interlocking Tiete rosewood, a rich cherry color that complemented the subtle tones of the cushions. Busts of ancient Romans sat in every corner of the room, and Jewel wondered if they'd entered Rick's private suite. She wouldn't have been surprised to find it so. Like the rest of the resort, the mahogany furniture, conservative king-sized, four-poster bed, and classic paintings depicting debauched virgins and devilish fauns all combined to create a rich and darkly furnished pleasure palace.

Jewel swallowed hard when she looked beside the bed. A portion of the wall slid back when Ethan flicked a switch, showcasing a variety of whips, chains, and sexual devices of which she'd much rather remain ignorant.

"Nice, hmm?"

Ethan left her to study the myriad devices; when he wasn't looking, she took a cautious step back.

"This is Rick's room, where we'll be staying for the next few days. He's been kind enough to lend it to us for your training. You really should thank him."

"Thank him?"

"Yeah." Ethan turned around, his eyes hard, his demeanor one she hadn't seen before. "You know, thank him. For giving you a job, for taking you in when you decided to run from a relationship gone bad. Or was that just another lie? Like the one about your ability to get off fucking for an audience, and with strangers no less?"

"What the hell are you talking about?" Jewel calmed her breathing but had no luck with her heartbeat. As Ethan neared, she felt like nervous prey near a hungry lion. Good Lord, but his eyes looked so dark as to be black, and she was slowly falling down that inky well into confusing but consuming desire.

"Don't you remember? You mentioned your unique appetites on the application."

What? What the hell had Uncle Tommy said to land her this job? He'd been emphatic that she not journey as a vacationer, so she knew he didn't want her here sexing it up. How the hell had their wires crossed?

"You seemed to like me well enough the other day." He reached out a hand and caressed her cheek before his touch grew more demanding. Gripping her chin, he forced her to meet his gaze.

"Well, Ethan, that's because I was so drawn to your stunning personality. You were just brimming with welcome and wit. I couldn't say no."

His lips twisted at her sarcasm. "You have a smart mouth, don't you?" He let go of her chin to find her shoulders, his grip strong but not painful. "But there are better uses for that mouth than insults."

His grin worried her, and Jewel decided she'd had enough of this game. She'd find that damned video another way, without succumbing to Ethan Reaper and his stupid "training."

She didn't like being manhandled, she told herself. She really didn't. And she surely wasn't becoming aroused from Ethan's domineering attitude.

"Let me go." She spoke calmly.

"Your pulse is racing a mile a minute." Ethan leaned down, his eyes on par with hers. Then his mouth was over her neck, sucking on the sensitive pulse point at her throat. He nipped hard, biting her, and she jolted at the erotic sensation. His hands remained firm, escape all but impossible unless she could manage a knee between his legs.

"No, no, baby. No violence." He shoved her legs apart, apparently reading her body language. "I'm in charge here. And you do what I say, when I say. That's rule number one."

"Bullshit," she rasped. "You're no trainer. From what I heard, you arrived a few weeks before I did as *security*. Now let me go."

He licked her neck before biting again, and she couldn't control a groan of delight.

"Your mouth says one thing, your body another. But either way, you're going to listen to me. I'm the master, honey. And you submit to me and me alone."

Oh, hell. She should have seen this one coming. A guy as big and brawny as Ethan would have no problems playing the "master" in his own version of some whacked-out domination game.

"Look, I—"

"Submit, or tell me why you're really here."

Why the hell couldn't he have conformed to stereotype? A man with that much muscle should have been high on testosterone and short on brains. Just her luck to find one with both testosterone *and* brains.

He didn't sound as if he totally bought her cover; she needed to act quickly. She might have been able to maneuver

Rick around, but Ethan Reaper was no one's fool. And Jewel didn't want to have to worry about him and the rest of Rick's security if it came to breaking into Denton's room.

"I'm here…" She paused, trying to come up with something better than the Denton/Ayers story. Dreemer's, Inc. promised confidentiality, so confiding to Ethan was out, even if she'd wanted to. Besides, she actually enjoyed the challenge he presented. He was hot, and he made her fight her own instincts. Besting Ethan would take a savvy mind, like stealing a pearl necklace right off its wearer's neck…

She glanced at one of the Roman busts and inspiration struck. "I'm here because I'm fascinated by the Mirvano Cup. It's amazing, so rare, you know?"

He stilled, and she wanted to congratulate herself, until she saw his face. All expression had fled, and his eyes seemed like fathomless pits of retribution.

"Say that again?"

Shit. It wasn't Mirvano. Her mind scrambled for purchase, and she tried to back away. Ethan, however, refused to let her go. They stood a breath apart, her head tilted to look up into his menacing gaze.

"Ah, the Mirvalo Cup? I just wanted to see it with my own eyes." Standing so close, he was making it hard to think.

Ethan relaxed a fraction, and Jewel readied to bolt. Maybe she could use one of those whips on the wall to ward him off until she could escape from the room.

"You mean the Mirvolo Cup?" he asked softly. His eyes were searching as he stared at her.

"That's what I said."

"Who do you work for?"

"Work for? No one. I'm a lover of Roman antiquities, and that cup's worth a fortune. Its history is priceless."

She tried to wiggle for room, but he wouldn't release her. His lips brushed her neck again, up toward her ear, and before she knew it Ethan was tonguing the sensitive shell. Heat shot through her body, fanning the fire in her womb. Dammit, was he buying her story or not? His touch was driving her out of her mind. Jewel grew wet, and wetter still when he began whispering erotic promises and future delights.

"You'll tell me everything I want to know, my Jewel. And in return, I'll teach you how to play my games. You'll beg me to come down your throat, baby, so many times that you'll forget what it's like not to suck my cock. And I'm going to ream that ass, to cream inside your hole and wash you with my cum. I promise. You won't leave this room until you've begged me to fuck your pussy, and fuck it hard."

He was breathing heavily, but then, so was she.

"And you'll call me 'Master' while you beg so sincerely on your knees."

"No way in hell," she rasped as his tongue made her knees weak. Who was she kidding? She wanted him in the worst way, and all they'd done so far was a little dirty talk and some ear action. She really had to get the hell out of here.

"Oh?" Ethan had her top off in a blink. His hands fitted over her breasts, and his mouth teased her lips. "You have great tits, baby. So firm and soft, with such pretty little nipples."

Jewel's breathing increased until she felt as though she were panting, yet she refused to give in. "Let go of me, you bully—"

"Master."

"—because I never have, and never will, call any man 'Master.' I'm not into that submission crap."

"Then why are you so wet?" He shoved a hand beneath her thong and swiped it through her slit.

She jerked, but his fingers refused to budge, and before she knew it he'd shoved one digit inside her.

"You feel good, baby. But you'll feel even better tied up. Ask your master nicely, and I'll let you come before I punish you."

She squirmed this way and that, but she still couldn't dislodge him. Instead she'd frustrated the hell out of herself by brushing her sensitive nipples against his chest. Ethan added a second finger, stretching her.

"Let me go," she managed on a groan as her body quickly rose toward climax.

"No, no. You don't deserve to come, not yet." He removed his hand, and she wanted to huff with simultaneous relief and frustration.

"Why are *you* training me, anyway? What do you know about this stuff? As the security guard, shouldn't you be monitoring the Mirvolo Cup?"

She could have sworn he smiled, but his lips firmed too quickly to tell. "That antiquity you're so interested in is safe, baby, a hell of a lot safer than your pretty little ass is right now."

Without warning, he threw her over his shoulder and started toward the bed.

"Now, slave, you belong to me."

Chapter Four

Ethan's heart wanted to burst out of his chest as much as his cock wanted to jump out of his pants. Hot damn, but Jewel made him so hard so fast, it was a wonder he hadn't shot his load when he'd shoved his fingers into her deliciously warm pussy.

The little liar squirmed over his shoulder, and her helplessness pushed him past his reservations. "Priceless antiquity," she'd alluded to. She was no more interested in the cup than he was a sexual trainer. He didn't believe she'd told the truth on her application, but he didn't think a thief as proficient as the one stealing from Rick's friends would be as clueless about the cup as she'd seemed.

She could, of course, be playing him, but he didn't think so. Regardless, he'd get his answers. The hard way. Using his free hand he shifted his cock through his pants material and, still uncomfortable, walked to the wall holding an assortment of restraints. Seeing several scarlet ties, Ethan went rock hard. And, there, a blindfold. Shit, he wanted this, badly.

Keeping hold of the wildcat over his shoulder took some careful maneuvering, but he grabbed a few silk ropes and had her naked, tied, and spread-eagled on the bed in five minutes flat.

She glared at him, her whiskey-brown eyes alight with anger.

Fuck it. He stripped off his own clothing, wanting some respite. The sight of this woman, bound and helpless before him like some pagan sacrifice, had him close to climax from the image alone. How many times had he dreamed of a lover like this? And she played the part of the outraged female to perfection. He'd never wanted a completely submissive partner. No, Ethan wanted to conquer, to dominate, and win his prize by earning it.

All of which, according to Rick's instructional DVD, had less to do with true D/s than with his personal fantasies.

Jewel jerked her arms and legs, trying to free herself, and he felt ready to blow. She was so fucking perfect. *A gift from the gods,* Rick would have joked.

And now, all mine.

Jewel's eyes lit with alarm as he stared down at her with such hunger, her gaze alternating between his imposing stare and his weeping cock. He lay between her thighs, his gaze centered on her exposed pussy.

"Wait a minute."

"No."

"But... Oh," she gasped, then arched into his mouth as he sought her clit. She tasted so damned good. Her juices were like honey, like sugar on his tongue. Her clit was plump, ripe with arousal, and he wanted to savor the experience. Ethan had never been able to enjoy a woman who was fully at his mercy, and to have Jewel here, as his, was like heaven on earth.

"Do you have any idea how sexy you are?" he rasped. "I want to eat you until you scream. Will you scream for me, Jewel? Will you scream for your master?"

"Screw you," she breathed even as she ground into his mouth again. "God, what are you doing to me?"

"So damned wet. You like being tied up, don't you, baby?"

He shoved a finger inside her as he licked her, and her breathing grew more and more choppy.

"Tell me, slave. What do you want your master to do to you?"

"Not…your…slave."

Ethan increased the pressure on her clit, shoving his fingers deeper to touch her G-spot. He felt her entire body clench, and he stopped, aware she teetered on the edge of climax.

"Oh, Ethan, more," she moaned when he slowed his fingers.

"Tell me what you want."

"Let me come."

"'Let me come,' what?"

She shook her head, thrashing on the pillows, as he brought her to peak again but not quite over. She panted. "You're a real bastard, you know that?"

The sexual frustration on her face increased his arousal. The fact that he was the fix to her problem, that he held the power to satisfy her, filled that void inside him that was always aching when it came to sex. His cock was wet from excitement, and he didn't know how much longer he could last. Each time he thrust his fingers inside her, he mimicked the action by thrusting hard against the bed sheets. The urge to fuck her lingered too close, and the scent of her desire only intensified his need to dominate the woman.

She had yet to call him her master, and he refused to give her the upper hand.

Inspiration struck as he glanced up at her mouth.

"Your master needs attention, slave." He licked his lips, savoring her taste, and leaned up. He crawled over her body, straddling her waist. When her eyes focused on his flushed cock, Ethan smiled grimly. "That's right. Suck your master, Jewel. Suck him so he can grant you the ease you need."

She licked her lips, her gaze both wary and wanting.

"Tell me, Jewel, why you refuse to say the words. They're just words, after all." He watched her, aware they weren't just words to her since she couldn't say them. She needed to be mastered, needed to give her control to another. He could see her desperate willingness to comply, even as she battled herself.

"You're not my master," she said quietly, looking disturbed. "I control my body."

"Do you?" He rubbed his shaft between her breasts, palming her nipples. He pressed callused hands over the beading tips, and she cried out as he rocked faster and faster, her hips bucking in a matching rhythm. "No, Jewel. I'm the master of your body right now." *And your mind.* "Give me what I need, so that I can give you what you need." He lowered to meet her mouth and kissed her tenderly on the lips.

She blinked up at him, confused, and bit her lower lip in indecision. "But I don't want to be anyone's plaything."

"Not anyone's plaything. *My lover*," he corrected. "Everyone else can fuck themselves. This is between you and me."

Her eyes widened, and he drowned in their honey depths. God, she pulled at him like no other, and he couldn't help wondering what it was about this stubborn woman that attracted him so much. Because the attraction went way beyond the physical.

Ethan wanted the sex so badly he could taste it. But in his mind, the sex would only open the door into Jewel's heart, body, and soul. He'd bind her to him physically, gain her trust and affection, and teach her to please him so that he could please her. He'd watched her these past few days while she worked, unaware. And Ethan found he wanted to be the one to make her smile, to make her laugh. The urge to please her outside the bedroom called to him as much as her body did. And though he didn't understand why, he wanted to savor the experience.

Jewel looked torn, almost as if she were finally taking his demand seriously. His heart raced as he waited for her response, wanting to hear her say it, just once.

"Just with you. *Only* you."

Ethan nodded, his gaze intent.

She took a deep breath. "Okay…Master."

He had to focus hard not to come, so pleased was he with her answer. As if she'd agreed to give him everything he wanted, her answer paved the way to a future he'd only dreamed about. Groaning with pleasure, Ethan leaned down, kissing her flush on the mouth. She opened under him, blossoming into the partner he truly desired.

Their tongues mated, hers retreating when his pushed forth. Her lips softened under his, accepting his aggression, his tenderness, and his building lust as she moved with him. Her breasts swelled under his touch, and he flicked her nipples, earning several moans out of his sexual slave.

He felt tense, ready to come at just the thought of her orgasm, before Jewel broke from the kiss with swollen, passion-stung lips.

"Fuck my mouth, Master. Please."

Needing to explode, he leaned up from the kiss and positioned his rock-hard cock at her mouth. "Very good, slave." Shit, this verbal game was making it difficult to concentrate on anything but ramming inside her heavenly lips. *Master.* He was her master. Oh, God, yes.

"Lick me dry first, baby. Gently."

Her small pink tongue darted out, her gaze intense on his as she ran her tongue over his slit, sweeping his precum with slow, delicious licks. Ethan closed his eyes, aware they were rolling back in his head. He began moving against her lips, pushing the crown against the velvet petals of her mouth.

"You taste so good, Master." Her voice was husky, and he opened his eyes to see her gaze was now glued to his cock. "You're so big, so hard."

He moved over her, and she licked him from his balls to his cockhead, her mouth hot as she pushed him closer to climax.

"I'm going to fuck your mouth, the mouth that now belongs to me." Ethan envisioned her in a collar, his collar, and pushed past her lips. "That's it, baby. Take it all in. Balls deep."

She accepted him, gagging a little, but she quickly pushed past the reflex. And before he knew it, she'd encased his entire shaft. He brushed the back of her throat, his excitement palpable.

"I'm going to come down your throat. And you're going to thank me for it when I'm done. Aren't you, slave?"

She nodded around his shaft, sucking and stroking with her tongue as if born to the task.

So hard and desperate for relief, Ethan felt his end approaching. And he didn't intend to hold back. The sooner he came, the sooner he could focus on Jewel, on molding her to his preferences, on swallowing her precious cum before stoking her to orgasm after orgasm.

Shaking, he thrust into her mouth. In and out, deeper and deeper.

She moaned and lifted her chin, changing the angle of her mouth over him.

"Oh, yeah," he rasped, fisting her hair as he thrust again and again. But he couldn't hold on any longer, not at the sight of her bound and helpless, taking his large cock inside her soft, ripe mouth. His fantasies made real.

"Good, very good, Jewel." His balls felt ready to burst. "I'm coming, baby. Swallow it. All of it," he groaned, and shot hard.

She took him, every last drop, leaving him empty and replete throughout his entire body. As he shuddered, leaning over her, he felt the stroke of her tongue as she licked him clean, and he couldn't move, taken with the image of her servicing him so completely.

"So good, baby. Now you're ready to begin."

* * *

Begin? Her heart was pounding, her blood racing, and her clit ached unbearably. She needed an ending, a climax, dammit. *Now.*

Ethan, however, climbed slowly off her body and lay on his side, propped on one elbow beside her, where she was unable to reach him. Jewel still tasted him in her mouth, and his flavor blurred her senses. So sexy, so unbelievably arousing. She'd never imagined how much pleasure could be had in giving to another.

His dominance released something within her, allowing her to be as wild and free as she wanted. And with Ethan, she more than wanted. Saying the word "master" had been difficult. Jewel felt like she'd surrendered to him, yet he didn't appear smug that she'd complied, only satisfied and sexually charged. The look in his dark eyes when she'd called him "Master" was permanently seared into her brain. So much desire, hot and real, and aimed at *her.*

Sucking Ethan, taking that long, hard cock in her mouth, she'd felt like a goddess. Drunk on his taste, on the trembling in Ethan's massive body that *she'd* instilled. For all that he'd been the one issuing commands, she'd been the one with all the power.

"It felt good, didn't it?" he asked quietly. He ran a hand over her flank, resting on her hip, his fingers tantalizingly near her shaved pussy. "Bringing me over like that. You took me all the way inside."

More than he knew. As if in swallowing his essence, she'd swallowed a bit of his soul as well. She couldn't explain it, but she felt irrevocably linked to the large man by her side. A man she really didn't know much about. A man who had tied her to a bed, who had done intimate things to her that she'd never attempted with another.

She flushed, and he grinned, his dark brown gaze trailing where his hand led. A large palm caressed her belly, then slid up to capture her breasts. He played with the soft flesh, flicking her nipples and cupping her breasts in a warm hand.

"Your body's perfect," he murmured. "You fit inside my hands as if you were made for me."

Jewel tingled, his words too near to what she'd been thinking for comfort. "Master?" She wanted to kick herself as soon as she said it. Now that he'd come down off his power trip, she'd meant to call him Ethan. "Master" had slipped out on its own.

"I love hearing you say that." His voice sounded thick, and she glanced down only to see his shaft rising again. "But we have a long way to go before I've fully captured your submission, Jewel."

She frowned. "Submission" didn't sound right. She'd have to explain—

"Master—*Ethan.*" He'd buried a hand between her legs, squeezing her clit with enough pressure to make it hurt. But the hurt was surprisingly good, and she couldn't keep from creaming his hand.

"Yes, baby." He released the pressure and slid two fingers inside her. "That's it. Feel the pleasure. But you can't come yet. Not until your thoughts and mind are on me, your *master.*"

Emphasis on the last word told her he wasn't happy she'd called him by his name. But, hell, calling him "Master" was beginning to feel natural. And that didn't seem to fit. She wasn't submissive. She'd never been one of those women to kowtow to a man. Yet he'd tied her up and ordered her to service him. And dammit all, she'd *loved* it. She'd found pleasure in the giving, a freeing sense of power she'd never before experienced.

But she now felt pleasure in the taking. Oh, did she. His fingers were thick and long, and kept prodding the once-elusive G-spot, which he'd quickly discovered. Unstoppable moans came from her throat, gurgling cries of need she could neither control nor suppress.

"That's it, baby. Let it out. Give yourself to me. But don't come, honey. Not yet."

She'd come when she wanted to, Jewel thought, turning to glare at him. The minute their eyes met, he stopped, and she groaned again, this time in disappointment.

"Now, Jewel, you're not playing the game. What's my name?" He teased her clit, one smooth thrust toward her womb with hard fingers.

"Come on, Ethan."

He removed his hand completely and it hovered above, the heat of his palm warming her cleft.

"Master," she corrected, sighing with pleasure when his digits entered her again.

"And who are you to me, baby?" His voice was as seductive as his touch, deep and throaty, as chocolaty smooth as his eyes. She stared at him, ensnared by the commanding glint of power in his gaze, by the strength in his arms, and the fingers that made her body sing.

"Your slave."

Her whisper made him smile, a gratifying grin that echoed in the firmness of his touch. "That's good, baby. Real good. And you should be rewarded."

Sliding down her body, he continued to thrust his fingers in and out of her, but when she felt his hot breath over her sex, she tensed in anticipation.

He blew a kiss over her clit before bearing down and taking the hard flesh in his mouth. Dear God, but the need to come built inside her until she wanted to scream her desire.

"Your pussy tastes so sweet. Like warm honey. And I want more."

Jewel moaned and shoved closer to his lips, gasping his name, *Master,* as she approached true bliss.

"You can't come yet, not until I allow it. Right, slave?"

Too caught up in his spell to care, she agreed. Hell, she'd have agreed to have her head shaved if he'd just put an end to this torment and let her climax...*make* her climax. "Yes, Master. Anything you say." She twisted her wrists in the dark red silk binding her.

"Whatever I want?" he murmured, his mouth full of her clit, his fingers sliding through her cream.

"Whatever you want."

"I want you to come, Jewel. Come hard, all over my tongue."

Groaning, she strained to get closer to him, to shove her clit tighter into his mouth. And then he was biting down, pleasuring her as his fingers brushed deep inside her. She felt the dam burst and exploded. Sobbing, she clenched around his fingers like a vise.

The orgasm was cathartic in more ways than one. Her body felt relief, finally, but so too did her tired mind. On the edge undercover, she'd been tense with sexual frustration, confusion, and unrequited desire for Ethan Reaper. On top of all that, she had yet to find a way into Denton's room, the wasted days sucking the energy and time she didn't have.

Now she finally felt as if she could relax. Her master— Ethan—would take care of her. As her breathing calmed, she flushed at still thinking of him as "Master." Once again in control of her body, Jewel had trouble ceding him so much power. Yet she reveled in the protection of his strength. Bewildered and embarrassed at having completely lost her mind, she turned to tell him she had problems with his authority.

And then he smiled at her. A genuine gesture of warmth, of caring. And her heart stopped for the split second it took to fall madly, stupidly in love.

"Better now?"

She nodded mutely.

His grin faded, and he stared at her as if trying to see all her secrets. "There's no shame in what you did, baby. I can tell you're still fighting it. But you don't have to. You know, deep down, what you did was right—right for you. I'm your master now, Jewel."

"But I'm not your slave."

He opened his mouth, clearly to retort, then closed it and narrowed his gaze. "No, you're not quite there yet, are you? But you're mine all the same. I control you in this bed, baby. Me and only me."

Some devil sparked her to respond, "But we're in Rick's bed, *baby.*"

"What's that?"

"You heard me."

Ethan's eyes darkened. "You don't know when to quit, do you?"

His gaze turned mean, and she felt an impossible flutter in her belly. Shit. Desire, strong and true, had her readying for him again.

"Maybe you want to be punished, hmm?"

"No, Ethan, I mean, Master, I'm good. I was just kidding."

Ethan said nothing. Instead, he loosened the restraints on her ankles and tossed her over onto her belly, the ties around her wrists long enough to allow such movement. Then he pulled her up so she rested on her hands and knees.

Both nervous and impossibly excited, she glanced over her shoulder, needing to see what he was up to. Deep down, she knew Ethan wouldn't seriously harm her. But she didn't know what he'd consider punishment. And the thought of the things he might do to her stimulated nerve endings in her body that should have been tired by now.

Rick's statement suddenly rushed back. *Now just imagine that fiery shade of red on her ass after a spanking, when she's coming around your cock.* Wet heat built between her thighs, anticipation spiking her reaction.

Then Ethan slipped a blindfold over her eyes, and she froze.

"Master?"

Her voice was shaky, but damn it, a blindfold? She recalled the dozen or more whips and cat-o'-nine-tails hanging on the wall. What the hell had she gotten herself into now? And why didn't her fear of what came next dampen her enthusiasm for what Ethan thought she deserved?

A rough hand slid over her left buttock, and she started. The blindfold heightened her other senses. The rasp of his hand over her ass sounded loud in the silence of the room. The feel of his palm, the harsh texture of hands used to hard work sliding over her silky- smooth skin, made her shiver. And his scent, the muted smell of spicy cologne and sweet, musky sex, had her mouth watering.

"Easy, slave." Shoot, he'd reverted to calling her "slave" instead of "baby." And worse, she found she was starting to like playing his sexual submissive. "You have to learn when to speak and when to remain silent. In my bed, wherever the fuck I sleep, you belong to me and no one else unless I decide to share you."

"Share me?" She squeaked when his hand came down hard over her ass, the spanking a painful slap against her tender flesh.

"Did I say you could speak?"

You son of a bitch. She fumed, remaining silent. Her ass stung from that wallop.

"Rick was right. What a pretty red." Ethan chuckled and massaged the stinging flesh, leaving an odd warmth in his wake. "You're mine, slave. Mine to take, mine to fuck, mine to share if I so please. What's wrong? I thought you liked looking at Rick. Don't you want a taste of that rich, blond playboy, like every other woman at the resort?"

Jewel shook her head but said nothing. Sure, doing Rick wouldn't be a hardship, and anybody with eyes could see his physical attraction. But Rick didn't make her heart race and her body tremble the way Ethan did. She'd fantasized about Ethan. Lord, had she.

"Good." Ethan rubbed her right buttock, squeezing her cheeks together around a hard, hot, and prodding cock. "Now talk, slave. Tell me, do you want me to give you to Rick?"

"No." No way. Rick made her nervous while Ethan made her hot. Only with Ethan would she feel safe to do whatever—

What the hell was she thinking?

Another slap, and she yelped, her right ass matching her left in the pain department.

Ethan rubbed the sting away again. "Stay with me, baby. I want your head here, in this game. What, thoughts of Rick making you distracted?"

"No, you big jerk. Thoughts of you," she retorted. *Uh-oh. Not smart.*

Jewel felt him rest the tip of his penis at her anus, and she froze. She'd never done it that way and wasn't sure she wanted to.

"Explain, now." He nudged farther, starting to penetrate, and she swallowed. He stopped, and the pressure eased after a moment, her anus parting to accommodate him. But the thought of him there scared the hell out of her. So why was she creaming *again?*

"I just… Sure, Rick's attractive. But I wouldn't touch him unless you were there with me."

He said nothing and remained still. She wished she could see his expression, because she didn't know how he'd take her next words, and much as she regretted it, the dam on her self-preservation seemed to have broken wide open.

She took a deep breath. "I don't know why, but I feel safe with you. Which is odd, considering you just spanked my ass," she added under her breath. When his palm stroked where he'd spanked, she quickly added, "I don't really want Rick. But if you wanted to, um, share me, I'd be willing to be with him if you were there with me. You know, like a ménage or something?"

Her face felt hot, and she knew she must have looked as red as the scarlet ties holding her wrists. *You should have lied, stupid. Ethan doesn't want to hear that you think another man's hot enough that you'd do him.* She didn't think she could be any more dense and chalked up her idiocy and blabbiness to sexual anticipation.

"So you want a threesome, hmm?"

He began caressing her, and she exhaled quietly. Apparently, she hadn't pissed him off with the truth. Thank God.

"No, I don't. I just told you that if I ever did have sex with Rick, it would have to be with you participating, too. And frankly, I don't see you sharing."

He withdrew the flesh pressing her anus, to her simultaneous relief and disappointment. "You don't, hmm?"

"I mean, you would if you wanted to. You said you would, but you don't want to share me, not yet anyway. I'm like a new toy, fun for the moment, right?"

"You're much more than a toy, baby. But I like your honesty. It's worth a reward…later. Maybe once you've been handed your punishment and taken it like a good girl. A good *slave.*"

She groaned.

He spanked her again. "What's that, slave? I didn't hear you."

"Yes, Master. Thank you for punishing me, Master."

"Very nice. I think you're trainable after all, baby."

Jewel gritted her teeth, wanting to call him every name in the book. And then he rubbed her heated ass and thrust her knees farther apart on the bed. The damned blindfold made her feel every touch with twice the sensation, and his powerful thighs between her legs felt as good as a caress.

"I'm going to fuck that ass soon, baby. Soon, but not now. Now you need something more to instill true discipline."

She shook her head, her hair cascading down her back and over her shoulders.

Ethan grabbed her by the strands and jerked her neck back. He leaned over her, his body pressing against hers, and turning her head, he met her lips in a brutal kiss. The minute his tongue penetrated her lips, his cock shoved inside her pussy with force.

She groaned at the intense pleasure, allowing him easier access into her mouth. A big man, Ethan had strength, and he used it without restraint as he rode her. His sheer energy made her wetter and wetter, and Jewel met his thrusts with an animalistic groan, true rapture only hampered by the hard hold on her head.

Ethan released his grip on her hair and pummeled into her, gaining better penetration with his hands now controlling her hips. "You belong to me and no one else. Understand?"

She nodded, joy rushing through her at the idea of being so possessed. As she turned away and stared into the blackness of her blindfold, she couldn't help feeling pleasure at her crazy situation. God, she felt so good, so incredibly sexy. That Ethan could want her so much... No one ever had before. No man had ever made her feel even a tenth of the feelings that Ethan did.

He rocked into her again and again, his balls smacking her clit, his thighs pressing against the backs of hers, dominating, claiming. And then he pushed her harder, touching the heart of her womb.

"Master," she cried, the sensations intense.

"Don't you dare come," he said through gritted teeth. "You'll take it and take it. And come only when I say so." His breathing was heavy, his words hoarse. *"Fuck."* He pulled out and came, shooting over her back. She could feel the hot jets of cum marking her skin, and felt indescribably let down that he hadn't released inside of her.

Oh, shit. That's way too weird. And submissive. And sexually slavish. What the hell? Maybe I am his to control, because God knows I'm no longer me anymore.

Chapter Five

Ethan had never come so hard before and wanted to melt like a puddle at Jewel's feet. Christ, the woman had him spinning in a million different directions far flung from reality. For a minute there, he'd believed the whole shebang. That she was his, his possession, his to control. No longer living a fantasy, he'd slipped into a sexual dream way too bizarre to be real.

And yet...she knelt before him, his cock still throbbing as he slid his tired member through her ass cheeks, stroking the last of his cum from his slit. Her back was a mess, awash with his seed. And the sight stirred him.

Mine.

Not questioning the impulse, he rubbed his cum into her skin, delighting in the sensual shivers from his still-frustrated *slave.* Ethan felt warm all over that she trusted him. She might not realize it, but she'd given him much more than he might have hoped, and in such a short time.

Any woman with a heartbeat desired what Rick had to offer, yet Jewel didn't seem to want it. And she'd told the truth. He'd read it in her body language and in her hastily blurted words.

Damn, but the thought of her anywhere near Rick made him want to break the man's legs and rip out his heart. Rick held a powerful sway over others, a mystique Ethan had yet to understand. Jewel Riser, if that was even her real name, belonged to Ethan. And as much as Rick made him wonder about things best left alone, he refused to share Jewel with the man. Boss or no boss. Ethan's interaction with Jewel went far beyond master and slave. And now, he had to question who'd mastered whom.

Incredibly, his cock rose once more, and he rubbed Jewel's firm ass, not surprised when she moaned softly. She was aroused and suffering. And he knew his punishments were working. Hell, he was a pussy for being so easy, but his heart softened at the thought of Jewel needing him.

"Are you thankful for your discipline, baby?" he asked in a gruff voice, knowing she had to be royally pissed at being used like this. The woman was upset, but the submissive slave that knelt before him reveled in it.

"Thank you, Master." Her voice was soft and reedy, and he knew what she needed.

Ethan left the bed. "Stay there, and don't move."

He glanced back and saw that she obeyed his command, her head hanging low as she tried to catch her breath. Her ass was red, her arms crossed helplessly before her, and the blindfold controlling her vision prodded his tired body into another state of unruly arousal.

Ethan returned to her with a small vibrating butt plug. Soft and pink, the toy made him think of his middle finger, save it was somewhat fatter and not as long. He'd told her he'd take her ass later, but he wanted to watch her reactions as he played with her before setting her off.

He found a small bottle of lube in the bed stand and slathered the coconut-scented oil over the plug's head. Placing a steady hand on the small of her back, he felt her shiver and smiled. This was going to be so damned good.

"Now, slave, we're going to incorporate some actual training. A good slave takes her master in every way without complaint." He couldn't help his voice from sounding so thick. He stroked her ass with the plug and watched her shudder. "Your ass is virgin, isn't it, baby?"

She paused so long he thought he'd have to make her answer.

"Yes," she whispered.

"Yes, what?"

She swallowed loudly. "Yes, Master."

"I need to prepare you, gently," he added, not wanting to scare her. "Anal play only increases the stimulation you'll feel when I'm fucking you. When done right, it can make your orgasm something fierce." He placed the plug at the small rosette of her anus. "Relax, slave, and take this inside you."

His words had her tensing, just what he didn't want her to do. But he wouldn't be denied. The eroticism of pushing that little pink cock inside her ass had him growing hard again. Beautiful, so beautiful, was all he could think.

"Push out. That's it, baby," he breathed as she moaned and took yet another bit of the plug.

Wanting more involvement, Ethan rolled onto his back and scooted under her thighs, staring up at her dripping pussy; her smooth lips made his mouth water.

Reaching around her hips, he lowered her to his face, careful to keep the tip of the toy inside her ass while he enjoyed her pussy.

"Just a small taste, to remind myself."

She gasped, and he slid the plug deeper as he sucked on her clit. He knew the dual sensation would intensify her orgasm. And the little witch deserved it. He'd blown so hard over her back...

"Oh, Ethan," she groaned, sounding lost. "That's so good."

He ignored the fact she hadn't called him her master, too taken with the sultry evidence of her need. Instead, he pushed the plug in a fraction more, pulling her clit between his teeth to distract her.

She shuddered and ground over his face, and he loved every minute of it. Her flesh grew tighter and tighter as he played. His hot breath, his tongue, and his teeth caressed and tormented her pussy until she was writhing and crying out his name, alternating "Master" and "Ethan" with such need he started shuddering with his own desire.

Leaving her pussy, he shoved to his knees and prepared to mount her. The sight of the ass plug aroused him even more, and he pushed it all the way in, pleased with her groan.

"Pleasure and pain, slave. Together, they'll make you crazy with lust. But we want the pleasure to far outweigh the pain, don't we?"

"Yes, Master," she breathed, pushing back into his raging erection.

"Beg me for the pleasure, slave. Beg me to give you what you really need." Shit, he was really good at this. And who knew she'd warm to it so much? This surpassed his fantasies, and he knew it had more to do with Jewel than with the image of any woman in such a position.

"Please, Master. Let me come. I beg you."

Her husky voice played over him like a silken caress, and he shoved his cock into her, sliding along the pressure of the plug, stimulating him more.

"Oh, oh," she cried and squirmed against him. "I'm so full. Please, Master."

"That's it, baby. Beg me."

"Please."

She shivered, and he decided to up her ecstasy a notch. Smiling, he leaned back to press the power button on the plug, groaning when she clenched him tight as the device began vibrating.

Her channel fit like a glove, and with some effort he forced himself to pull out, only to surge back inside, sucked deep into her womb.

"Please, Master, let me come," she begged.

Ethan heard her desperation, her voice hoarse with frustration. He slammed home a few times, his need upon him as well. But he wanted her to take him to bliss, for her to feel that giant wave before he took his pleasure.

"Come for me, baby. Come hard, and milk me dry."

She flexed as he pounded her, and then she was crying out and stiffening around him. She closed on him, her flesh urging his semen into her body with great rapturous pulls.

Inside her this time, as if he hadn't already climaxed earlier, he came hard, flooding her with his seed.

Ethan gripped her hips, frozen in the little death that stole every thought from his head. And then odd visions of ropes and toys, a flushed Jewel at home in his bed, took him higher. As if the sensations in his body weren't enough, happiness engulfed him in the presence of the angel, or rather, the sexy little witch, squeezing him tight.

"Master," she sobbed, wiggling her ass. "Turn it off, please."

He quickly did, not wanting to over stimulate her. Yet he kept the plug in, wanting her to get used to the stretched feeling. He would wait to take her ass, to claim what no man had ever touched before. The sheer ecstasy in the waiting would make the taking that much sweeter.

"Baby, you learn really, really fast," he murmured, and gently pulled out. He kept her on her hands and knees, however, and stroked her entire body until she finally stopped shuddering. With some regret, he slowly pulled out the butt plug. He slid it home again and pumped it inside her a few times, pleased at the lack of resistance around it. And then he withdrew the device entirely and placed it on the table beside the bed before removing her blindfold and untying her.

Realizing they'd fucked most of the day away, he decided to give them both a rest. Yet he couldn't wait to use the next few days to further her "training."

He owed Rick more than Rick would ever owe him. This time spent with Jewel was priceless, a dream made real. And Ethan had waited too long in his life to see such enjoyment. The fact that Jewel had met him stroke for stroke, climax for climax, and could go another round only further illustrated how perfectly they fit. Ethan planned to make the most of his time with her. Because being with her like this gave him ideas.

Anal, oral, whatever dirty, erotic thing he wanted, he'd ply her into playing. He'd make her his perfect lover, the ultimate sexual partner. His time on the island was limited, so he'd have to work fast. He'd solve the case for Rick, mesmerize Jewel with his sexual acrobatics, and somehow convince her to return to Seattle with him.

He grunted. If only she'd be as compliant out of bed...

* * *

Three nights later, a man wearing nothing teetered through the halls, apparently drunk. His hands and feet felt as though they belonged to someone else, his mind inebriated on the excitement surging through him. Yet he was clearheaded enough to know that what he was doing was wrong, utterly wrong, and extremely dangerous. No one fucked with Rick Hastings without severe repercussions.

But he'd timed everything perfectly. Right now, the man assigned to guard Rick's personal security servers shot out of the small room to take care of a sudden intestinal problem—compliments of a doped cup of mango iced tea. Though the guard had enough presence of mind to lock up behind him, he hadn't counted on anyone else having the proper password and keycard to enter the small room.

The intruder let himself into the room and quickly took in his surroundings. To his left were a rack of servers and digital equipment he had little interest in. The wall-mounted monitors to his right, however, made him take note. Several video feeds showed the open courtyard, pool, and common dining areas. Another smaller, desk-mounted computer screen remained blank, and it was on this that he focused. He sat down at the desk and pulled the keyboard close. Glancing down at the code written on his palm, he typed in the random numbers and letters he'd been given—for a small damned fortune—and stared in awe as the screen flickered and came to life.

The screen was sectioned into three views. In one, Rick and Elise were fucking like there was no tomorrow in a private Jacuzzi, a scene that both surprised and irritated him. In another, a prominent senator and his boyfriend—not his wife—were engaging in some interesting positions culminating in a messy release. Though stimulating, and with great potential for blackmail material, the images didn't interest him. He had his sights set on a bigger prize.

Thoughts of finally stealing Rick's prized possession, the Mirvolo Cup, refused to let him go. Ever since he'd seen the thing, he'd known he had to have it. Like the other objects he'd stolen, hell, even killed to acquire, the cup would tie him to the preternatural pleasures inherent in all of Bacchus's true artifacts. He could still remember the odd feeling he'd experienced after drinking from the cup and knew Rick's chalice, more than any other relic, had been the wine god's favorite.

Perhaps tonight he'd finally get his hands on the damned thing. He just needed to verify with his own eyes where the cup should be. Once assured Rick's room lay empty, he'd jaunt down the private corridor after turning off the security cameras and then, bingo.

But as he quickly scanned the lower view into Rick's room, rotating the hidden camera left and right, he was stunned at the erotic escapades in Rick's massive bed, a bed he'd once been invited into.

The new security man, Ethan Reaper, was fucking the shit out of some dark-haired goddess on her knees. He looked closer. *Holy shit.* Said goddess was Jewel Riser, the new hottie he'd been more than pleased to meet, and who'd mysteriously vanished three days ago. Damn, but he hadn't realized she'd been added to Rick's "dessert" menu. Uncertainty and anger confused him, and he focused on the screen. What the hell was Ethan doing in Rick's room? And who knew Ethan had such wonderfully wicked proclivities?

The intruder licked his lips. He'd met Ethan and been immediately intrigued, more so knowing the giant had been hired specifically to stand in his way. But he could never have imagined how delicious the guard would look during sex.

Reaper's taut ass flexed as he drove inside the woman's soft mouth. Groaning and grunting, the domineering man referred to the woman as his slave, and the watcher rubbed his own stiffening cock with pleasure. Rick had once been forceful like that. The one night Rick and he had screwed, he'd come so hard he thought he'd died and gone to heaven.

But after only one evening with Rick, he'd been banished to ex-lover status, both Rick and the Mirvolo Cup out of reach. In addition to the fortune it would bring on the black market, the cup was rumored to have mystical powers, powers the intruder knew to be true. He'd never before felt such sexual ecstasy as he had after sipping from it, and no matter how many lovers he took to his bed, he hadn't felt that earth-shattering pleasure since.

It was more than Rick. It had to be, he thought with desperation. Rick had no more interest in him since having had him, and he knew it was only a matter of time before the canny resort owner discovered his guilt. Yes, he'd been sloppy with Meyers. He never should have killed the man, but he hadn't been certain Meyers hadn't seen him in his private vault.

The screen took his attention again, and he stroked himself as he watched Ethan come over the woman's tongue. She thanked him repeatedly for the treat, and he wondered that he hadn't earlier sensed the submissive buried in her.

A sexy woman, Jewel Riser had an abundance of curves, a smart mouth, and a sense of humor. Unlike Ethan, who barely spoke and remained as expressionless as a rock wall. A ton of muscle, but not much upstairs, or so he had thought.

Hmm, apparently, Ethan had a lot more going on than first appeared. Glancing at the man's large, dripping cock, he smiled. Much more.

He panned the camera again, dismayed to find the Mirvolo Cup not in its usual place on the four-foot display table in the corner of the room. The table sat empty, and Ethan occupied the room while Rick took up with that slut Elise elsewhere. But the cup *had* to be in there. The million-dollar question was how to manage an opportunity to look around.

Filtering through resort images on the security feed, nervous excitement stole through him. Images of the VIPs sexing it up, thoughts about stealing Rick's most prized possession, and the imagined look on Rick's face when Rick knew he'd been bested—*by him*—all created a whirlwind of dark desire. Lust and longing filled him, and a wave of self-righteousness seethed. *I'll teach you to disregard me, to throw me aside.* He scowled at Rick, so caught up in Elise that the man couldn't see the truth when it stared him right in the face, day in and day out.

Pressure pushed his balls tight, and as he stroked harder, he coiled to release and made the decision to infiltrate Rick's room...tonight.

"What the hell?"

He turned, surprised. He hadn't heard the door open.

"What are you doing in here?" Peter Dancourt, the guard, asked in bewilderment.

"Waiting for you, lover," he purred and stood, pleased when Peter swallowed loudly and focused on his erection. The guard's eyes otherwise occupied, he missed the glint of silver that would have announced the intruder's real intentions. Three smart stabs and Peter gasped into death.

Staring down at his brawny ex-lover and caught up in the rush from having killed another man, he groaned and began stroking himself, finishing what he'd started earlier. He knelt down and aimed, and came in a stream over the deceased—a fitting tribute to a man who hadn't set him aside. A lover's last gift.

He smiled.

In a few days, DNA testing would prove him responsible. But by then he'd be long gone. A murderer, right under Rick's nose. If this didn't scare Rick, nothing would.

* * *

Jewel sighed and snuggled into Ethan's tight embrace. For three days straight he'd taunted her, tempted her, and shot her into so many orgasms she'd lost count. For a man bent on domination, he'd proved remarkably unselfish. She'd assumed, incorrectly, that he'd find his pleasure again and again, leaving her to wallow in frustrated misery. But Ethan had surprised her.

She knew a little about the D/s scene, from reading and talking with a few friends about the lifestyle. So she knew Ethan was anything but typical. He wasn't hardcore, thank God, and alternated too frequently to be a real Dom. Oh, he enjoyed her calling him her master well enough, but he seemed to like her resistance as much as he liked her giving in.

But, hello, her submission made him so hard and so thick, it was a wonder she could walk at all. She was glad of her contraceptive, or he'd surely have planted a baby by now. Jewel paused, and immediately shied away from tender thoughts of carrying Ethan's child. Literally shaking her head, she realized that for a woman who wasn't really into sex, she'd had more of it in her week here than she'd ever thought possible.

Even now her vagina felt deliciously used and a bit sore. Yet her ass remained as virgin as the day she'd arrived. She knew he was putting off the ass reaming she "so deserved" to draw out their excitement and anticipation. And damned if it wasn't working. Each time he mounted her, she wondered, would he do it now? And the butt plug he kept using on her, as well as his incredibly stimulating tongue, made her want it.

Wrapped in Ethan's strong arms as she was, her mission seemed so far away. They hadn't talked much, and she was both disappointed and glad. She wanted to know more about him. Hell, she was hungry for even a side note about his life outside the resort. But if he answered her questions, he'd likely ask her the same ones. And she didn't want to have to lie to him, any more than she wanted to listen to his lies. She'd caught snippets of his phone conversations with Rick, and Ethan seemed as concerned with Rick's well-being as his property...making her think he was here more to protect Rick than the Mirvolo Cup.

Jewel knew and understood the measure of value, and the stupid cup was priceless. Sure, she liked stealing to keep in practice. But with that damned cup...the pleasure to be had in its theft wouldn't compensate for the risk of discovery. And more importantly, she had no desire to violate Ethan's trust.

"You're thinking too loudly." Ethan chuckled and kissed the top of her head.

Warmth unfurled in her belly. "I'm curious about you."

"Oh?"

Hell. She desperately needed something more of him to hold onto... "Where are you from? And why are you really here?"

"I could ask you the same things."

"I'm from New Jersey, near the shoreline. And I'm Jewel Riser, waitress extraordinaire."

He didn't laugh as she thought he might; instead, he flipped her onto her back and leaned over her, staring.

"What?"

"You're a mystery, Jewel *Riser.* A woman who doesn't exist, in a place too wild for her own good."

"Doesn't exist?" She forced a laugh. "I'm right here."

"Please. I'm damned good at my job, Jewel. And no Jewel Riser has ever lived and worked in Jersey or any other state on the East Coast, unless you count an eighty-year-old grandmother of four."

Her pulse raced. He knew Jewel Riser didn't exist. She stared, wondering what to say.

"Can't you trust me not to hurt you with the truth?" he asked quietly, a flash of emotion in his eyes, gone so fast she wasn't sure she'd even seen it.

"I want to, Ethan." She surprised herself with the admission, and could see she pleased him as well. "But I don't really know you, either. Why should I spill my guts when you won't do the same?"

He said nothing, appearing thoughtful. Ethan shifted over her, pressing into her and effectively pinning her beneath him. That easily, she grew distracted at the sight and sensation of such raw strength. His biceps bulged, and his chest flexed, such a wonderful ripple of muscle that she wanted to lick all over…if she wasn't so exhausted from their lovemaking already.

As she thought it, Jewel flushed. *Lovemaking.* Could she call what they'd done lovemaking? Could a person be "loving" while tied to bedposts, sucking down her lover's cum while his mouth brought her to a violent climax? Yet Ethan's sexual play had softened after that first intense day. Though he was still Mr. Dominant, her master, he seemed to look on her with pride and affection, as more than a simple sexual partner.

His gaze now held that same admiration, and a hint of a smile. "That's what I like about you, Jewel. You're a real pain in the ass. Everything with you has to be earned."

She wasn't sure if that was a compliment, but his smile indicated it should be taken as such.

"I'll tell you the truth about me if you can tell me everything you know about Rick's cup." He pressed a sequence of buttons on the wall near the bed, and she watched in awe as the wall freaking *moved,* revealing a hidden panel, behind which sat Rick's blasted cup protected by an inner wall of glass.

"Crap. You would have to ask that." She grinned under her bluster, content to lay next to Ethan for the rest of her life—*the rest of the night,* she quickly corrected herself. "I know the thing belongs to Rick, obviously, and he makes all of his employees drink from it when they step foot on his island. He fills it with some funky wine that makes your head spin the minute you drink it, and he offers some wacky prayer to Bacchus, as if the cup's blessed, or something.

"The cup's old, I can tell you that. And those rubies and sapphires on the base are real, the gold authentic and probably between eighteen and twenty carats. Rick's so freaking in love with all things Roman that it shouldn't be a surprise he's devoted this room to Bacchus, the Roman god of wine and pleasure."

"That's all pretty basic. Anything else?"

"It's called the Mirvolo Cup." Jewel huffed and finally gave up on her earlier lie. "I don't know that much about Roman antiques."

"Well, that's the most honest you've been with me so far."

She sighed. "Look, I told you what you wanted to hear. Now tell me about Ethan Reaper, if that's really *your* name." Jewel desperately wanted to know more about Ethan. The more he told her, the better chance she'd have in finding some flaw so she could readily dismiss him when she left the island and returned to New Jersey. That way, thoughts of leaving wouldn't hurt so damned much.

"My name really is Ethan Reaper. I live in Seattle and run a successful security firm."

She hadn't expected that, but she supposed it fit. So why the hell was he here?

"Someone wants to steal the Mirvolo Cup from Rick, and we're worried about the danger to Rick's life as well."

She frowned. "Over the cup? Why kill him when someone could steal it easily enough?"

His eyes narrowed, and she realized she'd overstepped herself.

"What I meant to say is, why kill Rick? Everyone who knows the guy loves him."

"Including you?" His voice was quiet, intimidating, and yet sexy as hell. For some weird reason, the meaner he grew, the wetter *she* grew.

"Not including me." She sighed. "Look, I couldn't care less about Rick's Roman antique, and I don't wish him dead. I'm here, ah, let's just say I'm here on a confidential job of my own."

His interest seemed to intensify. His brown eyes deepened to black, and his body tensed, waiting for more.

"I'm not at liberty to divulge a whole lot. Suffice it to say, I have to get my hands on some damaging film that was taken by someone who's here."

He paused a moment. "Did he, or she, happen to take photos of a guest while they vacationed here?"

Ethan's question surprised her. She thought for sure he'd demand to know specifics right away. "Ah, yes, in fact, he did."

"Then, you have to tell Rick about this, Jewel. That is your name, isn't it?"

She flushed at his dry tone and frowned. "Technically, no. My name is Julia. But I've always gone by Jewel."

He studied her. "Jewel suits you."

"Thanks," she said sarcastically. "Glad you approve."

He chuckled and began rubbing her belly, soft, stroking swirls that comforted as well as stirred her senses. "Damn, but you're a real firecracker, aren't you? A firecracker out of bed, and a sexual dynamo between the sheets."

"You say the sweetest things." Jewel drew him down for a kiss, surprised when Ethan tenderly kissed her lips.

"Sweet? Just what every guy wants to hear. But seriously, Jewel. You need to tell Rick about why you're here. Trust me, I understand all about confidentiality. But Rick's fierce when it comes to privacy at this place. And if your boy has pictures of one guest, it's a sure bet he has pictures of another."

She hadn't thought about Denton possibly blackmailing someone else. Rick had high profile clients visiting all the time. Denton could really do some serious damage.

"So I guess your cover as a waitress was just that?" Ethan kissed her cheeks. "No fiancé? No dire straits? No addiction to public sex and orgies?"

"No." She flushed, caught by the warmth of his gaze. God, but he looked at her like he felt something more than lust, more than simple affection even. Jewel swallowed and shook her head.

"Good." He kissed her hard and gripped her hands over her head. "But for lying to me, you've earned more than a spanking this time, Jewel."

Lust flared, and she tried to protest, but they both knew she didn't mean it. Just as Jewel was about to confess how much he made her burn, how much he made her yearn for something more, an alarm sounded.

Ethan's gaze turned from aroused to menacing in a heartbeat. He quickly closed the wall housing the cup and shot out of bed, throwing on a pair of pants and his shoes. "Stay there. Whatever you do, don't leave this room. I'm setting it on lockdown. That cup stays here, and you with it."

She would have protested but then she saw the Beretta he tucked in the small of his back. Instead, she nodded.

"Be careful, Ethan. I wouldn't want any harm to come to my...master."

He slowly smiled. "I will, so long as Rick's treasure, and mine, are well guarded."

He departed in a blur, leaving her lying naked in Rick's bed, her mouth wide open. *His treasure?* She grinned from ear to ear. *Well, hot damn.*

Chapter Six

Ethan crouched over Pete Dancourt's dead body. "Shit." He'd liked Pete. In the three weeks since his arrival, Pete had been a consistent presence, knowledgeable about security and full of useful information about the island. But now he lay dead, stabbed to death, with someone's sperm staining his shirt.

What the hell did that mean? Had Pete and his killer been intimate? Was it a warning, that the killer had had ample time to kill Pete and stick around for some perverted jacking off? Or was the killer simply crazy, a sexual deviant wandering free around the worst type of resort for a criminal of his kind?

Rick muscled past the guards by the door and knelt next to Ethan. "Oh. Hell. Not Pete."

"Afraid so."

"What the fuck is on his shirt?"

Ethan sighed. "The killer and Pete were either jacking off before Pete was killed, or the killer did it after Pete's death. Either way, it's a little disturbing."

"Yeah, a little," Rick said sarcastically. He brushed damp hair from his eyes, and Ethan noticed his rumpled state.

"You just jump out of the shower?" He glanced back at Elise, also slightly damp and who remained tightlipped, her arms crossed over her chest as she waited by the door.

"You could say that. Man, I can't believe Pete is dead. He was such a good man to have around. Pleasant. Professional." Rick sighed. "At least he had no family to break the news to."

"The only good thing about this mess."

"Do you think our thief did this?" Rick asked in a low voice.

Ethan leaned closer, careful to keep their conversation private and continued as quietly as Rick. "I can't say for certain, but I've got a hunch he's behind it. And at least now we know it's a he." Ethan nodded distastefully to the stain on Pete's shirt.

"So is anything missing?"

"Not that I can tell. But the screen on the desk has been fiddled with. I don't know if he saw anything off your private feeds or not. Odds are, if he had the code to get in here, he might have been able to access your surveillance."

"Meaning he had access to see the cup."

The cup was in Rick's room. A room in which Ethan had been sure of his privacy…and Jewel's.

"*What?* You never mentioned video surveillance in your own room," Ethan whispered furiously.

"Oh, come on, Ethan. You don't think I'd leave the cup in plain sight without a digital trail of its whereabouts?"

"Plain sight? You keep the damned thing locked behind a secret panel in your wall."

"And sometimes I leave it in its case in the corner of the room. In plain sight."

Ethan flushed, realizing the thief might have seen his time spent with Jewel, and that Rick could see it later, in every excruciating detail, if he wished. As much as Ethan admired the open sexuality of Satyr's Myst, he didn't relish being the star of his own hardcore movie. And he knew Jewel would freak if she knew. "I want that video."

"Relax. You'd have to have my private codes to see what's taped in that room."

"Exactly. You might think you're the only one that has them, but if you recall, you told me where you keep your pass codes. I told you to get rid of the list, but if I know you, you just yessed me to death, and they're still there." Ethan shook his head at Rick's guilty look. "If I know about that sheet, I'm betting someone else might. Besides, a hacker won't care about codes if he can hijack your system." Ethan paused, his brain processing a mile a minute. "Security's been breached, and we have to face the possibility that the thief is not just a guest, but one of your employees."

"But you dismissed those suspicions. I thought you'd cleared everyone."

"I cleared your new folks, and the ones hired within the past year, when the thefts in your club first started. But way into his room and into his computer. After all, this was a pleasure resort, where sex seemed to occur at the drop of a hat. But she didn't plan on having sex with him to flush out Sophie's pictures.

"Oh?"

Tanya pouted. "Come on, Joshie. I thought we were going to fuck all night? And with Rick to watch." She reached down and grabbed Denton by the crotch.

Denton kept his eyes glued to Jewel, and she realized Ethan's polo molded to her breasts and hips, nearly brushing her knees. It was obvious she wore nothing beneath the cotton, and she blushed with misplaced embarrassment.

"Shy, honey? You're new, it's okay."

Bingo. "Um, yeah. You see, I've been undergoing some sexual, ah, help, the last few days to make me a better employee here. I'm afraid I'm not really ready for what you might have in mind." Her eyes flashed to Tanya, and she projected just enough temerity. "I mean, I do better one-on-one."

Denton grinned in understanding, and Jewel knew she'd managed to wedge a foot in the door to loosening his hold on Sophie Ayers.

She gave Denton a promising smile and finally felt as if she were doing her job. *Her job.* For four nights and three days, she'd been having sex and loving every damned minute of it. She'd turned into a raving nympho and had it bad for a domineering giant who referred to her as his slave and insisted she call him Master in the bedroom. Such a one-eighty from her stolid life just a week ago. Good Lord, Jewel felt like a different person altogether. So the reminder of

you told me not to look at the others, and like an idiot, I listened. My gut feeling tells me we're missing someone important."

"You definitely think this is the work of our thief, then. Not some random shot at Pete?"

Though Rick sounded hopeful, Ethan could see the man knew he was grasping at straws. "I can't explain it, but I feel a connection here, Rick. I think our thief must have distracted Pete in some way, because Pete took his job seriously. He wouldn't have let anyone in here without my authority or yours. And he had no way of knowing if I'd be checking on him tonight or not. I've been making random stops here all week. I mean, this place is cherry for anyone needing more info about the resort, and about you in particular. One look at the feeds in here and he'd be able to verify who's doing what where.

"I'm going to have Jacobs do another sweep, to make sure nothing electrical has been planted. We don't need the thief tapping into our own security while we flounder around looking for him."

Rick nodded. "I'll have to tell the staff about this." He stared sadly at Pete.

"I know. Just keep the details to a minimum. Tell them Pete died, and the circumstances are under investigation. Our thief's no fool; he'll know we're onto him. Hell, he left us a trail of breadcrumbs to follow. I just wish I knew why he's waiting to make his move on the cup."

Rick frowned and stood. "Maybe he's not." He punched in the codes, and they watched as the screen on the desk came to life. The computer showed three views. "There's my empty hot tub, the grotto where the senator is currently playing with his new 'house boy,' and…well, well. That's Jewel there, pacing and wearing your shirt, I believe. I like what you've done with the bed, Ethan," Rick murmured.

Several scarves remained tied to the bedposts, and an assortment of sex toys littered the bed table.

"Very creative. I bet Jewel loved them. The plug especially."

Yeah, she'd been really into that plug, and if Ethan had his way, she'd be into it again. But not until he could get a handle on this mess. As taken as he was with the brassy, black-haired witch, Ethan had to admit Jewel was a temptation. He needed to focus on this case, to reexamine past leads that had died, and scare up new answers.

Just then, movement in one of the shots on the computer screen grabbed him. A shadow that shouldn't have been there fell over Jewel, and she glanced over in surprise at something obscured by the camera's limited view. The shadow grew, and then the feed exploded into static.

Ethan was already moving, his heart in his throat. Fear spiked the adrenaline rushing through his body, and he raced without care, needing to find Jewel safe, to hold her in his arms and protect her from the threat spreading like a disease over Rick and that damned cup.

One thing was certain. Before the night was through, he'd have Jewel safe and sound in his arms again. And the intruder in Rick's room would wish he were dead when Ethan was through with him.

* * *

Jewel glanced up in surprise to see two people walking into a room supposedly on lockdown. Joshua Denton, of all people, and a beautiful, if drunk, woman teetering on high heels strode in like they owned the place. The woman wore a skin-tight, yellow minidress, complementing Denton's tan slacks and light blue polo shirt. He wore clothing befitting the veteran hosts of the resort, those whose sole purpose on the island was to escort—provide massages, pleasure, and general catering for—the guests. Jewel could only stare, stunned by his early return.

His pictures didn't do justice to his presence in person. She could definitely understand what Sophie Ayers had seen in him. Rangy and good-looking in a beachboy kind of way, Denton sported short brown hair and smiling blue eyes. H[e] had an island tan, obscenely white teeth against his dark[ ]skin, and the build of an athlete.

Denton stared at her as if another woman weren't [at] his side and clinging to him like a vine. "Ah, sorry. Tyr[e] told me Rick wanted Tanya and me to join him tonight." [He] looked confused, but not so confused that he stopped sta[ring] at her from head to toe. Denton licked his lips, his i[nner] gaze both bold and eager. "You must be new. I'm [Josh] Denton, and this is my friend Tanya. We're up for [some] sport, and what better way to introduce ourselves? [Why] don't we get more comfortable while we wait for Rick?["]

His hands moved to the hem of his shirt, an[d she] hastily stopped him.

"Hold on. I think there's been a misunder[standing] here." *Where was Ethan when she needed him?* S[tudying] Denton, Jewel realized she had to handle him just r[ight. She] couldn't come across as cold, not if she wanted to f[ind]

why she'd been sent to the island restored her balance like a shock of cold water.

And then Ethan burst into the room like a wild man, with Rick, Elise, and three other security guards hot on his tail.

When Ethan took a good look at her company, he frowned and murmured something to Rick. Rick motioned for Elise and the others to leave, then closed and locked the door behind them.

"Joshua Denton in the flesh. Welcome home." Rick smiled, as if nothing were wrong, and Jewel stared hard, wanting to know what she'd apparently missed, and how the hell Denton had entered a secured room.

Ethan cleared the anger from his face and backed away from Rick to remain protectively behind him. Jewel frowned. Obviously Ethan was playing the role of security guard and nothing more. The perfect employee.

Jewel watched with curiosity, feeling like the captive audience in a play taking so many twists and turns it was hard to keep track.

"I didn't expect we'd see you for another day or so."

Denton shrugged and rubbed Tanya's waist, apparently reluctant to tear his gaze from Jewel.

"I missed this place, and apparently, some action." He stared at Ethan and the door through which Elise and the guards had vanished. But when Rick simply smiled and said nothing, Denton shrugged. "I finished up my business early and found Tanya the minute I walked through the front door." Denton grinned at Jewel. "I have to say, I love your new girl. We were just introducing ourselves."

"Ah, Jewel. My precious little gem." Rick smiled, and Jewel smiled back, feeling as if she had a role to play as well. Rick joined her and hugged her to his side, his hands molding to her ass as if he had the right. Ethan didn't move, and Jewel kept the smile plastered to her face, wondering at Rick's game.

"Yeah, Jewel mentioned you've been helping her to adjust to life on the island." Denton chuckled. "Makes me think of my first time here, and how much you helped me."

"We do what we can." Rick bowed to Tanya. "Tanya, you're looking lovely as always. I see Josh is taking care of you tonight. But if I may ask, how did you two get in here? I thought I'd locked up behind me."

"The door was open a crack so we came in. You did ask us up here."

Rick's eyes narrowed. "I did?"

"Yeah." Denton frowned. "Tyrone told Tanya and me you wanted to see us, for a 'special get-together,' he said."

Rick's expression cleared. "Oh, that's the mix-up then. I meant I'd wanted to see you when you returned, thinking tomorrow. But I must say, Tanya's a wonderful choice of partner."

"So's Jewel," Denton added slyly.

"So she is." Rick grinned. "Right, well. I have a few more things to wrap up before I can call it a night. Why don't you take Tanya back to her room, and I'll order up a special menu just for the two of you. We're on for tomorrow night, all right?"

Tanya pouted but gave him a nod. Her hands on Denton stirred the man to quickly agree. Ethan moved to open the door, then stood back to wait.

"Later, Rick, Jewel." Denton gave Ethan a last, furtive glance before following Tanya out the door.

Silence descended, and Jewel wondered what the hell was going on.

"Take your hands off her." Ethan's words were quiet, and frightening in their intensity.

Rick squeezed her ass before letting go, and she took a shaky breath, wondering why she hadn't pushed him away as soon as Denton and his floozy left.

"You know, Ethan, both she, and you, are my employees."

"Fuck that. You gave her to me, she's mine."

Rick cocked his head and stared from Ethan to Jewel. "He taking good care of you, Jewel?"

She flushed. "Um, yeah." *Why the hell don't I just rate him on a score of one to ten? He's an eleven when he's hard, a fifteen when he's mad. He's so damned sexy when he's mean…and I am so incredibly perverted.*

Ethan scowled, his dark look sending tingles down her spine.

"So what happened?" Jewel asked quickly, reminding herself to focus on the mission.

Rick sobered, his eyes sad. "Pete Dancourt, one of my security team, is dead."

"Dancourt? *Dead?*"

Ethan stepped away from the wall, his stare brooding. "Tall guy, a little shorter than me, with bright red hair. Stabbed three times in the chest."

"Oh, my God. That's so sad. He was such a nice guy." Jewel remembered him. He'd had a nice smile, and unlike most of the people in this place, his stare hadn't lingered on her breasts the two brief times they'd spoken.

"Yes, he was." Rick sighed. "At this point, I think we can safely say that Denton wasn't the one who killed him."

"Why would you say that?" Ethan finally lifted his gaze from Jewel.

"Because he couldn't have seen the vid—" Rick paused at Ethan's hard stare. "What I mean is, he didn't know it was you, and not me, who'd been in here with Jewel."

"Yeah, or he could have been faking the whole thing. I still want to know how he got in here. If he's telling the truth, then someone else opened the damned door. But either way, he bothers me."

"I wonder why," Rick murmured, glancing toward Jewel.

"He takes a two-day vacation, his first in three years, right? Then he turns around and asks for another one, only to return early? And he just happens to walk into your 'unlocked' room right after Pete's been stabbed?"

"But he had Tanya with him."

"A nice, drunk alibi."

"I see your point."

Jewel interrupted. "Wait a minute. A man is dead, murdered? Who would do that?"

Ethan answered. "The same man after the Mirvolo Cup."

"We think," Rick added. "I see you've taken Jewel into our confidence."

"Hell." Ethan ran a hand through his hair. "She's not involved in this."

"I know."

"You do?"

"Obviously you wouldn't have told her if you didn't think you could trust her."

Rick's words warmed Jewel. Ethan trusted her. Maybe it was time to start trusting him. He had a lot on his plate, keeping Rick and that cup safe. Something Denton had said resonated, and she turned to Ethan, wanting to help.

"Rick?" Jewel chewed her lip in thought, stopping when Ethan's bright stare lit on her mouth. "Denton said something that made me wonder. He said Tyrone told him you wanted him up here. Seems to me like you need to talk to Tyrone."

"Yes, that's a very good idea." Rick glanced from Ethan to Jewel. "Why don't I see to that right now? Don't worry, Ethan. I'll take Elise."

"And have a second guard shadow you at all times."

Rick sighed again. "Of course. Why don't you two take some time to finish up in here? I'm afraid we'll have to move Jewel's training into your room, Ethan. Appears I have a date tomorrow night with Josh and his lovely lady."

"I want your 'surveillance' turned off, effective immediately. I'll turn it back on when I'm finished in here."

Rick shrugged. "Done."

"Actually, about that training," Jewel interrupted. "I think Ethan and I are about through." With Denton back, she needed to start working on him ASAP. She only had another week before Sophie's blackmail was due. Whatever feelings she'd garnered for Ethan were part of this fantasy world—a world she'd be leaving in a short time.

"No, actually, we aren't," Ethan said quietly, his gaze on Jewel. "Thanks, Rick. We'll wrap this up and head out of here in a few. She'll be with me, in case you need her."

"I assumed as much." Rick nodded at her and turned to leave, but not before she saw the satisfied gleam in his eyes.

Jewel caught a glimpse of Elise and two burly security guards before the door shut behind her boss. She could feel Ethan's stare burning a hole into her, and glanced up to meet his eyes. He stood aggressively, his arms crossed over his chest, his mouth a thin line of displeasure.

"Our training's not over until I say it's over."

She swore to herself. Now was not the time to be getting hot and bothered over Ethan's ego trip. His attempt to reestablish his dominance wasn't working. *It's not working,* she tried to convince herself. *Remember Sophie. Remember Dreemer's. Remember your perfect success record.*

Yet as she stood there under Ethan's stern gaze, she could only recall the feel of Ethan's hand on her ass, of his lips on her breasts, the taste of his mouth, and the steel in his cock.

Jewel shivered and saw satisfaction flare in his deep, brown eyes. She automatically stiffened her spine.

In a calm, even voice, she explained, "Ethan, I'm sorry for what you went through tonight. But I think you'll agree you have more important things to look after right now than me. You have a murderer and a thief, or maybe one and the same, to find. After all, you are responsible for Rick's safety, aren't you?"

She held her breath, pleased at the reasonable tone and wording in her carefully crafted manipulation.

Ethan nodded. "I am. And since there's nothing more I can do tonight for *Rick,* I'm going to plant myself in front of that cup until he returns in a few hours."

A few hours?

"Take off your clothes."

She needed to make a break now. Much as she wanted to stay with Ethan and not worry about reality, Denton had returned. A man had been murdered

"Didn't you hear me?" His voice softened, and his eyes narrowed.

Jewel tried to decide what to do. She couldn't possibly care that much for a man she'd only just met. And what exactly did she know about him? Ethan lived in Seattle. He was incredibly strong, intelligent, and surprisingly funny, with a will of iron. He owned his own security firm, and from what little he'd said over the past few days, had been in the Marine Corps a long time ago. Which fit with his macho, take-no-prisoners attitude and his ability to control any situation.

But what did she *really* know? His favorite color, movie, food? Ethan seemed to like seafood. And he ate like a horse. But what did her limited knowledge of the man truly mean?

She suddenly blinked up into his eyes and realized he'd invaded every inch of her personal space while she'd been woolgathering. "Ethan?"

Without warning, he grabbed her shirt by the hem and hauled it over her head. Tossing it to the side, he glared down at her. "Try Master."

Immediately, moisture pooled between her legs; her nipples hardened. He glowered and pinched one, the pain making her hotter.

"Ethan, come on—"

He kissed her hard, his tongue thrusting deeply into her mouth and stealing her last breath. He plunged in and out, and rubbed her nipple between his fingers. Cupping her other breast with his free hand, Ethan molded her, made her wanting and desperate for his touch until Jewel was practically climbing him to get closer.

He broke away from her mouth and stared down at her, his brows drawn tight. "Not Ethan. Master."

"No." Resistance was futile, but making him work to subdue her seemed to turn him on as much as it did her. Something about a man strong enough to force her compliance made her melt inside. And though Ethan could have used real force, the sexual torture he employed was much more devious because when he was through, she literally craved him. Would have crawled to him, and had only yesterday.

Before her "training," the thought would have shamed her, but now she wanted him to exercise that power, to show her she hadn't mistaken her trust in the man she'd met, who unknowingly held her heart in his strong hands.

His eyes glinted with hunger and with cruel delight. He rubbed his erection against her, pulling her into the hard evidence of his desire. "You're going to be punished for disobedience, slave. And this time, I'm done holding back."

Chapter Seven

Jewel quivered, almost undone by his rough handling and words. He'd thrown her to the bed and bound her after propping her on her belly over a silk-covered bolster. Once again he placed a blindfold over her eyes, and the waiting was killing her. She heard the rasp of clothing, overloud in the sudden silence. He moved around in the room, but she had no idea what he did.

After what felt like twenty minutes, she grew less aroused and more impatient. Did he have any notion of what foreplay meant? Leaving a horny woman to wait forever didn't exactly—

"Ow! Shit! What are you doing?" Her ass stung from where he'd slapped her.

"No talking." He slapped her ass again, stinging the other cheek.

"But—"

Another slap, and another. Her flesh was burning, yet she creamed, attuned to what the play preceded. Ethan rubbed her skin, his light touch arousing in the extreme. The contrast of care and punishment made her wet with desire. Jewel didn't understand how Ethan could arouse her so much. She'd never been spanked before she'd met him, and she'd never been turned on by scenes of spanking and dominance. Yet with Ethan, it only made the sex between them hotter, and dammit, more addicting.

"Apologize to your master."

His voice was deep and had her throbbing inside. He spoke directly into her ear, his lips closing around the sensitive spot on her neck just under her lobe.

"S-sorry."

When she said nothing more, he nipped at her and palmed her ass.

"Master."

"Good girl." Ethan ran that hand between her legs, sliding through her wet slit. He deliberately brushed against her clitoris, and she moaned, wanting more.

"Please."

"Oh, no, slave. You push and push, and now it's time for Master to push back."

The excitement in his voice spurred her desire, and more than anything she wanted to see his face, to see the hunger blazing in his eyes.

The bed dipped, and she sensed him in front of her. Something pressed her lips, something soft but wet. He prodded. Not so soft after all.

"Open your mouth."

She opened, and he pushed himself inside, his cock moist at the tip. Ethan kept moving, not giving her time to adjust to his girth. She gagged, trying to breathe while accepting him.

"Take it all. And do it now. I'm not waiting on you anymore, slave."

His harsh breathing excited her, and she groaned when he began fucking her mouth. He pushed deeper, slapping his balls against her chin as he rocked.

"Oh, yeah," he rasped, and rubbed his balls over her chin with his hand, encircling her neck with his fingers.

He tightened his hold and amazingly, she felt a swell in arousal.

"I could crush you, couldn't I, slave?"

She wanted him inside her, her pussy spasming with need. Ethan released his hold on her throat, petting her gently.

"I can do anything I want with you." He increased his pace inside her mouth, his voice thick. "And I'm going to. Open your mouth wider."

She did, and moaned when he withdrew. She felt him circle around her and smelled a faint hint of coconut.

The oil. She recognized the scent as the oil he'd rubbed onto the butt plug. Jewel licked her lips, expecting and even looking forward to the slight intrusion. He nudged her legs apart and spread her cheeks.

"Now you're going to please your master without a sound, aren't you?"

"Yes, Master."

"No matter how much it hurts."

Hurts? Oh, hell, he wasn't going to take her ass now, was he?

"Don't tense, slave. Relax." He grunted and began pushing, his thick cock stretching her comfortably, to a point. The plug had never gone so deep and certainly hadn't been as thick as what he now shoved inside her. And he gave no quarter.

"That's it, baby, take it all."

She panted and tried to push out, since pushing with her sphincter allowed him easier access into her body. Still, she felt uncomfortably full as he moved deeper and deeper. And her body burned, not used to such play.

"A little more. God, you're so fucking tight," he breathed, his hands gripping her hips. *"Yes."*

He rested within her, and she ached, wishing now she hadn't toyed with this idea. Somehow, she'd thought it would feel good, that the pleasure she'd experienced with the plug would be the same with him in her ass. But he was too rigid, too hard. And it hurt.

Ethan slapped her ass. "Don't move. Get used to me."

Get used to him? Hell, she wanted him out, and now. But she said nothing, determined to remain quiet. She could take what he had to give, and then some. *Master my ass...*

His fingers began playing with her clit, and she immediately jolted, moving his cock a fraction out of her.

"No, slave, I said be still." He rammed back into her, and she hissed at the pain.

At the same time it hurt, she realized it didn't hurt as much as it had. And the pleasure from his touch on her clit only added to the confusion in her body. Jewel wanted to move, wanted him to shove inside her as much as she wanted to avoid the pressure in her ass.

Ethan, however, took the decision from her. He began thrusting lightly, pulling out a little and pushing back in. And all the while he rubbed her clit, teasing the taut flesh as he fucked her ass.

"That's it. So good, baby. You feel so good."

And who knew, but so did he. After a while, the fullness within her felt right. If only she had something to clench in her vagina. She felt empty there, needing more. And then he withdrew completely and shoved something inside her channel—something not his cock. He pushed inside her ass again, stretching, stinging, yet the dual fullness had her frozen in blissful shock.

"Tell me now, slave, how does it feel?"

"I can't...oh, I'm going to come if you keep doing that."

He chuckled and slammed in hard again, his giant shaft rubbing against the dildo inside her, pushing it further as well. Returning his attention to her clit, he brought her quickly to the edge. "Don't come yet, baby. Wait for it."

She thrashed, her body screaming for release while he toyed with her. He let go of her clit and thrust slowly, all the way in, all the way out, and she wanted to scream. And then he did something to the dildo that made it vibrate.

"Master, please."

"You beg so sweetly, slave. Say my name again."

"*Master.* I can't hold back any longer."

He groaned and sped up the tempo, rocking into her at such a rate she knew he neared release as well. The feeling was incredible, knowing he was close to his end, that though

Ethan commanded her body, she commanded his. And she climbed with him.

"You'll come for me now, slave." He pinched her clit and thrust hard. *"Now."*

Helpless to resist, Jewel screamed his name as she came, trembling with the ecstasy of fulfillment. Ethan quickly followed, his shout as loud as hers, and he held her hips tight as he shot inside her. Within moments, cum slid down her legs, and she ached from clenching the dildo so hard within her pussy.

What felt like hours later, Ethan finally stilled inside her. "Yes," he groaned as he pulled out and thrust in one last time. "That was so fucking good."

Jewel sighed and hung limply over the small bench, completely wrung out.

Ethan stroked her back, then bent over and hugged her tight, cupping her breasts in his hands. "Tell me, baby. When is your training over?"

Bastard. But she felt too good to grouse. "When you say it's over." She paused. "Master."

She could feel his smile against her neck. "That's right, baby. So right." He leaned up and withdrew, removing the dildo as well. "I wish I had a camera. You have no idea how sexy you look like this, tied up, my cum dripping from your ass."

She flushed, yet the pleasure she felt from his words made her warm.

"Now how about we clean you up, hmm?"

Ethan left her and returned with a towel. He wiped her gently, then removed the blindfold and untied her. "Come on, baby. Let's shower and dress. Rick will be coming back soon, and I don't want him finding you like this."

In the shower, he treated her like a child, not letting her do anything. And truthfully, his care felt wonderful. So tender, he cleaned every inch of her before turning to himself. And as they left, he dried her off before finding her some clothes to wear.

"Where did you get these?" She recognized the short skirt and T-shirt as her own.

"I took them from your room a few days ago. I figured you'd need them when we left."

"Sneak."

He shrugged and finished dressing and tidying up the area, including cleaning the toys on the bed stand. Watching, Jewel sat like a limp noodle on the bed, and Ethan gave her a concerned look.

"Baby, are you okay? I wasn't too rough with you, was I?" he asked gruffly.

"No. But you did wear me out. I'm exhausted."

He grinned with relief and took her in his arms. Kissing her gently, he swept her off the bed against his chest.

Stunned, she stared at him, aware he'd never looked at her the way he was just now. Her heart raced as feelings burgeoned inside her, needing to be set free.

"Ethan?"

"Jewel?"

"I—"

The door opened, breaking the mood, and Ethan's smile turned into a frown. "Great timing," he muttered. He refused to let her go, and instead walked with her past Rick. "See you in the morning."

Rick nodded with a smile, and Jewel turned into Ethan's chest to avoid Elise and the guards' bemused stares.

As Ethan carried her down the hallway, she finally found her dignity and squirmed to get down.

"Keep it up, and I'll spank you right here in the hallway." Ethan kissed the top of her head. "Relax, baby. Let me take care of you."

She groaned her assent and snuggled against him, knowing she didn't really want him to let her go. Not now. And not tomorrow. And what did that say about her state of mind? Jewel was afraid Ethan had indeed claimed his slave, and for good this time.

* * *

Ethan spent the next two days working his ass off scrutinizing the staff's and guests' records. Through Jared in Seattle, he'd managed to land more detailed accounts of the staff's history, and now had another four suspects who looked like potential trouble. Thankfully, Jewel *Marciella* wasn't one of them. Jewel Riser, ha. Although, to give her credit, she'd gotten a "rise" out of him.

Hell. She was conducting her own investigation, one he needed to look into as soon as he took care of the more pressing problem of a murderer.

He sighed as he sat in Rick's office, using the time to organize his thoughts. To *try* to organize his thoughts. He and Jewel had left Rick's room, but Ethan had demanded she continue to "train" with him during the nights. Knowing she wasn't really into the whole sex scene, contrary to what her application had stated, had taken a load off his mind. He still wanted her to confide in Rick about her real reason for being here, but between Pete's murder, the thief, and trying to narrow down the suspects again, Ethan had his hands full.

And that wasn't counting his nights with Jewel.

He should have backed off a little. But Jewel got him so hard, so fast all the time. He couldn't be in the same room without wanting to have her. Watching her in the throes of orgasm was nothing short of heaven. And to know he'd put her there…it made thoughts of anything else pale, his focus completely on her.

That Ethan knew little about her personal life bothered him. But damn it all, he hadn't been able to stop himself from loving her delectable body. Time was running out, he knew. Before long, the case would end, and he'd have to leave the island. *But you have to catch that damned thief before you can leave,* his conscience asserted, *before he hurts someone else.* God forbid the killer do something to Jewel. He had to focus on the case. To catch the bastard, Ethan needed to be prepared. To stop fixating on Jewel. A seeming impossibility.

Ethan exhaled heavily. He glanced down at the files on Rick's desk and imagined himself back at home in his own office. Without Jewel. He didn't know what to do. Ethan couldn't possibly be in love with a woman he knew so little about. Sure, she fucked like a goddess and turned him on like no other, but he hadn't so much as dated her, knew nothing about her likes and dislikes out of the bedroom. So how could he be so twisted and superficial as to think he might be in love with a woman he'd only ever laid flat?

He didn't know, and the not knowing was driving him crazy. Every time he caught Jewel laughing or flirting with her coworkers and the guests, he saw red. Rick, damn him, knew the truth. That constant smirk on the man gave him away. But how the hell was Ethan supposed to concentrate when his woman was out there unclaimed? And therein lay the problem. In this fantasy resort, everything was allowed. So where did fantasy and reality separate?

Jewel was his slave...in the bedroom. Here in the resort, she worked independently, yet always had a special smile for him. But she remained her own person, strong, beautiful, and too damned self-sufficient. In his opinion, she seemed too available. Wearing that string bikini—thank God she still wore clothes around this place—she was a walking temptation. So who could blame anyone for looking when he had a hard time blinking around her?

Ethan growled and focused on the information in front of him. This obsession with Jewel was going to cost him. He knew it. He had trouble doing his job, didn't seem to want anyone else but her, and had a hard-on anytime she stepped in the room. Hell, anytime he thought about her.

He glared down at his tenting trousers and forced himself to read about Joshua Denton, to solve the fucking case. *Finally,* he was successful in shoving Jewel from his thoughts.

Denton had been an employee at the resort for three years. He did his job and did it well, a popular escort with the guests. He was a real ladies' man, but didn't have a problem screwing the male guests, either. There was nothing in Denton's file to indicate guilt, but something about the man bothered Ethan. And though Rick would have given him shit about being jealous of Jewel, Ethan knew it was something more.

His gut told him to keep an eye on Denton. That mess about vacations and coming back early smacked of trouble, not to mention Denton's allegations that the door to Rick's suite had been ajar. Ethan would stake his entire career that he'd locked the damn door. He was good at what he did; when it came to a lockdown, the door was locked. Period. Ethan sighed. He would get to the bottom of Denton after a more detailed search of the man's room.

The next file, Elise Tanner's, made him pause. Elise had been Rick's head of security for five years, as long as the resort had been open. In all that time, she'd been strictly professional, never bonding with Rick on a more intimate level than a handshake. Yet Ethan knew she and Rick had notched the old bedpost a few days ago. So what gave? Why increase the intimacy now? To throw Rick and Ethan off the scent? A distraction?

She had no apparent reason to want money. Elise had a hefty bank account, no outstanding debts, and no family issues demanding a sum of money worth anything the cup might offer.

Which left Jaz Henderson and Gus Ludrell. Everyone loved Jaz. He was the most popular of the waitstaff and a favorite to watch when it came to "games" in the resort. Jaz loved working at Satyr's Myst and was one of Rick's highest paid staff. He had a few gambling debts that he'd recently paid, debts that far outweighed anything his salary at Satyr's Myst could cover. But Jaz had managed to wipe them out, so he shouldn't have had any pressing need for a windfall of money.

Gus Ludrell, another of Rick's security, like Jaz, did his job and did it well. But Gus had been present when Meyers had been killed, making him a prime suspect. Not to mention the fact that Gus had slept with Meyer's wife and reportedly had a thing for collecting what others owned. From jewelry to property to people. Gus loved sex and the idea of living in a fantasy, and he had for three years. But he seemed to truly respect Rick, and he'd never had so much as a speeding ticket, much less a felony conviction.

Ethan shook his head. These four needed further study. The guests had been surprisingly easy to check off. None of them wanted their privacy shattered and preferred keeping a low profile while here. Murder and burglary would attract more attention than any of the guests wanted, including Rick's friends now on the island.

Last night, two of his Bacchus Club buddies had shown up. Evan Wood, a hotshot Hollywood attorney, and Jeremy Jones, a celebrity client and major art collector. Both men had motive to steal the cup, but none to murder their friend. Money was a powerful motivator, of course, but both men were extremely wealthy, as well as famous. They had no need for the type of money the cup would bring.

Ethan shook his head. No, it had to be one of the four staff he'd recently investigated. But which one? His head throbbed. Hell, he needed a break. Maybe now would be a good time to search Denton's room. According to the schedule, Denton would be occupied massaging the Taylor couple in the private cabana overlooking the ocean. *Perfect time for a little personal investigation.* But as he left the room, Ethan's thoughts turned to Jewel again, and he groaned, realizing he'd been well and truly snared.

Jewel smiled and batted her eyes, pleased when Denton approached her right away. She'd been working him for the last two days and had finally managed to get his attention. The damned female guests were all over him, especially Tanya, who seemed to wake every morning with a margarita glass in her hand.

"Jewel." Denton strutted to her side and made no effort to hide his interest as his gaze lingered over her breasts.

His orange and green tiger-striped trunks were the male version of her green suit, which consisted of three small triangles to cover the essentials and butt floss to bare her ass. Thank God for the Stairmaster at home.

"Josh." Jewel bit her lower lip, knowing how much that turned Ethan on. Denton was no different, and he stared at her mouth. "I've been looking for you. Tyrone gave me a break, and I was hoping you and I could, well, go somewhere and…talk."

"Talk, hmm?" Denton grinned, his eyes smoky with desire.

You'd think screwing anything that moved would have put Denton off sex for recreation, but apparently her lure was too strong to resist. Jewel wanted to grimace when he took her hand and kissed her open palm. Instead of feeling seduced, she felt slobbered on. But she smiled and tried her best to appear demure.

"I'm supposed to have an appointment in a few minutes." He looked over his shoulder at the cabana being readied by a few naked Myst girls, then shook his head. "Hold on a sec."

He left her only to return moments later. "The Taylors don't mind Sheila taking over. Come on."

They walked quickly to the third floor, what Jewel knew to be the bi floor. The staff and guests preferring adventurous, gender-friendly sexual partners resided here.

Denton punched in his code, which she committed to memory, and they entered. Much less plush than Ethan's room, Denton's room still looked comfortable. Decorated in an exotic jungle theme, animal prints and stripes covered the fabrics in the large bedroom.

The room held a king-sized bed, a standard in the staff rooms, as well as a brand-spankin' new laptop dazzling the small personal desk across the room. Jewel salivated. Now, how to get Josh out of the way so she could access his terminal...

"So what do you want to do first, honey? Oral, anal? Or maybe you just want a hard fuck, something more along the lines of what Rick likes?"

She blinked. Rick? Oh, right, she had supposedly been trained by Rick. But what the hell did he like? "Um, I thought we could talk." He frowned, and Jewel hurried to correct herself. "I mean, you could show me what you like. Tell me what you like. I'm supposed to please the guests, and everyone has a different turn-on, you know? What do you like, Josh?"

Denton's frown faded under a grin, and he sat on the edge of his desk. "Me? I'm a sucker for a good blowjob. Soft lips, a hint of teeth." He rubbed his fingers over the bulge growing between his legs. In the boxer trunks he wore, he looked very attractive, American-pie handsome, so she could understand the contrast of sexpot to boy-next-door as more than appealing to some. Yet she couldn't help comparing him to Ethan and finding him lacking.

Jewel realized he was waiting and wondered how best to go about this. She needed Denton out of commission. But she sure as hell wasn't sleeping with him. She didn't want him, and for all she knew, he had his camera up and running as they spoke.

She bit her lip again and stared around her, avoiding eye contact. "Can I tell you a secret?"

"Anything, Jewel." His voice rasped, his excitement clearly growing as he watched her.

"I want to see you touch yourself. In front of me. I, um, I really like that."

"Whatever you want. You want me to jack off? No problem." Denton untied the front of his trousers and released his straining erection. "So, tell me what you thought about Rick. He's big, isn't he? And what about that monster, Ethan Reaper? He's got to be huge. That whole don't-touch-me growl along with his massive size…he's got to have a huge cock." Denton grew as he spoke, his arousal telling.

A huge cock? You have no idea. "Wow, Josh. You're not so bad yourself. So big." *As if.*

"And getting bigger." He fisted himself while he watched her, his lids lowering while his breathing increased. "Rick took my virgin ass. Hell, I wasn't even into men, and he made me want it so bad. I did everything you could do to the man. I sucked him off, I took it in the ass, and it hurt so good." His hand grew into a frenzy of motion. "Oh, yeah, that's it. Watch me, Jewel. Your eyes, your mouth. I can just see you going down on me, sucking my cum."

"Yeah, sure. That's right." Ick, when would this end? After her time spent with Ethan, the sight of so much sex around the resort only made her think of doing it with *him*. But standing around with Denton made her feel dirty, and she decided to leave before the situation grew out of hand...so to speak. "Oh, no."

"Yeah, it's gonna blow. Why don't you get on your knees and swallow it down?" Denton moaned, his balls tight, and his cock flushed with arousal. "You've got me really hard, honey. And I'll bet your pussy's wet from watching me, huh?"

Not surprisingly, it wasn't. "Uh, I don't think so. I just remembered Rick wanted me in his office this morning by eleven. And it's almost eleven fifteen. He's not going to be happy." She took a step back.

"Not yet." Denton startled her by grabbing her before she could leave. He jerked one of her hands from her side and put it around his hard shaft.

She flinched, and he smiled. "That shyness is so sexy. I want you to take me in your mouth. Let me blow into you, sweet."

"I don't think so." She grimaced, and Denton's smile turned sly.

"What's wrong? You a dick-tease, Jewel? Trying to sucker me with that shy smile and those thick lips?" His lips quirked as his eyes brightened. "Or is this what Rick taught you? Start reluctant, draw them in. Make the guest take you hard, overpowering you?"

Crap. His cock leaked under her hand, and she quickly took it away.

His eyes turned flat, and his smile soured. "Oh, I get it. If it's not Richie Rich, Rick Hastings and his millions, you don't want it. On your knees, bitch."

Okay. This was now officially out of control. Jewel had no problem using force. "Bitch" was one word that really pressed her buttons. And Denton's attitude left a lot to be desired.

"I hope you're getting this on camera," she whispered.

He looked startled. "What?"

"On camera. You know, the way you filmed the others?"

His face darkened and flushed, the once-handsome boy-next-door now a blackmailing thug with a point to prove. "You little bitch. Which one of them hired you? Who are you working for?"

Them, he said. Just great. Ethan had been right. Denton was after more than Sophie Ayers. Now to work this from another angle. "I'm supposed to be working for the senator." It was just a guess that Denton would have set up the most vulnerable client in attendance. And by the look in his eyes, she'd hit pay-dirt. "But you have such a nice setup in here. Give me a share, and I'll make sure you get your money."

In his anger, Denton began stroking himself faster. "You're going to suck this down, and then we'll talk about a deal. I'm doing the fucking here. Now, on your knees, or do you want me to rape you, after all?"

The hard excitement on his face had her taking another step back. Just as he lunged for her, the door behind them opened.

Chapter Eight

"What the fuck?" Ethan growled, staring in obvious shock as Denton knocked her to the floor. She felt Denton nudging against her and scowled, really disgusted.

"A little help here," she grunted before her assailant was lifted off of her and thrown into the nearest wall, which was unfortunately near his desk.

"Watch the computer."

Denton cursed as he regained his feet and managed to tuck himself back into his shorts, glaring at Ethan and Jewel. "You're in on it together?" He flew at Ethan this time, but Ethan sidestepped him easily and spun, shoving the smaller man to the floor. He punched Denton in the back and flipped him over, pressing into Denton's neck. Denton gave a hiss of protest before his eyes rolled back in his head, and he passed out.

When Ethan stood, he quickly shut the door to the room and locked it. His eyes were two dark pits of rage as he stepped over Denton's unconscious body. Jewel swallowed loudly, aware she was in deep—

"*Shit.* What the hell is going on in here? Please don't tell me you were meeting Denton for a quick fuck." His anger turned to full-out rage, and for the first time Jewel felt a stirring of fear.

"No, no. Nothing like that. Denton had it in mind for a...for some fun. I just wanted his computer."

Ethan's anger simmered, his fists clenching and unclenching.

"Honest. Ethan, this is the guy I'm here to investigate. He's been blackmailing some guests, and in particular, my client."

"Why should I believe you?"

"Because loverboy turns me off. For the first time since being on this island, I'm not in perpetual heat."

Ethan glanced down her body, relaxing a fraction. So she was stunned when he yanked her to him and thrust a hand between her legs.

"Ethan, really," she huffed.

"Damn. You weren't kidding." He removed his fingers, and she glared. Kissing the scowl off her face, he surprised her by smiling. "So Denton doesn't do it for you, hmm? Good to know."

"Glad you're so pleased. Now can I have a go at his computer before he wakes up?"

Ethan shook his head. "Don't worry about dickless, here. You take your time."

While she set about cracking Denton's computer, Ethan tied up the jerk. After a few minutes, she entered the hidden files on the computer and began searching for a backdoor around his password. She easily breached his firewall and scanned for any file containing Sophie's name on it.

"Wow. You're pretty good at that." Ethan stood over her shoulder. "Took you no time flat to infiltrate his security. Not bad."

"I've had a lot of practice." She tried not to be distracted by the larger-than-life male at her back. "Damn, but Denton has more than a dozen folders in here. And look at this. He's been making money off of these people for years." Searching by date, she found Sophie's file and glanced over her shoulder. "I need you to turn around."

"For Christ's sake, Jewel."

She frowned. "We promise confidentiality to our clients. Turn around."

He swore but did so, and Jewel watched the video unfold. Holy cripes, but Sophie Ayers had quite an imagination, and a real knack for leather. Jewel took a deep breath and deleted the evidence.

"Dreemer's, Inc., right?"

Damn, he was good. "Maybe."

"Please. Give me some credit."

"Fine. I work for Dreemer's. Happy now?"

"Not as much as I plan to be when we get the hell out of here," he muttered.

She took a few more minutes to thoroughly search Denton's files for any more mention of Sophie Ayers. At least the computer was clean. Now if she could only be as sure that he hadn't made any backup videos.

"Can I turn around now?"

She ignored the exasperation in Ethan's voice. "Yeah, but I'd like to look through the rest of these files with Rick's help." Ethan swore and scowled at mention of Rick's name. "Oh, Ethan, get a grip. I'm not getting my kicks from this. I want Rick to ID the other victims on these videos, so he can contact them and set them at ease. And there's no telling what backup discs Denton's already made."

"Okay," Ethan said after a moment. "But you and I are going to talk about this. I don't understand why you didn't tell me you suspected Denton in the first place. I could have given you access to his place without a problem."

"But it's my job to help my client. Not yours. And we did promise her—"

"Discretion, I know. Hell, Jewel. I run a securities firm. I know all about big words like 'discretion.'"

She flushed, and he glowered.

"We're going to talk about this, at length, later tonight. And don't let me catch you straying from Tyrone's sight again. He's one of the only people I trust that's completely innocent of any wrongdoing around here."

"So Rick talked to him about what Denton said the other night?"

Denton groaned, but they ignored him.

"Yeah. Tyrone heard from Jaz, who heard from someone else, that Rick wanted Denton. We can't trace the original source of the order, and I'm still not sure how that door was unlocked when I personally set the lock myself. But since Denton's story checks out, someone else must have unlocked the door."

"That is odd. Jaz, huh?" She couldn't see him as the guilty party. She genuinely liked him.

"Yeah." Ethan glanced at Denton's still body and lowered his voice. "He's someone I'm looking into. Look, Jewel, I'm having a hard enough time tracking down a master thief and suspected killer. I don't need to be worrying about you getting raped while I'm at it."

She stared. "He wouldn't have raped me, Ethan. Relax."

"Relax?"

Uh-oh. His voice had gone decidedly gentle. Never a good sign.

"He had his dick out, ready to shove it into you. And the asshole was almost on top of you when I arrived. Tell me why I should calm down. Unless you wanted Denton to give it to you. Did you, Jewel? Did you want another man? Tired of me already?"

"Get a grip, Ethan." She snorted, perturbed that she found his jealousy arousing. "You touched me. I was bone-dry. What does that tell you? I'm here to do my job, nothing more."

"No, baby. You're here to do whatever *I* tell you to do. Now I'm telling you to head back to my room and climb onto my bed, where I sleep. And where I'm going to fuck you senseless. Don't stop on your way. I'll be right behind you."

"Ethan—"

"Go, now. I'm calling Rick in to deal with this."

She glared but turned. "Don't forget the laptop," she reminded.

"Get the hell out of here."

*   *   *

Ethan thought he heard her mumble "asshole" but couldn't be sure. The alternating spouts of rage, jealousy, and pure arousal made it hard to be clear about anything. The little fool could have been hurt by Denton, a man larger and stronger than her. Hell, the bastard had been hard and ready to fuck her, yet Jewel told him she'd had everything under control.

Sure she did.

He should have felt bad for testing her, for measuring her arousal. But he couldn't help the relief filtering through him. She really hadn't wanted Denton, and why he should feel so damned reassured by that fact only added to his worry that he'd fallen head over heels for the stubborn little witch.

"What the hell?" Denton slurred, groaning as he shook his head.

"Can it, asshole. The boss will want to talk to you." Ethan dialed Rick's line and explained the situation. Rick and three guards would be arriving posthaste.

Ethan stared down at Denton in disgust. "Got greedy, hmm?"

"Shit. Let me go, and there's a cool half mil in it for you."

"Forget it. But you know what?" Ethan leaned down and punched Denton hard in the gut, earning a wrenching groan from the man. "You go near Jewel again and I'll rip your balls out and feed them to you, one at a time. You hear me?"

Denton was still trying to catch his breath, but he nodded vigorously.

"Good." A knock at the door interrupted them. "Rick's here, and he has some questions, which you'll be happy to answer in complete detail, isn't that right?" Ethan put his foot between Denton's legs, and Denton babbled, eager to please.

Ethan left him to open the door, and Rick entered with his men, looking extremely pissed. As the guy stood over Denton, Ethan felt a chill wash over him at the look in Rick's eyes.

"Josh, Josh. This isn't going to be pleasant."

Denton's eyes widened, and Ethan smiled, pleased to leave him in capable hands. The guards around Rick grinned with menace, and Ethan knew Rick had apprised them of the situation.

"I have some business to take care of in my room. Call me there when you're done, Rick. And I'll be taking the laptop with me."

Rick nodded, his fury focused on Denton.

Ethan gathered the laptop and pointed out at least one hidden camera he'd noticed in a wall vent—a common enough place—to the guards. As he left, he heard Denton spilling his guts in a rush.

Pussy. Ethan shook his head. One mystery had been solved. Now he only had to ferret out one other unpleasant mess from the island...but *after* he'd seen himself that Jewel was indeed okay. He left the third floor by the stairs and had just entered the first floor hallway when he felt a presence behind him. Curious, as no one had followed him down the stairs, and he hadn't heard any doors open in the hallway, Ethan turned to see who was there...and took a tremendous blow to the head.

He stumbled and tried to defend himself when a second blow struck him senseless. His last thoughts were of Jewel as he blacked out.

Jewel frowned at the clock for the fifth time. Granted, taking care of Denton and the blackmailing pictures was important, but if Ethan thought she'd agree to sit on her thumbs and wait all day for him to return, he had another thing coming. Hell, she'd already wasted the afternoon on his domineering ass.

She was due to serve the after-lunch set at two and had just enough time to return to her room and change before she was late. *Come on, Ethan.*

Huffing, Jewel took another turn around his room, looking for anything she hadn't yet studied. While waiting for Ethan, she'd given in to her curiosity and had found more to like about the dratted man.

A photo, tucked away in his little black book, of him and a friend, both with shorn hair and wearing Marine Corps green, showed he could indeed form a healthy relationship with the same sex. Rick not withstanding, Ethan tended to boss everyone else around, and she knew it had more to do with his personality than his job.

The black book held a ton of phone numbers, several of them women's numbers, Jewel noted, and all but three had been crossed through with an emphatic "don't call again" printed in clear black ink by their names. Ethan didn't seem to have a steady girlfriend at home, and she liked that he wouldn't have such hot sex with her when committed elsewhere.

His writing was precise and easy to read, contrary to the man himself. She wished she understood what went through his convoluted mind when he gave her those breath-stealing looks, the ones that made her want to scream out "I love you" like a fool.

He kept his room neat, actually put his dirty clothes in the hamper and tucked his shoes away in the closet instead of leaving them lying around. Her brother did that, and it drove her nuts. Ethan had family as well, two brothers that she'd read about in a letter from his mother, also tucked into that black book.

She thought it cute that he'd kept a letter from his mom, dated several months ago, and was pleased to see Ethan shared her familial values. According to his mother, the woman was still dying to see grandchildren, and as the eldest child, Ethan was holding up the works.

Jewel sighed. How familiar that sounded. And speaking of familiar…

Spying Ethan's cell phone, she picked it up and dialed her uncle, who was probably worried silly, considering she hadn't contacted him since she'd been sequestered with Ethan for her "training." But, hell, who could think when a sexy dominant had you tied up, aching from a bazillion orgasms?

"Uncle Tommy?"

"Jewel, where the hell have you been?"

Funny, but he didn't sound all that concerned, and she had a sneaking suspicion he knew a lot more than he'd been telling her.

"I've been tied up and was nearly killed," she lied.

"What? Rick never said anything about—"

"Would that be Rick Hastings, the man to whom you apparently told I was into group sex and liked to watch?"

"What?"

"Yeah, someone put down on my application that in addition to my desperation from losing my fiancé, I like to have sex with a lot of men and in public."

"Hell." He paused. "I knew Nick had seen something when he was in here last week. He accepted your going way too easily. It had to be him."

"Oh." Nick was *so* going to pay when she went home. "Well, sorry for thinking it was you."

"I merely told Rick to keep an eye on you, and that you were there checking on a potential blackmailer for me. Now if you happened upon some fun in the sun, who am I to forbid you? And, no, I don't want to know anything about it. Frankly, the idea of you being old enough to have sex is turning me gray, and like I said before, your mother would kill me if she knew I'd sent you *there.*"

Jewel took the phone away from her ear to stare at it. So her uncle *and* her brother had set her up. She didn't know what to think, then decided the hell with it. She'd met Ethan, so she couldn't be too upset with her family.

"Jewel?" Her uncle yelled through the phone.

She quickly put it back to her ear. "Sorry I haven't called recently. I've been very *busy,* "she drawled.

Silence.

Grinning, she added, "I found and deleted Sophie's files from our blackmailer's laptop, and am in the process of scanning the rest of Denton's computer to erase any trace of

Sophie Ayers's name." *As soon as Ethan gets his sorry ass in here.* "Tell her not to bother showing up next week, unless she wants a tan. Oh, and I wouldn't be surprised if Rick, *your buddy,* gives her a call. He had no idea anyone was blackmailing clients from his resort, and according to Ethan, Rick takes that kind of thing very seriously."

"Ethan?"

"My personal bodyguard." If only he were in here guarding her body right now. She could really do with some personal attention.

"Oh, um, right. Okay, then. Let me know when you have the rest of the files, and I'll book you on a flight—"

Jewel didn't hear the rest of what he said. Sudden panic overtook her at thoughts of leaving when her "relationship" with Ethan had no semblance of order. Though they'd screwed every which way from Sunday, she was still in the process of learning more about him. And the damned autocrat lived in Seattle, on the *opposite* coast. How the hell would they develop anything further, separated by thousands of miles?

"Jewel, did you hear me?"

"Don't book me a flight. I'll make the travel arrangements myself. I'm not sure how long Rick might need me here to serve his clients."

"Please tell me you're not saying what I think you're saying." Her uncle sounded sick.

"Come on, Uncle Tommy. Rick's losing Denton, and he'll have to replace me as well. Despite what Nick wrote, I'm a hell of a *waitress,* and I work the lunch and dinner shifts while most of the others are out, ah, entertaining the guests here."

"Oh." Uncle Tommy cleared his throat. "Just check back and let me know what's going on. And don't wait four days this time, or I'll have Rick take it out of your pay."

"Ha, ha. Very funny." A pounding on the door distracted her. "Okay, Uncle Tommy. Gotta go. Love you."

Jewel disconnected and quickly put the cell phone and Ethan's black book—minus that picture—back where she'd found them.

Ripping open the door, she frowned. "It's about damned time...Jaz?"

"Jewel, hurry. Ethan's been hurt, and he's asking for you. He won't let anyone help him until he sees that you're okay."

She left the room without question, following Jaz quickly down the hall and around the corner. In no time at all they reached Rick's suite, and she watched anxiously as he entered the right codes to access Rick's rooms.

He held the door for her, and she rushed in, looking for Ethan. But to her surprise and chagrin, she found no one but Gus, another security guard, standing by the empty corner mount where the cup sometimes sat, his face grim.

Shit. This spelled trouble, and she knew Jaz was one of the suspects on Ethan's list. "Where's Ethan?" she asked calmly, forcing innocence into her voice. That Ethan still hadn't returned to her worried her more than anything, but she resolved to play it cool and let these two think they held the upper hand.

"Ethan's tied up, you might say." Jaz grinned, his smile looking much more sinister than sexy. "Now, Jewel, don't pretend ignorance. I know all about you, thanks to Ethan and his handiwork. You have quite a reputation at Dreemer's, Inc. And from what I saw of your work on Josh's computer, I can only imagine you're quite the computer tech."

"Jaz? Not you?" she held on, trying for dismay and not the anger frothing her thoughts.

"Sorry, baby, but as sexy as you are, and without a doubt I'll treasure the image of Reaper shooting into your mouth, you don't come close to the prize I'll have once I possess the cup."

She purposefully ignored his comment about watching her have sex, knowing she'd freak out later at thoughts of her intimacies with Ethan being viewed by a wacko like Jaz.

"Did you kill Pete?"

Jaz shrugged, and she noted Gus's scowl with interest.

"It had to be done. But I was quick and as gentle as could be. Peter, unlike some others, respected me. Peter loved me."

"You told me it was an accident, that you fell into him during a struggle and the knife slipped."

Jewel stared from Gus to Jaz.

"I lied." Jaz smiled, the expression doing nothing to warm his cold, flat gaze. "Gus, it's us against the others. We have to remain strong, together." Jaz grabbed her arm and walked over to his friend, dragging Jewel behind him.

"Gus, why are you doing this?" She had to know. Money or power? She'd bet on the former.

"To get back at Rick," Jaz explained, his gaze fixed on Gus. "Everything was fine until Rick started doing Elise. Poor little Gus has been in love with her since the moment he set eyes on her. But she never had anything to do with the people working here, not even Rick. Until a few days ago. Then, Gus had a meltdown, and gave me the codes I needed."

"But no one was supposed to be hurt." Gus glared at Jaz, staring hard at his hand gripping Jewel's arm. " I'm sorry, Jaz, but I'm out. Take the damned cup. Take whatever you want. But I'm leaving, and Jewel's coming with me." He grabbed her other arm, but Jaz took that moment to shove a fist into Gus's stomach, punching repeatedly. Except his fist held a knife.

Jewel dazedly wondered if he'd used the same knife on Pete.

She stared, aware Jaz had released her, but she was too caught up in the shock of what he'd just done to move. She'd never before been so close to death, had never seen a man killed before her eyes. Television and movies didn't come close to the sad brutality of such violent waste.

"Don't worry, Jewel. I would have killed him regardless of your involvement." Jaz sounded like himself, charming and pleasant, while he held a knife, no, a dagger, dripping with blood over Gus's unmoving body.

She felt dizzy for a moment, caught in the grip of a nightmare made real. Jaz handled her gently, and she was more than aware of the weapon in his free hand, just waiting for the moment to plunge again into solid flesh.

"You get that cup for me, and I'll let you go. And trust me when I tell you that your massive lover, Ethan, really is okay. I like him, and I like you. We share something in common, all of us. We're just pawns in Rick's sordid games."

Bitterness pooled in Jaz's deep brown eyes, and Jewel shook her head, overcome by a sudden, unwelcome empathy.

"He hurt you, didn't he?" she murmured.

Jaz clamped his lips together and pulled her toward the bed. He touched the same buttons Ethan had worked previously to unveil the cup, and they watched in silence as the wall moved, showcasing the glittering cup surrounded by thick glass.

"I can't touch the Mirvolo Cup until the security around it is completely dismantled. I know you don't have the codes, only Rick does, but with what you can do with security systems, I figure you'll find a way around this particular problem."

Jewel gnawed her lower lip, intrigued at possibly beating the system, as well as stalling for help to arrive before Jaz finally lost it and stabbed her, too. Gus groaned, drawing her attention, but Jaz shook his head.

"Ignore him. I stuck him hard and deep. He'll bleed out. Unlike Pete, I don't want Gus's death to be easy." Jaz snorted. "Traitor. You know, Jewel, it's true. Never trust a man."

He pointed her to Denton's laptop that he'd plugged in for her, and to a small black bag on the bed. "Tools you might need to overcome the system. I know what I'm talking about. For the last year I've been pilfering from Rick's closest buddies. But I don't have quite the finesse you seem to have with computers, and this prize needs a savvy hacker. It's really too precious for words that you arrived on the island when you did. I thought I was going to have to force Jacobs to help me. Unfortunately, he's straighter than your boy Ethan."

Jaz sighed while she sat down at the desk to begin working on the laptop. Luckily, Denton had tapped into Rick's security long ago, so she had the software needed to invade the home server.

"From the beginning I knew why Ethan was here, but he did a decent job and distracted Rick from what was right under his nose." Jaz sneered. "I'm just another employee. Too much a nobody to allow into Rick's precious Bacchus Club, even though I was good enough to fuck all night long."

"Bacchus Club?"

"Rick's manly group of perverts. A bunch of millionaire executives and Hollywood A-listers who collect ancient artifacts rumored to have belonged to Bacchus. You know who he is, don't you?"

"He's a Roman god."

"The Roman god of wine and debauchery. Dionysus to the Greeks."

It felt so odd to be conversing normally with a man who'd just admitted to killing one man, had stabbed another, and who most likely meant to kill her as well. The scrambled lock holding the cup behind a glass wall only made the situation that much more surreal. A challenging system Jewel was actually enjoying trying to crack, while under the surveillance of a charming madman.

"So why can't you join the Bacchus Club?"

Jaz left her side and began to pace, twirling the dagger in his hands. "I tried talking to Rick about it a year ago, and he politely brushed me aside. After our time together in here, in this very bed, I had assumed, incorrectly, that he loved me. The things we did together..."

She glanced up to see Jaz's puzzled face.

"I have sex all the time, but I've never made love like that. A love where you and your partner are suddenly one. You know what I mean?"

She thought of Ethan and nodded.

"But to Rick I was just another fuck. And after he let me drink from his precious Mirvolo cup. We drank together, shared some wine. And Rick babbled something about 'those that Bacchus favors.' Hell, Jewel, he should have favored me. Everyone loves me." His voice rose, and she turned away, staring hard at the screen in front of her, trying to appear invisible. *"Everyone loves me.* Everyone but that fucker Rick Hastings."

He sounded on the verge of a sob, and a surprising welling of sympathy filled her. "We all love you, Jaz," she said softly, tearing her eyes from the computer. "You were my first real friend here."

Jaz calmed as he stared at her. He even managed a smile. "You were so naïve and still are. Like a fish out of water here. You should leave Satyr's Myst, Jewel."

Yeah, if I'm still alive to do so, I will.

"Did you get what you needed from Denton?"

Startled, she stared at him. "I did. But how did you know about him?"

"I've known about his activities for years. I helped him once or twice, but blackmail is such a tasteless crime. No passion, no morals. There's no excitement in it. Do you know, I stole from Rick's friends, and each time it drew me, like a drug I couldn't get enough of."

"I know the feeling."

"You do, don't you?" He smiled with warmth. "I almost thought about giving it up after Meyers. John and I had shared a wonderful evening—which is how I normally made my way into the Club-goers' grand estates. I fucked my way there." Jaz chuckled and rubbed at his crotch. "But John was a light sleeper, and he caught me leaving his vault. Empty-handed, of course, as I'd stashed this dagger elsewhere. But if he'd told... Well, I couldn't have any suspicion, you know?"

Jewel nodded, her attention as riveted to him as to the server she was trying to infiltrate. She managed to crack the first and second levels of defense, but the next was proving more difficult.

"I don't understand why you stole from the group, though, Jaz. Why not just take what was Rick's and be done with it?"

"Because I needed to know."

"Know what?" Damn it, this layer was a real bastard. She needed more time and more tools to do it right, without tripping any safeguards.

"That the cup itself held the real magic."

She stopped and turned to face him. "The real magic?"

"Rick felt it, and others have, too, I know. I've heard them talk about it. But I felt nothing more than a small tingle. Just an all-consuming love with Rick that night. A love that can't possibly be natural after what he put me through."

Jewel wondered. She'd felt that same tingle, but in her it had been more powerful, like a haze of desire that wouldn't quit her blood. But magic? She couldn't possibly think herself in love with Ethan due to some insane talk about a magic cup...could she?

"You know, don't you?" he asked slyly. "Is that what draws you to Rick, too?"

"No."

"Really?" His gaze hardened. "Because I know Rick's taken with you. Even after fucking Elise, he still wanted to do you. I could tell."

"Elise? The head of security?" Funny, but stalwart and serious Elise hadn't seemed Rick's type. Petite and dark-haired, she seemed way too somber and professional to screw around with a playboy like Rick Hastings.

"Don't play coy, Jewel. I like your innocence, but innocence and ignorance aren't one and the same. I saw you taking Ethan, saw you licking his big cock. Ah, there's that blush; that's so sweet. So how was he? Did he taste as yummy as he looks?"

Jewel didn't know what to say. Instead, she turned back to the computer, praying Rick or Ethan would stumble upon them. Ethan—who was currently "tied up." She'd refrained from thinking about him because she didn't want to doubt that he was okay. Any other thought was unacceptable. No, Ethan would be here soon. She just had to distract Jaz long enough to let her *master* do his damned job.

And if he didn't hurry it up, Jewel promised herself she'd tie *him* up when this was all over.

Chapter Nine

Ethan grunted in pain as he finally managed to saw through the remainder of the ropes chafing his bloody wrists with a shard of sharp glass. He took care of the knots at his ankles as well, but when he tried to stand, the small janitorial closet he was stashed in spun.

Pressing a hand to the back of his head, he felt it come away bloody. Great. He closed his eyes and inhaled deeply, forcing his eyes back open to better understand what the hell had happened.

Jewel, was all he could think. *I have to get to Jewel.*

The memory of leaving the stairwell and being bashed in the head slowly returned, and Ethan focused on standing tall and clearing his mind. Blotting out the pain, he breathed evenly before attempting to open the door.

It was locked, of course. But the screwdriver set on the second shelf to his right quickly took care of that. When the door swung open, Ethan did his best not to plow down the half dozen guests staring at him in horrified fascination. He recognized a few of them, then quickened his pace when the familiar face of Elise neared.

"Have to reach my room." He coughed through a dry throat.

"You look like hell." She wiggled her way under his much-heavier body and managed to turn him around all the same. They moved quickly, thanks to her sturdy strength, and reached his room in minutes.

"Jewel." Ethan heard the panic in his voice and forced himself to remain calm. *Overcome the fear, the danger. See the true course and steal your victory.* The mantra had served him well enough overseas, and it would serve him as well here, with his woman in danger.

Elise swore. "Ethan, what the hell's going on? I can't find Rick, and Gus and Malcolm have been out of contact for the past hour."

Ethan entered his room, hoping to find Jewel on his bed, where he'd told her to wait for him, only to find it empty. He sank down on the bed and gave an involuntary groan.

"You're lucky your brains weren't bashed in," Elise said softly.

"Thanks, Elise. Tell me more good news."

She frowned. "I think Gus is the one who stole Rick's codes. He's been acting odd lately, and I saw him in Rick's office the other day when he had no reason to be there. But Gus turning on Pete makes no sense to me."

"Me, neither." Ethan rose and wobbled, but glared at Elise when she tried to steady him. "We need to find Rick right away. You track him down, and I'll head to his suite.

The Mirvolo Cup is our other vulnerability." Not to mention Jewel. "Our thief will strike there as well as at Rick. We cover them, we should be okay. Pull everyone if you have to, but find Rick and do it as discreetly as possible."

Elise nodded, never questioning. Ethan liked her, then recalled she was still on his suspect list even as she left his room. Shit. More complications. He tried to shake off his dizziness and wiped some blood out of his eye when a rivulet blurred his vision.

I'm so going to paddle Jewel's ass for leaving my bed. The thought cheered him enough to leave the room and reach the server closet that Pete used to man. With the new codes Rick had inputted to ward off more undue intruders, Ethan punched in the numbers and entered the small room, ignoring the frowning guard who was manning the station. He was dimly aware of the man leaving him alone. Focused, Ethan sat and entered another password and watched the desk-mounted monitor come to life. What he saw scared the hell out of him.

Jewel sat across from Jaz, a determined yet scared look on her face. Gauging her expression, he knew he needed to look no further for the guilty party than Jaz. But he still wished he knew why the man had done it. Why kill Pete? And why go after the Mirvolo Cup? Motives led to understanding, and it was always a good thing to understand one's opponent.

Ethan's vision blurred again, but he pushed through the pain, determined to reclaim Jewel and put a stop to Jaz's madness once and for all. Armed with little more than a throbbing skull and an overtaxed body, he muscled his way down the hall toward Rick's suite, only to be intercepted by Rick, Elise, and a dozen hulking guards.

Rick held up a finger for silence and pulled Ethan back down the hallway toward the nearest room, the others following closer behind. Once inside, Ethan stared in amazement at the gadgets strewn over the furniture.

"Shh, listen." Rick turned up the volume on one of the devices, and Ethan blanched when Jewel's and Jaz's voices mixed.

"Why are we waiting?" Ethan demanded, but Rick forced him into a seat.

"Because I need to time this just right. Jacobs, come here."

Jacobs nodded and sat by Rick. Ethan didn't hear what Rick told him, but the large security expert smiled and began typing.

"Look at Jewel, Ethan."

He did as Rick asked, wondering why he couldn't understand what was happening. Impatient, he stood. Rick mumbled something to the men behind him, and Ethan scowled at the guards suddenly surrounding him.

"You're in no shape to interfere. Somebody patch this man together while I take care of the mess I created. Now watch, Ethan." Rick pointed to a giant plasma screen on the nearby table. "We're going to get Jewel and the cup out of there safely."

Rick murmured something else to Jacobs, then turned to Elise. The look on Elise's face was surprisingly guarded. Then Rick kissed the breath out of her before walking out the door.

Apparently, Elise would have gone after him, but she, too, was held back. Ethan was startled to hear the petite woman swear like a Marine.

"Elise?"

"Dammit. Let's watch, Ethan, as Rick the Magnificent plans on saving the day. The jerk." Her eyes misted, but she blinked hastily.

They stared at the screen while Ethan mentally scrambled to find a way out of the room without falling on his ass. Jewel needed him, and he needed more than life itself to see her safe. And as Rick entered the viewing screen and found himself face-to-face with a murderous Jaz and a bloodied dagger, Ethan realized something else. In all his years of service, he'd never lost a man. And he didn't plan to lose one now.

"Fuck Rick." Ethan shook his head. "Jacobs, you're the computer expert. Find a way to send a message. You six," he said, blinking to keep the large guards in focus. "Follow Elise and take charge of the perimeter..."

* * *

Jewel swallowed audibly as she stared past Jaz to an apparently unarmed, pleasant-faced Rick Hastings. *Are you nuts?* she mouthed, knowing she and Jaz had been watched from the security cameras in the ceiling. She'd been told as much through the laptop when an easy, basic computer code had intruded while she'd been unscrambling that third, impossible layer of electronic defense.

"Jaz?" Rick said quietly. "I see a man facedown in the corner. What's going on?"

"Oh, Rick." Jaz turned around and sighed, pulling a gun she hadn't noticed before, and motioned Rick farther inside. "I hadn't wanted you to find me like this."

"Sure you did. You're a smart man, Jaz. If you'd wanted complete anonymity, you'd have stolen that cup a while ago and done it right out from under me."

Jaz smiled at the compliment, staring at Rick like a starving man, and Jewel was startled to see how much he was still in love with Rick. She glanced at Rick, but his gaze remained locked on Jaz. Slowly, subtly, Jewel noticed that Rick placed himself between her and Jaz. The fact that Ethan still hadn't arrived began to shake her confidence.

"How's it going, Jewel?" Jaz asked, a dagger in one hand, a pistol in the other.

"I'm getting closer." *Jacobs,* she typed. *What the hell is Rick doing in here? And where's Ethan?*

A flurry of crazy characters popped up on the screen, giving her a headache reading through them. Tired of wading through the jumbled script, she made sure Jaz's attention was centered on Rick before entering a few commands to make reading the type easier.

Ethan's fine, a jackass as usual.

Thank God. He was all right.

Do whatever Rick tells you, and whatever you do, don't excite Jaz. Let Rick distract him. We'll be in momentarily. Is that a gun in Jaz's hand?

Yes, and a dagger in the other——the one he probably used to kill Pete, and the one he stabbed Gus with.

She typed slowly, keeping a puzzled, frustrated look on her face so Jaz would assume she was still working.

Okay. I'm going to release the final bar on the cup. You were close, but nowhere near to unlocking it in time. Just pretend you're having a genius moment.

Jewel inhaled softly, nervous. What if Jaz decided to kill them once he had the cup in hand? At present, he was talking softly to Rick in a sick, lovey-dovey voice. Whatever hold on sanity Jaz had possessed prior to this afternoon, he'd surely lost it after stabbing Gus. Hell, maybe he'd lost it after stabbing Pete.

"You know I never meant to hurt you, Jaz, don't you?" Rick took a step closer to the man, but Jewel saw Jaz's fingers tighten around the dagger. Oddly, Jaz didn't seem as concerned with the gun as he was with the other weapon, and she realized he was waiting for Rick to step within range, then whammo, he'd thrust hard and deep.

"Jaz," she said loudly, standing to grab his attention. Both men turned to her as one. "I did it. I broke the security."

Jaz smiled, his face alight. The door on the glass casing slid open with a soft buzzing, and in seconds, the Mirvolo Cup stood without the encumbrance of a barrier.

"Rick, grab the wine."

Rick shared a frustrated glance with Jewel and shook his head. He grabbed a bottle from a small minibar and returned to Jaz.

What was he doing? Jaz had his attention centered on the damned cup. Now, while he was preoccupied, they ought to be racing for cover. But, no. Rick stood with a sad expression on his face as he stared at Jaz. Well, if he wasn't leaving, neither was she. Jaz didn't seem to want to hurt her, and she'd be damned if she'd leave Rick alone with a crazy man. Granted, she was no Amazon, but together, they might be able to overpower Jaz enough to get their hands on his gun, at the very least.

"Pour it." Jaz put down the dagger and reached for the cup. When his fingers closed around it, a strange glint lit his gaze. Jewel watched the odd ceremony, bemused by the strange shadow clinging to Jaz. Almost as if death loomed near... She shivered and saw Rick stare at her, his eyes unreadable even in the bright light of the room.

"Bacchus favors me. Say it, Rick. Say, 'Bacchus favors you, Jaz.'"

Jaz waited, the pistol upraised in one hand, the cup in the other. The rubies on the cup's base glinted like drops of blood over the gold, and Jewel wondered at her fanciful imaginings. The unnatural stillness in the room only added to her unease, and she took a step closer to Rick as Jaz raised the cup.

Rick used a corkscrew to open the bottle while Jaz closely watched. He stood within a breath of Jaz and filled the cup with rich red wine. "Why don't you let me hold the chalice, Jaz?"

"No. You won't take it from me, *lover,*" Jaz spat. "This is just killing you, isn't it? You're always so in control, always so damned possessive of this fucking gold cup. Well, watch as I possess what you treasure most. More than a man, more than that whore Elise. More than the love that could have been yours," Jaz said bitterly.

"Jaz, I'm so sorry... But you don't know what you're holding." Rick tried to persuade his ex-lover; Jewel wanted to kick him.

Let Jaz have the damned cup already. Let's get out of here and leave this mess for security to handle.

"Fuck you. Now the magic is mine." Jaz kept his eyes and his gun trained on Rick while he swallowed mouthful after mouthful from the gleaming chalice.

At that moment, the room erupted into chaos. Ethan and two men burst through the door while Elise and several others crashed through the windows bordering the eastern and western walls of the room. Jaz started at the noise and suddenly stumbled. That quickly, Ethan was on him, knocking the gun from the other man's fingers. But Jaz somehow managed to escape his hold and lunged at Rick in a shocking burst of speed.

"You mother fu—" Jaz shrieked as spittle flew down his chin. He stopped abruptly and began seizing, then fell to the floor. His body flailed uncontrollably before he gurgled one final time and stilled on the floor.

Jewel gaped in shock, barely aware of Ethan's arms around her. But as he leaned heavily against her, she realized she was holding him up as much as he was trying to comfort her.

"Oh, my God. Ethan, are you all right?"

"Fine," he said hoarsely, and kissed her hard on the mouth. She noted the dried blood on his face, the matted hair, and stained clothing. Blood, too much blood and death. Then she looked at Jaz's still form on the floor. "What the hell happened to him, Rick?"

Rick shook his head, a haunted look in his eyes. "I always handle the Mirvolo Cup for a reason. The cup has its own defenses, the least of which is a very deadly poison known as tanghin. When I found the cup, I had it extensively tested."

"It's in the cup?" Jewel stared, horrified. She'd sipped from that thing only a few short days ago.

"It's released into the cup if you don't press the correct sequence of stones before gripping the handle." He smiled sadly. "Bacchus didn't favor Jaz. I tried to tell him that, but he wouldn't listen."

Jewel felt like she was watching a bad soap opera. Glass covered the area; one man lay dead on the floor while another groaned, near death, under the care of the guards. And Ethan, her hero, looked like death warmed over.

"Come on, tough guy," she said, taking a deep breath. "Now that you've rescued me, how about we fix that gaping head wound?"

Ethan half nodded, then chose that moment to lose consciousness and took her to the floor with him as he fell.

* * *

Ethan woke to a splitting headache and an arm across his chest. To his relief, Jewel snuggled against him, safe and warm, and undeniably naked. Despite the pain at his temples, his body stirred, and he wondered at his own fortitude.

"Hmm?" Jewel kissed his chest and yawned. She rose on her elbows to look down at him. "Finally awake again. Do you know your name?"

"What?"

"Come on, Mr. Dominant. Your name. And where do you live?"

He rattled off the answers and gently probed his skull, wincing when he felt the tender spot behind his head.

"Easy, Ethan. Jaz must have whacked you pretty hard. You've been in and out of it for over twenty-four hours. But don't worry, we took you to the hospital and they did a CAT scan. No brain damage. Good thing you have such a hard head."

"Where..."

"You haven't had a reason to use it, but Rick took you to his fully staffed clinic available on the other side of the island. They mostly do cognitive research, or something like that, but I wasn't really paying attention when we were rushing you over there."

He wasn't so groggy he didn't appreciate the tartness of her answer. "Worried, hmm?"

"Of course. It's not every day your knight in shining armor passes out and takes you down with him."

Ethan closed his eyes and felt his face heat. "Sorry."

She laughed and stroked his chest. "Don't worry about it. Elise and Rick pieced together for me what happened. But I'm still not over my mad at Rick. What the hell was he thinking to just walk into his suite with Jaz waving a knife around?"

"He was doing what I should have done. Protecting you."

"No. It was more than that. I think Rick truly liked Jaz and felt guilty he'd dumped him. But, man, Jaz was way over the deep end."

Ethan couldn't help reliving his fear of when she was stuck in that room with a maniac by her side.

"It's not all bad, Ethan. At least Gus wasn't willing to kill anyone. He exercised poor judgment, sure, but he's no killer. They flew him to Nassau for help, and last I heard, he was just leaving the ICU at Princess Margaret Hospital."

"Good."

She was quiet a moment, and he opened his eyes, wanting to see her. Jewel stared at him, her light brown gaze speculative.

"What's wrong, baby?"

"I just think it's weird that all of what happened centered around broken hearts. My client obsessed over a younger, handsome man, thinking herself in love, but got blackmailed instead. Jaz really just wanted Rick to notice and love him again, and Gus turned on Rick because he was jealous about Elise. For such a noble emotion, love seems to be a real asskicker. You know?"

The look she gave him made his stomach tighten. Love. Yeah, he knew all about it. The question was, did she? And how to bring up the subject without looking like a complete moron, especially since they'd basically met only a week ago. How many people fell in love that quickly?

His mouth felt dry. "Jewel? Would you mind grabbing me a glass of water?"

She scrambled to her feet, and he caught a glimpse of flushed breasts and a firm, round ass. Unfortunately, she returned from the bathroom wearing his shirt. "Here, take this. Some pain reliever for your noggin."

Ethan swallowed the pill and downed the water in one gulp. "Do I have you to thank for stripping me naked?"

She grinned. "Yep. Rick left you in your underwear, but I thought you'd be more comfortable sans clothing."

"Thanks." He felt clean except for the gritty taste in his mouth. And, damn, but he wanted to kiss her. To that end, he swung his legs over the bed.

"Where are you going?"

He flinched against the pain in his head but made his way to the bathroom and closed the door behind him. He emerged feeling refreshed—empty bladder, clean teeth, and clean face. Too bad he wasn't up for a shave. But from the look on Jewel's face, she liked him just fine.

Ethan sat on the bed again, propping himself against the headboard, and drew her to him.

"So what now?" she blurted.

"Now we make love, slowly for a change."

She blushed and glanced down at his growing erection. "Honestly, Ethan. You were nearly brained to death Thursday. Take it easy." She glanced away from him. "I meant, what are you going to do now? I imagine you need to head back to Seattle. With your business and all…"

"Yeah, but I'm in no rush." He dragged her over his hips, her knees straddling his groin, and hugged her tight, inhaling the subtle fragrance that was all Jewel. "I guess you're heading back to Jersey, right? Back to Dreemer's, Inc. What is it you do, exactly?"

She began stroking his chest, small circles of feather-light touches that had him hard and aching in seconds. "I work for my uncle. I'm an investigator, kind of like what you do, I guess, but I normally work more behind the scenes. This case was pretty different from what I normally do."

"Which is?"

"Computer investigations. And on occasion, I've been known to help reacquire items our clients have lost or had stolen."

"What, as in repossessing stuff?"

"Ah, yeah. You could call it that."

"Or as in stealing stuff? You seemed pretty confident that a thief could easily steal the Mirvolo Cup, despite the security. You almost did it yourself."

She huffed. "If I hadn't been pressed for time and if I'd had my equipment, I'd have bagged the cup my second day here."

"Oh?"

"No offense to Rick's security." She eyed him slyly. "But his electronics need work. That coding was child's play."

"You don't say." He'd seen the modifications Jacobs had made and been impressed. Then again, Ethan knew more about physical security than the electronic type. He hired the eggheads at home to take care of the IT side of things. Not to mention Jared had a real knack for computers. "You know, Jewel, I subcontract a select group of folks like you to work for H&R in Seattle."

He kept his voice light, conscious she'd tensed. "Maybe you might think of branching out."

She said nothing, but she raised her eyes to his again. He quickly removed the shirt she wore that blocked her from his view, trying to handle his chaotic thoughts.

Why was this so awkward? "In fact, this job has probably tired the hell out of you. So much physical exertion, the stress of lying to your master..."

She frowned, and he grinned, pleased at the way her nipples puckered. God, she was so beautiful. She made him ache in so many places, namely, his overemotional, maudlin freaking heart.

"Your point, dear Master, who fell over the slave he was supposed to be protecting?"

Ethan scowled. "Low blow, Jewel. My point, you little witch, is that you should take a break after such a hard case. Come out to Seattle and relax for a while. I'd be happy to show you around town."

Jewel stared at him. "Is that an official invite?"

He felt on edge, tense. "What if it is?" Okay, so that came out much more harshly than he'd intended. "Come out and see my town. You'll like it, baby, I promise."

Before she could deny him, he kissed her. Softly, with all the emotion caged up inside of him. She sighed into his mouth and twined her arms around his neck, so careful not to hurt him.

His heart raced, and he settled her firmly over him, his cock pressing against her heat. "Have I ever told you how much I love the way you taste?" He kissed his way down her neck and cupped her breasts, marveling at her perfection.

"You're sexy, smart, so beautiful, and all mine." *Mine. I claim you.* And he showed her by chipping away at her kiss by kiss, caress by caress. Whereas before he'd taken her forcefully, this time he asked with his body. Both hesitant yet firm, he urged her responses with tenderness.

His lips sought the hollow of her throat, and he sucked her passionately. She was moist over him, and he found her wet heat with light petting, drawing his fingers over her clit time and time again as he made love with her mouth.

Rubbing his chest against her breasts, he made her moan. Sucking the tight beads of her nipples with warm, giving kisses, he made her sigh. And when he slowly eased into her narrow channel, he made her cry out his name, her eyes shiny with emotion.

Ethan thrust slowly, the effort not to slam up into her almost exhausting. But her sighs and moans as her climax built firmed his resolve. She took more and more of him, and the gradual orgasm took on a life of its own. When they finally crested together, she lay panting against his chest, their bodies still joined.

His fingers teased her hair, stroking with possession, with affection, and more. He hugged her to him tightly, not wanting to let go. When she glanced up at him, he opened his mouth to tell her how much she meant to him...

Except the peace and hesitancy that had been present before, now mirrored in her eyes as fear. And Ethan had a bad feeling he'd made the biggest mistake of his life by showing her how he felt. Without the stricture of their sexual games, his emotions had clearly reached for something that wasn't there, missing their mark yet again. And it was all the more painful this time because he'd finally fallen in love.

Chapter Ten

A month later

Jewel stared glumly at the picture of Ethan and his friend that she'd swiped before all hell had broken loose. The most cowardly, selfish act she'd ever perpetrated, against a man who'd done his level best to save her from herself.

Ethan had held her so gently, so carefully as he'd thoroughly made love to her. No artifice, no master/slave games. Hell, his heart had been shining there in his eyes. And what did Julia Marciella do? The idiot ran away from the best thing that had ever happened to her. Some "Jewel" she turned out to be.

Ethan hadn't said another word. He hadn't seen her off to the airport or even said good-bye. And she felt like the biggest jerk that walked the planet for turning down what could have been a wonderful thing.

So what that she'd fallen in love with a man in a week's time? She'd been away from him longer than they'd been together, and she'd been miserable every minute without him. She couldn't sleep, couldn't eat, was bitchy to her family and her friends—those she hadn't lost by being such an ass, that is.

Jewel sighed and ran her thumb over the image of his hard face. She felt her eyes welling again and angrily blinked back tears. Nothing seemed to help. Working provided no relief; it was only something to fill the hours while she thought about Ethan. Her family constantly worried over her, so she found avoidance the key there. Nick and her uncle had even stopped haranguing her at the office because she cried every time they tried to be nice. Had she not known better, she might have thought she was pregnant. Lord knew she'd made love with Ethan enough to get the job done. But she'd just had her period, and her implant remained firmly in place. And *that* made her cry. No babies with Ethan. No seeing Ethan. No more "Yes, Master" with Ethan. Jewel sniffed and tossed another empty box of tissues in the trash.

"That's it!" Her uncle stormed into the room and slammed the door behind him. "You and I are going to have a long talk, missy."

Jewel scowled, knowing she looked ridiculous with red-rimmed eyes and a stuffy nose. *Really threatening, Jewel. Maybe you can drown him to death in tears.*

"Don't give me that look. Let's get it out, right now. You've been a complete basket case since you returned, and according to Rick, sources close to Ethan Reaper say he's in the same boat. Grouchy, arrogant, and a real pain in the ass to be around." Uncle Tommy huffed. "Looks like you two are a match made in heaven."

She stared at her uncle, again amazed at how much he always knew. "How—"

"Rick sent me a few e-mails, and I have to say I'm liking him more and more. He mentioned he thinks you're an idiot for letting love pass you by. According to the grand master of sex and salutation, as Rick likes to think of himself, I quote, 'Jewel is a smartass who needs a strong man to keep her in line. And none come stronger than Ethan Reaper.'"

Her uncle rubbed his hands together and then took a small piece of folded paper from his sport coat. "This is Reaper's current address. I put a blueprint of his home in your car, as well as an overlay of his security. I figure if you take the flight I booked for you tonight, coach, with layovers, you can make it to Seattle by tomorrow morning. That should give you time to clean yourself up and stop being so damned weepy. Honestly, girl, have some pride."

Jewel snickered around a sniffle. "Sorry for dragging you down."

"Good. Now go put yourself and this poor man out of his misery." Her uncle sighed and stared around him. "I suppose I'm going to have to give this office to Danielle. She'll fight Nick for it, but she's meaner in the end. Promise me you'll call and visit often, and I expect you to do Dreemer's proud. You're the first to launch our West Coast branch. So give H&R a run for their money." Her uncle's eyes twinkled. "Steal what you have to, just don't get caught."

The family motto.

Jewel rose and hugged her uncle tightly. "I'm sorry for being such a wuss, but I never expected to fall in love. And he's such a major pain, Uncle Tommy."

He grinned. "I know. I've done some research, and he sounds like a real S.O.B. I like him already. Go steal his heart like a real Marciella, and make sure he knows you're getting married here, by the shore. Your mother will never let me hear the end of it if you get married somewhere else."

"Mom agreed to all this?"

He nodded. "She loves you so much, honey. And it's been killing her, killing all of us, that you've been so unhappy."

"I know. I was trying to convince myself my feelings were just leftover from the job. But they won't go away. I have it bad."

"Just like your father. He mooned over Felicity something fierce."

She smiled, thinking of her father. "He did, hmm?"

"Oh, yes. And Felicity, a true work of art, made him bite, beg, and steal into her good graces. Let's just hope your man is a lot more forgiving."

"Oh, he's not, not at all. I can't wait to grovel."

* * *

Ethan grimaced. If Jared called him an asshole just one more time, he was going to beat the snot out of the pansy-assed college boy, Jared's pending fatherhood be damned. It wasn't his fault Marcy had threatened to quit yet again.

And he'd told Mike and Steve he'd take this weekend's shift, so why were they complaining about all the work they'd been given lately? Since he'd returned from hell on earth, Ethan had taken on three cases in the span of a month.

He'd pulled overtime and then some, making the agency some primo bucks in the doing. High profile, too. Caught a celebrity stalker and a corporate spy soaking his company for millions.

Too bad the successes did nothing to soothe the huge ache in his heart. He felt tired and cranky all the time, and Jared could go fuck himself if he couldn't handle his own tender feelings.

"Pussy," Ethan muttered, as he let himself into his dark house. Once again, he'd returned long after the sun set, and the bleak, empty atmosphere suited him to a "T." Greenlake usually gave him a sense of peace, but lately, the damned ducks made him want to go hunting. Cheerful assholes ran around the fucking lake trail at all hours, and his neighbor was two more muffler shouts away from getting his ass handed to him on the hood of his '66 GTO.

Grumbling to himself as he slammed his way into the hall, Ethan shoved his mail aside and dropped his keys on the table in the entryway. He didn't bother turning on a light. Instead he felt his way into the kitchen and grabbed a beer. Sucking down the bitter ale, he climbed the steps to his bedroom, forgoing a dinner he didn't feel like eating.

Jared's wife had been nagging him again today. "You're losing too much weight, Ethan. Tell him, Jared." As if Ethan needed to hear that he looked as good as he felt—like shit. Hell, ever since coming back from that godforsaken island, his life had swirled down into a whirlpool of never-ending despair.

Ethan thought about Jewel, that little witch, all the time. And his nights were the worst. He had the most erotic dreams, constantly waking to wet spots in his bed. Wet spots.

As if he were some horny teenager instead of a damned thirty-five-year-old man. His brothers had thought his heartache was funny, until he'd punched Hale in the face and nearly broken Trevor's arm. Now they avoided him like the plague. After another swallow of beer, Ethan admitted he couldn't blame his brothers for doing so.

Groaning, he realized tomorrow he had to show up for the family dinner or his mother would do as she'd threatened and move in with him until he sought professional help.

Hell, the only professional help he needed was from a real "professional." Maybe then he'd stop coming on his fucking bedsheets.

Groaning at his thoughts, *always of Jewel, dammit,* Ethan flicked on the bedroom light…and froze.

He blinked several times and barely noticed dropping his beer.

There, in the middle of his bed on unfamiliar black satin sheets, lay Jewel, naked save for the black leather collar around her neck. Scarlet red rose petals lay strewn around her figure, and the contrast of the petals and the black sheets made her skin glow like the pale moonlight just outside.

"Ethan." She smiled, and he swallowed around the lump in his throat. Joy burst through his being like a ball of pure light, and he had to force it down, remembering how they'd parted.

She didn't flinch at his scowl, like everyone else at work did. Instead, she rose to her hands and knees and crawled to the edge of the bed and knelt there.

Pulled as if on invisible strings, he met her there, standing directly in front of her, an inch from her blessed skin.

"What the hell do you want?" Ethan wanted to smack himself as soon as he'd spoken. But he didn't intend on going through the pain he'd already suffered again.

"I missed you, Ethan."

"Right." He snorted.

"I can't sleep. I can't eat. All I can think about is you, how you feel, how you sound, how you taste."

She tugged at his shirt and unbuttoned it from collar to waist. Bastard that he was, he didn't have the heart to stop her. The minute her fingers grazed his chest and tugged at his nipples, he got the mother of all hard-ons.

"I'll ask again. What do you want?" Christ, he sounded hoarse.

"I want to tell you how sorry I am." She teased the snap of his jeans, now tight against his jutting erection. "When you made love to me that last time..." She paused and unsnapped him. "I was so scared of what I felt. I couldn't believe I could feel love for a man I'd just met, who I knew little about...it was overwhelming."

His breath came in fits and starts when she slowly lowered his zipper. And then the word "love" penetrated, and Ethan zeroed in on what she was saying.

"You made me feel things, made me want things I never had before. I mean, I had sex with you in public. And I'd never been so turned on in my life."

He barely stifled a groan when she set him free, lowering his jeans and underwear to his thighs.

"It was safe when it was all a game. Master, slave, and all the positions under the sun." She took him in her hands, and he was helpless to prevent the moisture pooling in his slit. Shit, he could see how hard her nipples were. Her tits were killing him. So were her soft hands. But the worst...she'd said she *loved* him.

Ethan groaned.

"You can't know how sorry I am for the way I left you." Jewel glanced up, and he saw tears in her eyes. "I love you so much, Ethan, and I want to show you how sorry I am. I've wanted you in so many ways since I left. But most of all, I just wanted to see you again."

She stared at him critically, and wonder of wonders, she grinned at what she saw. "You look terrible. You've lost weight."

He frowned, but before he could say anything, her hot little mouth engulfed him in one long suck.

"Shit." He moaned and couldn't help thrusting into her mouth. "Jewel, baby, what are you doing to me?"

She sucked him hard and licked him with her tongue before answering. "I'm loving you, Ethan. And I'm begging for you to accept my apology...Master."

He rasped her name and began fucking her mouth, needing the comfort and warmth that only Jewel could provide. Staring down at her, he watched as she took him in and out, only a collar on her delicate throat to shield her flesh.

Wrapping his hands in her hair, he moaned her name, how much he'd missed her, how much he loved her as he pumped. All too quickly he came, unable to resist the temptation of her heat.

"Swallow it, baby, take me." Ethan shuddered into her mouth, spewing with a great cry.

When he could finally catch his breath, he rubbed his hands in her hair and pulled her gently off the bed to her feet on the floor.

"I'm sorry, Ethan. I should never have left the way I did."

"No, you shouldn't have." He didn't let the elation he was feeling show on his face.

"I, um, I'm ready to make things right. To make an honest man of you."

His heart wanted to explode. The woman wanted to *marry* him. What he'd been fantasizing about for a solid month was suddenly very, very real.

"Or not, if you'd rather just have the sex."

Still he said nothing, enjoying the desperation on her face that slowly transformed into delightful anger.

"Look, you bastard, I know I was wrong. But I love you, and you're stuck with me. So if you have some other floozy hanging around, dump her. You're mine. And I love you," she added again, for solid measure apparently.

Ethan began laughing, he just couldn't help himself. And suddenly she laughed with him.

"Oh, baby, I've missed you so much." He hugged her to him, wiping the tears of mirth and happiness from his eyes.

"Me, too." Jewel laughed when he picked her up and tossed her on the bed.

In seconds he'd stripped out of his clothes and settled on top of her. "Look, if I promise not to make love to you so gently any more, will you stay with me?"

She flushed. "Actually, I loved what we did that last time on the island. I was such an ass for running from you."

"From us," Ethan corrected, and rubbed his hand over her collar. "Shit, Jewel. Do you have any idea what it was like to see you naked in my bed wearing only a leather collar? I jerked off to that image for a solid month while you were gone, and I still had wet dreams."

Her eyes danced. "Really? Me, too. Oh, not of me in a collar, but of being with you again. I love your muscles. The way you smell." She inhaled the spot at the base of his throat, making him shiver. "And especially the way you taste."

He groaned and pushed against her, his cock at half mast. "Give me a minute. You took my strength with that pretty little mouth. Damn, baby, you made me come so hard I about lost my mind."

"And after that knock you took a month ago, you don't have much left to lose."

"Very funny." Ethan laughed with her, so happy he wanted to shout. "Now about this honest man stuff—"

"No pressure. It's a yes now or later. Doesn't matter to me when you say it, so long as you say it."

But he could feel her tension. "For the record, *I'm* proposing. And you're going to marry me. That's final."

"You're so bossy." She grinned from ear to ear. "But just so you know, we have to do it in New Jersey, or I'm disowned."

"Oh?"

"Yeah. And you're marrying into a family of thieves."

"Figures." He shook his head, his eyes twinkling. "Both my brothers are cops, my dad's a retired Fed, and I'm a prior Marine."

She laughed. "Oh, good. Family get-togethers will be sooo much fun."

"Yeah." Ethan stared down into his future and wiped a happy tear from her soft face. "You know I'm going to milk as much apology out of you as I can."

She sighed with contentment and hugged him. "I know. I deserve it."

"We both do, baby. Remember, Bacchus favors us."

Jewel laughed, and he joined her, determined not to forget Rick on the wedding list that he planned on drafting just as soon as Ethan finished making proper love to *his woman*.

"Jewel? If you're really sorry, you'll come in with me to work tomorrow. You see, everyone's been blaming me for being such a bastard lately, but when I show you off, they'll understand."

She grinned. "That's what they said about me at work, too. You know, Uncle Tommy was right. We really are made for each other."

And the next day, when she passed the Marcy test, he knew he'd found a winner.

~ * ~

Marie Harte

Marie Harte is an avid reader who loves all things paranormal and futuristic, but especially all things romance. Reading romances since she was twelve, she fell in love with the warmth of first passion and knew writing was her calling. Twenty-three years later, the Marine Corps, a foray through Information Technology, a husband and four kids, and her dream has finally come true. Marie lives in Georgia with her family and loves hearing from readers. To read more about Marie, visit www.marieharte.com and check out her blog at http://www.marieharte.blogspot.com.

TITLES AVAILABLE In Print from Loose Id®

A GUARDIAN'S DESIRE
Mya

ALPHA
Treva Harte

COURTESAN
Louisa Trent

DANGEROUS CRAVINGS
Evangeline Anderson

DINAH'S DARK DESIRE
Mechele Armstrong

GRACEFUL SUBMISSION
Melinda Barron

HARD CANDY
Angela Knight, Morgan Hawke and Sheri Gilmore

HAWKEYE ONE: DANGER ZONE
Sierra Cartwright

LEAVE ME BREATHLESS

Trista Ann Michaels

MANACLED IN MONACO

Jianne Carlo

STRENGTH IN NUMBERS

Rachel Bo

THE ASSIGNMENT

Evangeline Anderson

THEIR ONE AND ONLY

Trista Ann Michaels

THE COMPLETENESS OF CELIA FLYNN

Sedonia Guillone

THE PRENDARIAN CHRONICLES

Doreen DeSalvo

WHY ME?

Treva Harte

Publisher's Note: The print titles listed above were previously released in e-book format by Loose Id®.

LaVergne, TN USA
19 January 2010
170398LV00002B/89/P